Safer
Than Houses

SAFER
THAN HOUSES

FRANCES FYFIELD

LITTLE, BROWN

LITTLE, BROWN

First published in Great Britain in October 2005 by Little, Brown
Reprinted 2005 (twice)

Copyright © Frances Fyfield 2005

The moral right of the author has been asserted.

All characters in this publication other than those clearly in the
public domain are fictitious and any resemblance to real persons,
living or dead, is purely coincidental.

A CIP catalogue record for this book is available
from the British Library.

HBK ISBN 0 316 72764 4
CF ISBN 0 316 72765 2

Typset in Plantin Light by M Rules

Printed and bound in Great Britain by
Clays Ltd, St Ives plc

Little, Brown
An imprint of
Time Warner Book Group UK
Brettenham House
Lancaster Place
London WC2E 7EN

www.twbg.co.uk

For Michael Sells

ACKNOWLEDGEMENTS

With many thanks to Dr Pat Rapley, Senior Scientist at the London Laboratory of the Forensic Sciences Services, for her generous help on the subject of Fire investigation.

All mistakes are my own.

Take care of your fire and candle,
Be charitable to the poor
And pray for the dead.

Night-watch curfew

PROLOGUE

Bang, bang, bang. Worse than the sound of a gun.

It was, as Jane Austen described, a good address, had been once, and perhaps, unfortunately, might well be so again. Tucked away in Bloomsbury, that area of art, literature, science and Bohemian respectability, lit with verdant green squares, Bedford, Russell, Georgian houses sitting around like grand old ladies knitting, feet firmly planted on the ground. There, there were tall, wide doors, reached by steps, flanked by curved iron railings, places of visible reception rooms, drawing rooms and significant chandeliers, panelled and painted walls, old societies, and learned activities within. A place of contrasts. Into the squares, like a spider's web, led the smaller streets of terraced houses, places of less certain fortunes. In Jane Austen's times, the second-grade families and hangers-on might have lived here, without benefit of a carriage, on the outer skirts of the West End, enduring a comparative lack of riches, and in later times, downright poverty in a dozen different manifestations. Now he lived in a half of a house, or more aptly, the greater fraction of a long skinny building, with himself in as uncertain a condition as the street. And he lived with a heavy-footed monster.

Dump, dump, dump. Crash.

He looked up at the ceiling. The plasterwork was old and uneven. It had always been like that, but never before had that thundering footfall, more hoofs than feet, dislodged a flake of plaster to fall on his upturned face like a flake of dry snow. *Gerrummph, gerrumph, gerrumph,* the sound of foot-steps, grinding above his head, undeterred, undrowned by the sound of Handel on his CD player, the very notes preaching harmony and sounding like a nonsense. Pictures on the walls, old, wood panelling, lovingly restored, the whole edifice crooked and wonky and sturdy, despite the creaks, the makings of a fire in the grate, which he could not light, because she complained and banged and said it seeped smoke into her room. The pocked mirror above the redundant fireplace reflected a face he no longer recognised as his own, shiny with tears.

He could go down to the lower ground floor, to the elegant kitchen with the old fire range and food and warmth, but the sound of the television would still penetrate, and the stain on the ceiling would remind him of the Devil. Three times her bathroom had flooded, though the merciful eccentricity of the plumbing had diverted the water not into this floor, but down into the haven of his kitchen, where the ceiling sagged, brown and stained, and he had brushed out the water into the dark garden in his vigorous way. He was not old, yet; he felt he had aged a hundred years.

The footsteps resumed; the TV boomed. His head felt fit to burst, unable to take in any other, internal sound. He unhooked his coat, opened his own door and tiptoed out into the passage he shared with her, towards the front door they also shared. He would go out for a walk; there was nothing else to do. He had once been described as the perfect guest, and he was not old, yet.

Outside on the steps, he closed the door quietly behind himself, of habit. He was a quiet man who also liked to talk; she knew that. The Satanic creature owned the top half of this house; he owned the rest. They were supposed to live like neighbours, in peace, security, and civility, and she was intent on reducing it to rubble and his soul with it.

The cold turned his breath into vapour. He could hear the distant traffic in the square, humming and rumbling, imagined buses depositing people at the dozen hotels that stretched along what everyone knew as Hotel Row on the far side, saw taxis and cars taking the world out and back on a Saturday night. Another life was audibly out of reach and he wished the traffic would detour down here instead of devouring itself up there. He craved noise outside; silence within. He took hold of the cold iron railing, which he loved at least as much as he loved all inanimate things, and began to descend the mere three steps to the pavement. Encountered a wet polythene bag on the second step, and fell. She must have left it there.

Buckled, more than fell. Twisted over on his foot, heard a distinct sound, like a *twang*, steadied himself, gripped the railing, and sat, slowly. He did not need to examine it to know something was broken; only bones made such a sound. Metatarsal, probably. He sat for a while. You bloody fool.

Then he fumbled for his mobile phone, beginning to shiver. Shock. Needed to get back in, tested the weight, tried to get up, not good. Bones were bones. Fingers cold, breath steaming his glasses, eyes inside specs not doing good.

3

Nine . . . nine . . . nine . . . *I am not that old, but I am very thin, these days.* He sat where he was on the cold step, waiting for the ambulance. In an area of hospitals, they were never far away. He remembered how the Devil had said that the existence of hospitals in this part of the world had come up as a local health hazard on the survey of her flat. All that medical waste and all those chemicals, spouting into the air. Traffic'll kill you first, he said, remembering it, waiting for the ambulance, which took a time, all the same.

They were kind, but busy. He was not young, but not old enough for special consideration. Busy night, things not what they were, guv. Can we just leave it, and you go to Accident and Emergency in the morning?

The door behind him opened as they prised off his shoe.

The woman stood, in all her splendour, capable and dependable, with her iron hair held back.

He needs strong tea and sugar, they said. And that foot strapped up. Pointless taking him to Accident and Emergency at this time of a Saturday night. Big queue.

I'm his neighbour, she said brightly. I'll look after him.

He thought he shouted, No, no, no, but no sound emerged.

They took him back up the three steps, following her directions, into the hallway. Yes, she was saying, kindly. I know what to do, we don't need to trouble you. The foot needs ice and elevation, crêpe bandage, treatment tomorrow. I'm a nurse, you know.

They left him on the chair in his own hallway. The soul of geniality, she showed them to the front door, and while she did so, Henry hobbled the necessary steps to the open door of his flat, got inside, and slammed it shut behind him. Leant against it, double locked it, listened at the keyhole. There

4

was a pause before he heard the front door bang closed, and after a moment, her voice, horribly close, the feel of her breath though the keyhole.

I'll look after you, she said. And laughed. Then he heard her heavy, slow footsteps going back upstairs.

Without the coat, he might have shaken himself to pieces. Why the hell had he not screamed at them to say, take me away? Because shouting and screaming was unnatural for a quiet man who could scarcely murmur protest at the best of times, although he loved to talk. And he could not afford to go, and leave her here. She would flood his house, kill his cat, claim his territory and leave him homeless. Instead he was a prisoner.

Shock gave way to pain and weariness. He sat huddled in his coat, until he managed to bump his way downstairs into the kitchen, travelling on his bottom, looking for the old crêpe bandage which lived in a drawer and the frozen peas in the freezer. He was highly practical and knew what to do. After some fumbling around, he sat with the rogue foot propped on a chair, feeling it throb. The cat watched, unhelpfully. He lit a cigarette and watched it glow, wondered if it was true that everyone was capable of murder, laughed, as if he had been tickled. Then wept.

He had always been the perfect guest, even in his own rooms. A bachelor, an effete who loved women and was timid of them at the same time.

What kept him going now was the vision of a woman, coming indoors and hugging him. He would be like the princess who slept for a hundred years, only he was a prince. It was the princess who would come along and break the spell of this passive horror, by hugging him awake. She would lead him away to a place of safety. He dreamt of being kissed awake, and then hidden away. She would bring back his nerve, and dispel the spell.

On the other side of the city, near, but far, a robust old lady held an unpleasant one-page letter up to the light of her ancient standard lamp, the better to read it from the comfort of her armchair. The urge to tear the paper into small pieces was certainly strong, but on mature reflection she decided it could all wait until the morning, since emergencies were always the inventions of men.

CHAPTER ONE

Dear Helen of Troy, Lady of the Lake, slayer of a thousand suitors' hearts, oh lovely jubbly jellybean babyface . . .

She tucked the card back in the envelope. It was a talisman to brighten the day, even a day like this that was part of a succession of days that began dark, paled into grey and then became dark again. Days when she wanted to remain under the blankets, imagining the sound of the sea and the deliciousness of sleep. Never going out. Sarah Fortune shook her head and kissed the page. Thank you, she said, silently: thank you for reminding me of jellybeans, and how to be cheerful for Dulcie.

She sipped her tea. The Fountain restaurant at Fortnum and Mason on a Monday was the perfect venue for watching Dulcie Mathewson proceed over the floor towards her with a certain regal clumsiness. Dulcie's handbag rivalled any held by a duchess; it was a sharp-edged block of leather which doubled as a weapon, and when she sat, it required a seat all of its own. It looked as if it should contain something live, like a chihuahua, or a cat.

'You look wonderful,' Dulcie said, seating herself heavily and pushing back her delicate chair into the one behind at the next table, without apology. 'Wonderful, as usual. I do love that colour on you,' nodding deference to a rust-coloured scarf of silk petals. 'But you do look a little *peaky*, now I come to observe. Is that Earl Grey? Give me China tea. I suppose it's too early for gin.'

Sarah regarded her fondly. It was difficult to resist hugging Dulcie, but Dulcie did not always like it, not in public.

'How are you, Dulcie?'

'Blooming, as you can see. Never better. Or as good as I damn well can be without Ernest. Can't believe it's nearly two years since that ghastly funeral. Now it's one damned committee after another. Not enough time for shopping. By the time I've finished with the arts committee, the legal charities wotsit and the hospital trust, thank God I've no time for grandchildren either. Little bastards.'

She laughed, refreshingly loud and long. The adjacent group began to leave, perhaps exactly as they intended, although Sarah was not sure. She never knew if the ripples created by Dulcie were a natural result of her presence, or contrived. There was nothing Dulcie did without a purpose, although not necessarily one fully defined in advance. She had a way of clearing space.

'That's what you get from once being a magistrate,' she boomed, reaching into the handbag, which did, indeed, occupy its own seat like a lady-in-waiting. 'Everyone's looking for a bloody chairman or treasurer, and I'm in. Chief Nit. It's also what comes from being a lawyer's widow.'

A status Sarah Fortune also enjoyed, although differently.

The family at the next table were halfway across the room, fanning out as they fled. Dulcie poured and drank the tea, laced with sugar. The bulk of her was both soft and solid, and Sarah was ridiculously pleased to see her. Her sheer presence was a reassuring blessing. She might always want something done, and that made no difference.

'That's better,' Dulcie Mathewson said, spreading herself. 'How sweet of them to go.'

'So give me the good news first,' Sarah said.

'Right. Ernest's stocks and shares have held up well, all things considering. Poor darling, he'd have turned in his grave if he knew about current politics, or the way the firm went, which was only the way it was going before he had that last heart attack. Nothing to do with the bacon sandwiches you used to buy him, dear. Kept him sane.'

Dulcie took off her glasses and rubbed them with her napkin, thoroughly. Sarah thought briefly of her office on the top floor of Ernest Mathewson's legal firm, where, for a decade, she had once been the ever-junior lawyer who would never make partnership, all complicated by the additional, self-created, unofficial responsibility of *looking after Ernest*. And thus she had met and collaborated with Mrs Dulcie Mathewson, wife of the bemused senior partner, Ernest himself. She had also known their son, Malcolm. There was always a pang of nostalgia, rather than regret, when Sarah thought of Malcolm, and she often wondered if that was because the loving, followed by the leaving of him, had lost her the opportunity of having Dulcie for a mother-in-law. It seemed a lifetime ago, instead of a mere six years. With the uncanny ability, honed over long acquaintance, to read her thoughts, Dulcie beamed at her.

'No need to ask after him every time, you know. I'm far

better off with you as a lifelong friend, and so are you. Malcolm's inherited some of his father's pomposity, now he's a father himself, and you'd have hated one another by now, as well you knew. Such a sweet little wife he has, as I told you. Can't talk to her. This ghastly subservience. Your own career, my dear, has been so much more *innovative*. Do let me know when you need more clients. All those committees; I meet suitable candidates all the time.'

'Fancy you criticising deference in a wife,' Sarah said. 'You used to treat Ernest like Lord and Master.'

'We all have to *pretend*, you of all people know that. It's the art of maintaining control.'

'Fools are more hard to conquer than persuade,' Sarah quoted.

'Oh Lord,' Dulcie said, tipping the teacup over her nose. 'If you take men for fools, you're really in trouble. I think I need a new hat.'

'You don't need a hat. No one *needs* a hat.'

'You never know. I anticipate at least three funerals and one Buckingham Palace garden party this year. That kind of thing, you might like to come to the latter. Anyway, need and want is the same thing.'

She leant forward over a comfortably spread waist, practically resting her large bosom on the table. 'You do realise, Sarah, that after two years of the widowhood business, spending money's still a marvellous novelty. It's taken up until now to sort everything out. Ernest always had me scrimping and economising and now I've got oodles. Never felt secure before. I'd rather he was alive, of course, but the only compensation for death is the opportunity to behave quite differently. He gave me the freedom, the dear man.'

'I suppose my benefactor gave that to me,' Sarah said,

adjusting her scarf, sensing Dulcie's desire to move on to the next thing. 'I still can't get over him leaving me a *flat*. A bunch of flowers, maybe. Not a whole apartment.' The scarf was an impossible confection of silk leaves in rust and black, appliquéd to thinner silk, looking like a rag from a distance, and on closer view a work of art, lying nonchalantly on her collar bone. Dulcie's handbag seemed to leap back into her lap, unbidden.

'Well, you did look after him, dear, and you did deserve it. Ernest had some very nice clients as well as some nasty ones,' Dulcie added, not wishing to dwell on it. 'Such a good old judge he was, to give you security. Unheated garrets and mort-gages really aren't any good to the creative soul, are they? And isn't it wonderful to be left something in a will? Preferably a lot. I shan't mind dying when the time comes, if my death invests someone else with choices. At least dear Ernest had the sense to tie some of it up, so I can't spend it all.'

'You could do up the house,' Sarah suggested. 'Modernise a bit?'

Ernest would have vetoed that. Nothing was ever renewed in Dulcie's house after she got her way the first time on account of being a bride. He hated that kind of change, and so did she.

'Can't be arsed,' Dulcie said. 'I'd rather have a dog than an electrician. Let's get frivolous.'

They moved, adroitly, to the ladies' fashion floor, where Dulcie assumed rather more delicate movements in the vicin-ity of clothes, tucking the handbag inside her coat to avoid it swinging from her shoulder and knocking things over. She had a horror of being required to pay for something she had merely damaged. They admired the hats, without enthusi-asm, since none had the extravagance to fire Dulcie's imagination, and besides, she had changed her mind about what she wanted. That was the whole point about shopping. A new coat would be better, dear, but the coats on display in late February were fitter for spring than for the raw, damp weather outside.

'Why is it always impossible to buy something to wear *now*?' Dulcie complained. 'Who the hell wants a cotton coat *now*? At least charity shops don't make you think of summer when it never happens. Wait a minute, look at this. That would look lovely on you.'

She paused by a charcoal-grey coat, long length, fitted, flaring below the knee, high-necked, soft, light wool which swung like silk as Dulcie attempted to lift it from the hanger. A tired assistant loomed at her elbow as she began to tug at the wire cable that anchored it to the rail through the sleeve, and if madam would wait, she would unlock it.

'Oh, very funny. They lock up bloody coats now. Put chains on them as if they were delinquents. What do they think they're going to do? Escape?'

'We were looking for a coat for you,' Sarah said, shaking her head.

'We were just *looking* for the hell of it, Sarah. Do as you're told.'

Sarah shrugged into the coat. It was panelled into seamless seams, so that, left undone, with hands in the pockets, it slouched like an arm-in-arm friend, and swung lazily. With a dozen buttons in the same fabric fastened up the front, it neatened itself into formality, looking almost judicial, the elegant lawyer's coat, commanding respect, slightly severe if only it were not so soft. Unaccountably, Dulcie's eyes filled with tears.

'Turn round,' she said, fishing in her pocket for a capacious handkerchief and blowing her nose. Sarah turned, a brief pirouette on high-heeled boots which she wore like slippers, to run down any road. Sarah, always ready for flight. Dulcie loved her so much it hurt. She knew it was returned in equal measure, not that either of them was likely to say so.

'Ernest always loved to see you in charcoal grey,' she said, in between blowing her nose. The assistant retreated and left them alone. 'He said it suited you best. Better than black. He'd phone me to tell me what you were wearing each morning, and then you'd phone me to tell me what state he was in during the afternoon, so I'd know.'

Both of them mourning him. 'He did love clothes, didn't he?' Sarah said. 'And he was right. Grey suits me better now. Soft dark grey. The new black.' She began to take off the coat. Even in the warm room, it felt chilly to be without it.

'I wish you were my daughter,' Dulcie burst out. 'And I'm also bloody glad you aren't. You'd scare me to death with worry, to say nothing of envy. I really wish I had your career. What are you doing, taking that sodding coat off? It belongs to you. This coat does not wish to remain imprisoned on a rail,' Dulcie said. 'It would be cruel to it.'

'It's lovely . . .' Sarah said, slowly.

'. . . Too severe? Too warm? Too classic? Not the right label? Not right for your image? Grey, rather than black? Doesn't fit right? What's wrong with it?'

'It's . . .'

'Too dark, too impractical? Prefer it in red? You're mad. *What's wrong with it?*'

Dulcie was roaring. The assistant stayed away.

'It's too expensive,' Sarah said. '*Way* too expensive. That's the only objection. Yup, I have my glittering career, but that's

13

not exactly cash rich at the moment. Maybe I'm getting too old, but—'

'Too *old*? Are you barking mad or what? You've only just started. You've been working at a discount again, haven't you? And anyway, *I'm* buying the coat.'

'I can't let you do that,' Sarah said, evenly.

'Bollocks. Ernest paid you peanuts all those years ago. He exploited you. He put you in danger with Charles Tysall, *twice.*'

'He never meant harm to anyone, and he gave me a client base, and I owe you both, rather than the other way round . . .'

'Got bugger all to do with *owing*,' Dulcie bellowed. 'And I'm nearly thirty years older, and much, much bigger than you, so WHY CAN'T YOU JUST *TAKE* SOMETHING?'

She tore the coat out of Sarah's arms and strode to a till. Sarah followed, protesting, overruled by that resonant, magisterial voice. 'Are you saying my money's not good enough? Call a doctor to this woman. She needs treatment. I'm trying to buy her a coat she wants, and she won't let me. What kind of daughter is that?'

The coat was wrapped in swathes of tissue and an unnecessarily solid, huge bag, as if to give it space to breathe. Mrs Dulcie Mathewson's card was presented and accepted and no one referred to the price. Hurrying to leave, as if they had stolen the thing, they collided with each other in the door; Dulcie stopped and beamed.

'I've been longing to do that for years,' she said. 'And now, let's have a drink.'

It was dark outside; February dark, head-in-oven time of year, Dulcie said. The windy rain gussied spitefully on the corner as they turned left and left again. 'Should have bought a sensible hat,' Dulcie grumbled, patting her abundant grey-rinse curls which shone blue in the streetlight. It was the sort of musty dark which seemed endless, in which Sarah felt she needed to move from one sanctuary to another. They moved on an automatic route, both knowing where they were going, without discussion. Dulcie wondered if she was the only person in the world who worried about Sarah Fortune. The soft lights of the Lamb public house beckoned through the nasty drizzle, the figured windows half obscured by the window boxes full of straggling winter greenery which had given up the fight to survive. Inside, at the far end of the L-shaped bar, there were a couple of regulars to whom the same applied. Two men nursing pints looked as if lunch was a distant memory, tea a complete irrelevance, and life might begin again when the crowd came in after working hours. Not long to wait. Dulcie sighed with pleasure. Both of them felt more at home. Dulcie tipped her head at the fat man slouched at the nearest end of the bar, and looked Sarah straight in the eye.

'I'd rather die a virgin,' she whispered.

It was the sort of unreconstructed pub which ignored its rich environs of retail therapy, as well as the pressure to serve food, and instead went along with catering for those in urgent need of strong drink, served without flourish or style, consumed in a dark corner. The bar was solid mahogany, embellished with ornate shelving above, and the fat barman with a seen-it-all expression leant through the gap and then turned his back, avoiding eye contact. The prevailing smell was old beer, tinged with the sweetness of spirit, cigarettes and cleaning fluid. You could cut it with a knife.

'Two large gins, please.'

Sarah elbowed Dulcie aside in order to pay, and Dulcie allowed it. They retreated to the high stools flanking the window ledge and looked out at the rain, Dulcie, at least, feeling an enormous sense of achievement. Sarah raised her glass.

'Thank you,' she said, 'for my ridiculously expensive, gorgeous coat. I shall wear it with pride and joy, to celebrate my fortieth birthday.'

'Time to be ambitious. At least you've grown up enough to accept a gift graciously.'

'Oh come on, Dulcie, I do that all the time.'

'But not usually from a woman. You prefer to earn it, I suppose.'

'Of course.'

Dulcie leant forward and sipped her gin. Mother's ruin. The first sip of a gin in a pub like this was absolute nectar. The stuff was never the same at home, even if the mixture was stronger, which all went to show that the alcohol content had little to do with the pleasure.

'Sarah, dear, do you remember Henry Brett? Friend of Ernest's. That shy man. The expert in something useful. Used to come to dinner with us. He always looked in need of a feed.'

'Henry Brett? I remember the name, but I don't think I ever knew him. I know, wasn't he the one Ernest got in to advise on the firm's art collections after I left?'

Dulcie nodded. The art collection had been a bad idea. Ernest had used a lot of experts on that and in various insurance cases, never thought they were worth the money, and always evaded paying them.

'Ernest used to get me to feed him in lieu of payment. He was the sort of academic type who could never send a

16

bill, that man. Lives alone with a cat. Ernest cheated him. A bit.'

'And?'

Dulcie stroked the condensation on the outside of the glass, lovingly.

'He wrote to me so sweetly after Ernest died. I tried to keep in touch after that. Like I did with several people Ernest owed money. I liked Henry. He was the perfect guest. He used to bring flowers already arranged in water, so that you didn't have to put down what you were doing. Can you imagine? But now when I phone, he doesn't reply. He's either in trouble or maybe he's ill or something and is too proud to say. It would be like him.'

Sarah sighed. Dear Dulcie, the networker.

'What could *I* do for him?'

'Oh, just knock on his door and find out if he's all right,' Dulcie said airily. 'He doesn't live far from you.' She slipped a card with an address into the bag with the coat. Always trying to fix her up. Then she banged down the gin glass on the smeared surface of the window ledge. Outside, the rain stuttered to a halt. She turned her eyes on Sarah. Dulcie's eyes were pale blue and shrewd.

'You would tell me if there was anything wrong with you, wouldn't you?'

They could lie to one another with fluent ease.

'I'm a very lucky woman,' Sarah said. 'And there is absolutely nothing wrong.' She hesitated. 'You know I'd do anything for you, don't you?'

Dulcie kissed her, gruffly.

'If I didn't think you'd kill for me, I'd never have bought you a coat.'

★

It was not entirely true that there was nothing wrong on either part, although never anything wrong between themselves. The gift left Sarah slightly light-headed. Leaving Dulcie to take a taxi to her own upholstered house in Kensington, a place full of hummingbirds and floral decoration, Sarah missed her. The tube was over-warm and rush-hour crowded; uncomfortable, and no room to look at the faces. She did not want to go home, and that was worrying, because home was everything, the bedrock of life. Although not exactly where the heart was. Her heart was all over the place.

The foyer of the block of flats where Sarah lived had been subject to a facelift and she preferred the old wrinkles. The carpet with its geometric design had gone, although the mirrors remained. Fritz the doorman was on holiday, which was part of the problem, because he was not there to intercept the letters, which lay in a heap on his desk. It was the wish of some of the residents that the public spaces inside this potentially grand mansion block be revamped to reflect a certain status. Sarah preferred the slightly tatty gloom which had once existed. The lift worked every day, now, which was also a change. The foyer was lonely without Fritz, even though he was absent more often than present. Sarah did not really belong in a place which had a doorman at all, but then her home had been an inheritance. A gift of staggering generosity; only now, as is the way with all over-generous gifts, it seemed that somebody wanted it back.

She could see the letters for the whole block, sitting on the foyer desk, caught in the mirror, as soon as she was through the heavy plate-glass doors. It would take a tank to get through those doors. She padded across the rich carpet, of which Dulcie would thoroughly approve, towards the desk,

and began to sort through the letters, hoping there was nothing addressed to herself, delivered by hand in the afternoon,
the way they were. But there it was, lingering amongst the
bills for Flat 16, the circulars for 11, prominent in its handwritten glory, her address loud and clear in black felt pen.
How rare to get handwritten letters instead of emails. She
tried to conjure up the other letter which she had read while
waiting for Dulcie, and take courage from it.

Oh lovely jubbly jellybean babyface.

The letter she opened now was the sixth in succession,
and was certainly devoid of affection. This letter-writer had
more control with words.

> *Dear Miss Fortune,*
>
> *How aptly named you are. You have what is
> mine and I want it back. I've explained this to you
> before, and you've ignored me. You could have left a
> letter for me to collect, as I asked. What I have in
> mind is a perfectly straightforward transaction,
> which won't leave you entirely penniless. After all,
> you've looked after the place for me for three years,
> and I owe you for that.*
>
> *Alas, you will not listen and it seems to me you
> need persuasion in order to see reason. I am watch-
> ing you. I regret the necessity of letters like this, when
> ALL I WANT IS JUSTICE.*
>
> *Accidents can happen.*

She turned and faced the plate-glass doors, which led out
to the busy road, where she knew she was spotlit. Just in case
he really was there, she put up two fingers and pulled a face.
Then she took the charcoal-grey coat from the posh bag,

shaking it free of tissue wrapping, and tried it on in front of the big mirror which allowed Fritz the doorman to see who came down the stairs at the same time as he could see who came out of the lift. A better, bigger mirror than she had in her flat upstairs. The coat swung, soft and light. She buttoned every single button; it still swung, like a suit of fluid armour. Let him watch, if he watched. Let him get blood on this. This was given with love. She picked up the coat bag, her own coat, and the letter, and took to the stairs. Three floors. Big doors in here. Accident-proof. Home.

Since the first letter had arrived, before Christmas, she had tried to walk up and down stairs, with a modicum of dignity, as if she was being watched. She knew her own value, as well as the complete uselessness of fear. Opening her own solid, double-locked door, to go into the familiar warmth of home, she was realising that the letters had got to her, because he was, quite simply, getting better at it. As if he knew that there was very little which made her nervous at all, except the strangeness of this silly persistence. She was guessing it was an old man; no one else wrote letters, except lovers. The letters were the equivalent of mere whisperings in the dark, picking at a scab until it bled, turning a scratch into a scar. They made her own scars, the visible and the invisible, itch.

They worked despite her own determination; they worked against either sense or reason, because she was not a great believer in luck. This was her flat, her name on the deeds and a lease of a hundred and twenty years. She closed the door against the world, went down the corridor to the end room, hating herself for moving in that direction against her own will. Put the letter with the rest on the desk, next to the single

spare bed with its white coverlet, and looked round a comfortable little room, the smallest in her flat.

She was afraid of nothing but her own conscience. She
simply disliked anyone who was cowardly enough to hide
behind anonymity. If this was an aggrieved brother of the
dear not-so-old judge who had left her the flat, let him say so.
Until he spoke clearly, she would ignore it. The severity of
the charcoal-grey coat looked fine with the frivolity of the
petal scarf. Her red curls looked good with both. Sarah
Fortune found the hat she usually preferred to an umbrella,
plucked Dulcie's handwritten card from the mounds of tissue
left in the coat bag, and went back towards the front door.
Dulcie's errands always came first. Hesitated, then stopped,
with her hand on the latch.

It was no good playing anyone else's game. There had
been enough disruption here. If someone was pretending to
have a right to her flat, let him prove it. He would have to do
better than that. Deluded people got worse if you responded,
smaller if you ignored. She knew, but all the same it would be
nice to know who it was.

Dulcie's geographical notion of what was near, or far, was
never very informative, and depended on a map peculiar to
her own mind. By near, she meant nearer than Kensington.
A cab stopped. Cabs stopped for a woman in a coat like this.
A coat like this spelled affluence, authority, and the promise
of good manners.

Dulcie was right: Golden Street was near; she really could
have walked, even though it was a thousand miles from
home. Near and far. The scale of everything changed en
route, from large and grand, to small and discreet, and back

again, as if some city-centre planner was playing games. No street the same; she loved it.

Golden Street was inaptly named, possibly with a sense of either optimism or irony attached, to reflect the fact that not all the streets of London were paved with gold. Original lampposts, Georgian fronts to tall, irregularly handsome houses, some of the windows boarded. There was a yellow glow from the lamps which illuminated the windows parallel with their height, the light scarcely reaching the uneven surface of the pavement. An almost Dickensian street, even to the nip of frost which had entered the air, solidifying the leftover rain; Georgian, bastardised by Victorian, then by twentieth century, and now by the twenty-first on one side only. The left-hand side of the street was more or less original; the opposite side was swathed in scaffold and flapping tarpaulin, the renovation or destruction or replacement hidden from view. On the Georgian side, several of the houses bore depressing neon signs, advertising cheap hotels, suggesting old lodging houses and mean rooms by the hour. Betwixt and between were the other houses, similar but not identical, which had no discernible identity and nothing to define them as homes. A deadish street in the evening, despite the hum of traffic from the square; a throughput of single pedestrians, at least one a minute, hurrying along on the way to somewhere else, then a throng of young, like a flock of noisier birds, passing through to the brighter lights at the other end. A mews, leading off, halfway down, and lots and lots of litter, which informed Sarah of the century she was in. A plastic bottle fetched up against a step, a glove on a railing, old flyers stuck against a lump in the pavement, a half-eaten sandwich, and a burst plastic sack on a doorstep, shedding paper, as if someone had just moved away and left the detritus of a short office tenure. A street of rentals and dubious, undecided ownerships, waiting on fate.

Sarah squinted at the address on Dulcie's card in the yellow lamplight, fumbling through the petal scarf for the spectacles which were usually worn round her neck on a silver chain. Dulcie's writing, like her directions, was bold and authoritative although not always clear. She favoured green ink, bad in this light. Number 16, surely. It was a street with eccentric numbering, jumping from 2 to 5, 11 to 15. None of the houses, except the Lotus Hotel, had a name.

She had turned off a busy thoroughfare, where traffic hurled itself round one of the larger squares. Looking at the road before her, with its row of parking meters and a smattering of parked cars, she imagined she could hear the sound of horses' feet and smell manure, rather than the flap of the tarpaulin on the hidden piece of progress on her right and the lingering smell of rain. She began to walk, uncertainly, squinting at the address. The street did not feel sinister or unsafe. It felt old and tired, waiting for something to change, as it had changed before, again and again, in a long career. Her feet in the high-heeled boots sounded sharp. Dulcie had given her the second talisman in the form of the gorgeous coat. She was invincible. *Jubbly jellybean babyface*.

Drawing level with a house with no visible number, Sarah paused. Light flooded from the doorway at the top of a short flight of badly worn steps. On the top step, a man sat, oddly, since he looked as if he was trying to bar the door itself, lying with his back to the jamb and his legs extended across the open threshold. He was wearing a short, dark-coloured jacket, a suggestion of a white collar at the neck, and the protruding legs were very thin. He had one shoe off, and one shoe on, and seemed to be examining a foot. A cat sat at his feet, defiantly bored and ginger.

She had the impression, and no more than that, that he was neither young nor old, and it was not himself which drew attention, but the hallway behind him, shining out in a vivid dark turquoise green, lit by a small sparkling chandelier which looked as old as the street. She stopped and stared at him. She might have passed on by, except for that gulp of colour and the fact that he was whistling. Sarah held on to the railing, peered at him and cleared her throat.

'Excuse me . . .'

When Dulcie ever attempted to describe Sarah, she would always try to explain that the girl had a voice with a laugh in it. You know, she would say, as if that was the next thing she was going to do, laugh at herself, as if everything was ridiculous. A seductive voice.

'Yes?' the man said, unfolding the arms which crossed his chest and folding them again. 'Yes, I might *excuse* you. Provided, unlike some people, you would tell me what for. Or why the hell I should.'

A nice voice, the voice of a teacher, perhaps, full of injured innocence. All the same, Sarah found this over-wordy response made her defensive.

'I'm asking you to *excuse* me for interrupting you, but only for long enough for me to ask you a question. I have a reason for the question, obviously. I'm looking for a house and for someone, but there is absolutely no reason at all why you should answer.'

Old windbag. She found herself looking at the foot. As her eyes adjusted to the light, she could see it was black and bruised. Also, as her eyes travelled towards his face, she could see that he was following the direction of her gaze, and smiling. The irritation died. It was a nice, clear face.

'How terribly rude of me,' he said, in the same mild, carrying voice. 'You say excuse me, in your pleasant voice, and I invite a debate. On a doorstep in a cold street in London. What a prat. Forgive me, but life has been more than a little irritating recently. What I should have said is *how can I help you?*'

She found herself going up the steps, attracted by the manner of him. The colour of the hallway behind him had a mesmeric quality, rich colour and light, beckoning one towards it. This had to be Dulcie's Henry, Ernest's expert in art, with a hallway to match. He had a courtroom voice and a serious face. Ernest had often chosen people for their looks. She crouched level with the cat.

'Is this your house?' she asked. 'Do you know this street?'

'Two questions in one. Yes, it's my house. *Part* my house. I am the only person I know of my age who still lives in the house where he was born. Yes, I know this street, or I did know it, once.'

She leant forward to touch the cat, which remained indifferent, and then withdrew her hand. It was impertinent to stroke a cat without permission either from the cat itself or the owner. As if cats were ever truly owned.

'Do be careful of your coat,' he said. 'I haven't swept these steps in a while. May be damp, also.'

'Do you know Henry Brett? Or if not, do you know which house is number eighteen? Could be sixteen, mind.'

He swung himself round so that both legs were inside the threshold. He placed the barefooted leg over the other one for support, and cupped his chin in his hand. A pedestrian passed by, without looking either left or right.

25

'There's only one Henry Brett,' he said. 'Why do you want to know?'

She shrugged as if it did not matter. This was surely Dulcie's Henry, and he did not look well.

'An old friend of his asked me to look him up and find out if he was all right.'

'A kind person, then.'

'*She* is, yes, extremely.'

'Well, there you have it. This is number sixteen. Do you know the time?'

The cat moved suddenly, without pausing to stretch, jumping over where the man's feet had been and darting into the green-blue hallway. Caught in the light of the chandelier, it was more the colour of mustard. Henry Brett cursed under his breath and began to scramble to his feet with surprising agility, pulling himself up with both hands clutching the doorframe, without putting weight on the bare foot, resting the heel on the ground.

'It's about seven fifteen,' Sarah began.

'Doesn't matter, doesn't matter, I don't need to know any more. She's coming back any minute, the cat always knows. I've got to get in quick, oh *bugger.*' He stood clutching the door, shaking, suddenly losing direction.

'Here, let me help.'

'Yes, please.'

She took his left arm and put it round her shoulders and he let her take his weight. He was thin and wiry, strong, but helpless, wanting to move quicker than he could.

'Which way?'

'Here, just here . . . Shut the door, quick.'

She kicked the front door closed behind them. Together they shuffled forward down the turquoise corridor to an open door on the left. Ahead of them she noticed a flight of stairs, with carved banisters and a fine newel post at the foot. The carpet beneath her feet was thick enough for Dulcie's taste, but she could see it was stained with peculiar white marks, as if someone had dropped bleach.

'Quick,' he muttered. 'Oh please, quick.'

Impeded by his tremor, they reached the inner door and went inside, where he shrugged her off, pushed the door shut behind them and hobbled into a room on the right. She hovered, uncertain, puzzled, intrigued, surely finding out more about Henry Brett sooner than Dulcie had intended. The room was dark, apart from the yellow light from the street outside, and the brighter light streaming in from the narrow hall behind her, lit by another chandelier. Sarah could see a dining table, flanked by ornate high-backed chairs, wooden shutters drawn back, and all she could hear was Henry's ragged breath. A car passed; then there was silence. She could smell old wood and wax. He was grasping the back of one of the chairs with both fists white in the light, breathing like a train. His face, in profile to the light from the window, was pale and terrified. It was very warm in here, heating full blast.

'What is it?'

'Shhhhh . . .'

In the near distance, she heard the front door of the house slam. Henry whimpered. After three seconds there was a loud knocking on the inner door, a pause, then a softer knock and a wheedling voice.

'I know you're there, dearest. How's the foot? I wish you'd let me help you. Don't want gangrene, do we? Ah well, suit yourself.'

Heavy footsteps plodded up the stairs. In the near distance, another door slammed so hard, it seemed as if the house shook. The footsteps continued over their heads. The man Sarah knew as Henry began to weep. Sarah touched his hand; it was icy cold. He took his hands from the chair and moved a step towards her, and she caught him, arms round his chest, his head landing in her hair, and there they stayed, in a long embrace, until his legs began to buckle and his trembling was less. She said nothing until he spoke. 'Oh, oh, that's lovely.' He sank into one of the chairs. She pulled out another in the semi-dark, opposite him, picked up the bare foot and tucked it into her lap, swathed in the folds of the open coat. Then she took his icy hands and began to chafe them warm. The weeping choked into silence, and he gave a great juddering sigh.

'Oh,' he said. 'I dreamt of this.'

She waited. She was good at waiting.

'What did you dream of?'

'Being hugged. Where do you come from?' he asked, bewildered. 'What do you do?'

She continued chafing his hands, feeling long, bony fingers, and callused palms. The palms of a man were the judging of him. Workman's hands. She judged a man by almost everything except the shape of his body. Judged by manners and voices, and mostly instinct. Sarah smiled at him.

'I'm a tart, Henry,' she said. 'I hug for a living. Now perhaps you can tell me what all this is about.'

CHAPTER TWO

There were gold stars on the ceiling. The body lay on the couch, without moving. Eleanor yawned.

There were a dozen kinds of bodies, three dozen, five dozen, in endless permutations, none ever looking like another, distinguishable by size and surface area, or whether they came into the category of sleepers or talkers. Some days, Eleanor thought she would actually prefer them to be dead, because they would be less of a nuisance. Mrs Hornby, with her thick neck and spongy back, was due in half an hour. That was the real problem. Eleanor would have liked to be able to choose her clients. Earning a living as a massage therapist could go to hell, and it made her feel bad to skimp on the sleepy patient she was treating simply because she was dreading the one who was coming next. The room smelt sweet, as dark and comforting as a womb, inviting secrets and sleep, designed to promote calm and help karma. Deep red floor, thick curtains of the same colour as the midnight-blue ceiling with the small gold stars which sprang into life when she turned on the light and they opened their eyes. A fantasy room, with a little touch of glitter, like the one she had wanted as a child. Exposed to broad daylight, it was a mixture of cheap effects and second-hand plumes which no one but she herself would see. Only the massage table was new.

Eleanor craved a forbidden cigarette. She wore ethnic cotton trousers for ease of movement and credibility, wanted silk, satin and high heels. She preached sound diet and positive attitude, preferred to eat crap, smoke and drink, and actively wanted something else carcinogenic to do, like sunbathing. She was depressed. Let the man sleep. He was breathing the even breath of a man without dreams, and surely would not notice that she had stopped touching him.

To be frank, she was sick of the touching, stroking and kneading. Grief made her sick of it, everything made her sick of bones and flesh. Sod those little gold stars. She was a long way from that first flush of idealism; the belief that she had in her hands the alleviation of pain, the dispensing of comfort, the curing of lives and the giving of hope. A creative healer, without years of wasted medical training which turned out pig-headed doctors.

She thought of Sasha, her partner, lover, friend, who had broken her back on a medical career. Been sued by that bitch. Lost and spurned, and spurning all who knew her.

The client breathed deep and quiet. Eleanor got up and twitched the curtains. Still daylight out there, not that he would guess. Massage therapists did not get sued, but there were still obligations to a kindred kind of Hippocratic oath, despite all the nod, nod, wink insinuations people still made about her kind of therapy. She could not abandon a patient; she was not allowed to give up. There were other rules, such as do not hurt people, try and make them better, tell the truth, as if truth was ever welcome. Like saying, yes, these aches and pains of yours are because you're too fat. Or, your doctor should have referred you for therapy long before he operated on your back, not long afterwards. The trouble was always getting people too late, and even more to the point, getting all these poor sods with twisted bodies, their pain, both actual and imagined, as real as a wound as well as a symptom of something wrong with their lives. Undiagnosed malcontent, grief, anxiety, wrong turnings, no choices, disappointment, loneliness, stupidity, things which could not be changed unless recognised and often not even then. Bodily distortion, great and small, the symptom of something else. After fifteen years, Eleanor thought that the problem with the majority of her patients started with their hearts and their heads and became locked in their limbs. To these she gave respite in the form of an hour to themselves, relaxation through touch, and the chance to talk. Or sleep. It was a second-rate version of being loved.

Face it, she told herself. You have never actually cured anyone of anything.

You have reached the point of boredom and disillusionment. You don't even want to try for a nice patient you like and you can't get rid of a patient you loathe. She made a desultory attempt to swipe the oil from the back of her sleeping man, and kneaded her knuckles into his shoulders.

She wiped her hands before turning up the light. Oil made everything sticky. At the end of the day, when they were gone, she would go through with the unethically chemical spray and paper towels, especially the lavatory seat in the loo next door. This was her domain. A dark room and a loo, and God help her, Mrs Hornby was next.

'Turn over, there's a love. Time to wake up.'

31

She liked them to wake up and see the stars gathering light as she turned up the dimmer switch as a gentle reminder that she wanted them out, time being valuable. He turned, and she struggled for a moment to remember his name.

'Wasn't asleep. Just resting.'

'Oh.'

'Always used to pretend to be asleep when I was a kid. Kept the old man off me.'

He bent his back off the narrow massage table, state of the art, adjustable, and reached for his toes, curling over an abdomen flatter than a piece of wood. Four stomach curls in a second, with his hands behind his head.

'Gonna tell me to drink water, are you? Gonna want thirty quid for doing next to nothing?'

She sat still, silent and ashamed.

'Sorry,' she said.

'Don't matter, doll. I've only come in twice, because someone told me it would be good for me, stop me twitching, and you're only round the corner. It's nice in here.'

He was stocky with muscle rather than superfluous flesh, yeoman build, with broad shoulders, from which his distinguished, disfigured face rose on a surprisingly long neck. When he turned towards the side light, he revealed a profile of startling attraction and an eye of piercing blue. When he turned his head towards her, she could see that it was a jigsaw puzzle of a face, with healthy skin to the left, contrasting with the shiny, thin skin on the right, dragged tight around the other eye, which was paler and watered in the cold.

'It was you who was dozing off,' he said, kindly. 'I suppose you thought it was a waste of time, getting as far as my feet. Still, you loosened up my shoulders something lovely.'

He was completely uninhibited in his dressing, which he

did so fast it put her in mind of someone on the run, used to making a swift exit from naked to clothed in two seconds. The speed was second nature; like a lover found in a husband's bedroom, or a soldier called to battle. The former image sat more easily with the man she now remembered only as Alan who worked in the Hotel Belvedere. At first sight he was far from ugly, normal, even handsome from three feet away, giving an impression of huge strength which was both reassuring and threatening. The plastic surgery on the facial burn was successful by any standard, but concentrating on him for the first time, Eleanor guessed he did not feel the same. He did not feel cured. His face satisfied a surgeon, but it was a pale imitation of a previous face and he disowned and despised it. His shoulders stiffened and ached, his back bent sideways with the weight of that face; his fists clenched and he held his breath in the effort to turn away from his own reflection, because it was not what it was and he was not the same man. His sleep was disturbed because the grafted skin itched to be scratched and he could not rest it against a pillow and it felt unreal, like tissue paper. He might ache out of sheer resistance. Using his fingers, he combed his thick hair into shape.

'To be honest, love, this massage business isn't really for me. Feel a bit silly. I'd be better off being out there, touting for business.'

'I thought you worked in the Belvedere.'

'That's my bread and butter, yeah. You still need the jam, don't you?'

He seemed relaxed and easygoing on the surface, fully dressed now, peeling off money from the roll in the top pocket of a fine cambric shirt, turning to look for his coat. She noticed he was beautifully dressed. Clothes mattered to him.

'I'm sorry,' she said. 'Keep the money. I didn't do you justice.'

'Nah, take it, doll. We've all got to live. I didn't mean to be rude. And I could get used to pampering, only I can't really afford it.'

She took the money. There were still minutes to go before the hour was up. Eleanor felt that she did, at least, owe him a little conversation, and suddenly wanted to distract herself from the fact that Mrs Hornby would arrive in fifteen minutes precisely.

'I don't suppose the pay's much good in the hotel world, is it?' she asked. 'Must have glamorous moments, though. The Belvedere's pretty smart.'

She did not know; she was guessing.

'There isn't much glamorous about dossing in a hotel, doll, and looking after so-called security. The five stars it's got are worth as much as those on your ceiling.' He grinned, emphasising the jigsaw effect of his face. 'They come and go, you know, same old, same old. Thieves and drunks everywhere.'

She opened the door from the magic room and felt the draught down the corridor. The chipped paint on the other side and the bare passage leading out were a better indication of Eleanor's precarious status than the interior of her rented room. Rents were cheap here, but not cheap enough. He made a brief bow, gave a small wave.

After he had gone, Eleanor tidied the room, dismissing the thought of another failure. She was thinking how tempting it would be to sprinkle sand on the couch for Mrs Celia Hornby and trying to pull herself together, while instead she unrolled fresh paper. The man had worn good aftershave, which left a lingering scent, stronger than the oil. Eleanor was trying to recall how she had explained her hatred of Mrs

Hornby to herself, trying to make herself think it through. Right, she hated Mrs Hornby because that woman had wrecked the career of Sasha Anderson, and had thus, at one remove, wrecked their entwined lives. Sasha had operated on Mrs Hornby to explore a cyst on an ovary. She took the sickly ovary out. Strictly speaking, she should have woken her up and asked her permission first, but it was safer to do it her way. The patient was past childbearing, but it was still a technical breach of the rules. Mrs Hornby had screamed and ranted and sued, secured a large settlement out of the health authority and Sasha's reputation was mud. No one wanted to employ a female gynaecologist who cost money. She had slunk away to another city where she was not known. It was the end of the affair. So why keep treating her now? Eleanor had asked herself in the quiet of the swimming pool. I can't give up because I hate her. She was here first. It would be unprofessional. I go on because, foolish though she is, she actually *listens* to me. OK, she doesn't believe the diagnosis, but she believes I can make her better. Perhaps I enjoy the power. She almost allows herself to be hypnotised. Perhaps I enjoy punishing myself. And I don't any longer have so many devoted clients that I can afford to turn one away.

That was the real truth. They were stuck with one another, only it was more than that.

Mrs Hornby didn't know the Sasha connection; why should she? She was entirely self-obsessed. She had a life of self-imposed misery which she spread like an infection. Eleanor pulled back the curtain, peered out, and saw her coming down the street. She had a doughy face, like porridge. She was thin, but carried her fat in pockets slung around her, had the profile of a pug dog. Her straight hair was pinioned beneath a metallic headband. She was guilt personified. No doubt about who she was.

These days, Alan had a few doubts about what he was himself, never more prevalent than when he had to say, *I can't afford it.* There was something very unmanly about that, just as there was about wanting your own body to stay as good as it could be at fifty plus. Being a man was difficult. Whatever else it involved, it required cash. Still, he was on his way to a late breakfast and maybe a bit of business, so maybe he was turning a corner. He needed to turn that corner, go back to what he had been. A man. There were not too many good male role models in his life. It was the women who counted. His mother had told him what a shit his father was, although that was perfectly obvious from the bruises Dad inflicted. His gran, with whom Alan had worked the East End market stalls when he was five, told him what a useless old sack his grandad was, which was equally obvious from the fact that Grandad never moved out of his armchair until he finally shifted himself into bed and died. But he had been kind, which told Alan that kindness alone was not enough to make a man, any more than brute force was. Pack leaders had to have more, and to keep the admiration of women you had to have much, much more. Alan's moral compass came from an anarchic peer group of street kids, the elder statesmen of the local criminal fraternity for whom he had run errands; then the market traders at Columbia Road and beyond, selling everything from plants to bric-à-brac, and most of all, his gran. Gran told him cash was king and you never turned anything down. Learn a good trick; do it again and again.

He stroked his face and walked on. No, he must keep his

pride. To be a man, you had to be able to make money and turn a trick; you had to be able to fix and mend, although not always at the first time of asking. You had to come home at night, but not every night. You had to be able to fight without losing and not get caught, have the element of the brute about you, but not all the time. You had to owe no one. Forty years down the line, Alan was still trying to work out the proper ingredients of the kind of manhood to which he had aspired, which other men respected and women adored, and he had only got as far as realising that the two could not be reconciled. The only thing which was equally important to both was looks and cash.

He was anxious, and that was a bad habit. Nervous that the man would turn up at the meeting place, and depressed at the prospect that no one would, ever again. If he hadn't got the looks, he'd got to have the cash.

He stood outside, a few steps away from the door of the house where Eleanor had her room. It was the kind of mish-mash street he liked best. Looks were everything, keep up appearances, but then there was the puzzling fact that he felt he was a nicer man himself since he lost his face, although not that much nicer. Made him notice more, instead of wait-ing to be noticed. Couldn't afford niceness. Not many choices left, but at least he had something good. He had London to live in, and a woman friend. Women needed favours and they needed looking after. He loved women, all women, almost without exception, and he was in danger of needing one in particular.

Henry had forgotten that he was nervous around women. He had been prowling round, like his own cat, exploring her territory with her permission. He touched the door, then raised a fist, and knocked on it gently. The contact of his knuckles made hardly a sound. Sarah found him, listening for an echo.

'Fireproof,' he said admiringly. 'Two inches thick and fire-proofed at the back. And just look at that lock.'

He held the door wide open for Sarah's inspection. She looked at it.

'Not only the lock, but the bolts into the frame, see? It'd take twenty minutes to get through this with a sledgehammer. It's a proper safe room. No messing about here. All done to a very high standard. Lovely.'

'I think it's hideous.'

'Why?'

'The necessity's hideous. A room within a home where you can lock yourself away? Like paranoid millionaire stuff. Or an Egyptian queen in her sepulchre. I've ignored it. I never close doors, you see.'

'You knew it was there. You talk in your sleep.'

'Nonsense.'

'You do. Although it would be stretching a point to call it intelligible. And I was too charmed, too safe to listen, but you did mention a safe room. You said, *he needs a safe room*. In my vanity, I thought you were talking about me. I could never have thought that a woman like you really existed. You took me to hospital. You listened to my gabbling while we waited for the doctor. Then you argued with the doctor. You brought me home and filled me with gin and put me to bed and hugged me. And you've let me sleep all day long. I'm not a new man. I'm a severely traumatised, nervous, shy man, but I'm immeasurably better than I was. I suppose I should go home to my cat. You must have known you had a safe room. It's inconceivable you didn't.'

'You do use far too many words, you know. No, I didn't. There was always this small room at the end, and far too many locks all round, as far as I was concerned. I didn't buy this flat, you see. No one showed me round, or anything like that. I was just told it was mine. And I arrived. Then I ceased to notice the details I didn't need. Do I really talk in my sleep?'

'Not enough,' he said.

'Come on,' she said. 'There are better things to see in this flat than the spare bedroom, even if it is safe. And I'd like you to tell me again what you've told me so far. Otherwise Dulcie Mathewson will kill me.'

He followed her down the corridor which bisected her flat, into the living room. It was becoming afternoon dark again; whenever was it not dark? She walked like a dancer. A prance in the step, like the laughter in her voice. And she talked in her sleep. He never knew a tart could be like this. A carer, in need of caring.

'Dulcie,' he murmured. 'Dear Dulcie. What a treasure.'

There was a small sketch on the wall nearest the living room which fronted her apartment. A man on a bicycle, pedalling away, with his hat blowing off behind him. Charming. Henry, as he now knew himself to be, after weeks of confusion, was wondering how to pay for services rendered in this perfectly comfortable, slightly down-at-heel apartment in a block rather too grand for it. The two did not match. The exterior was pretentious; her interior not.

'Sarah,' he called after her. 'I can pay you in paintings. Things, not money.'

She was in the kitchen, pulling a cork out of a bottle.

'I've already been given a coat,' she said. 'And the cat has enough to eat for another day. We'll get pizza.'

'I must go home,' he said.

'Not yet. It's early yet. And yes, if paintings are what you've got, that'll be fine.'

He liked the room, although he knew that in another life he would have been appalled by it. Nothing quite finished, nothing to the highest standard, and yet the comfort. A fire, some mock gas fire, mimicking long-alight coals, framed the room, false but disarmingly cosy. One enormous painting, squashy chairs and the sofa, on which he sat, suddenly tired and bewildered, wondering quite what it was he had said the night before, and the morning after, regretting none of it but wishing it had been clearer, to himself, let alone his hostess. That was a good word, hostess. It reminded him to be a good guest, within a different set of rules. No other hostess had ever encouraged him to talk so much and then, injured as he was, taken him to bed.

He had told her about Mrs Hornby, but probably not in order. He had told her, in the hospital queue, about how it was his house, and she wanted it. He sighed, accepting wine, looking around with pleasure. Sarah Fortune might have been lacking in the finer points of taste, but she knew how to hug and she was not a bully. He felt sublimely privileged, and he was not used to it. And there might have been a chip out of the crystal glass she offered him but it was good crystal. Life was difficult for a snob. There was a virtue in non-antique furniture. He could place his foot, festooned in the sort of moon boot he associated with an astronaut, on to her sofa. She stuffed cushions beneath it, raising his skinny leg to hip height. Then she lay down next to him. It was quite unlike any tart's parlour he had ever visualised, and for all that, the room he liked best was the safe room. A pretty little bedroom, high above the world, safer than houses. That was the room he wanted.

'I'll remind you I was once a lawyer,' she said, at just the right time for the warmth of her body and the warmth of the fire to penetrate his skin. 'So, Mr Pedantic, *one* tries to deal in certainties. I got it all, about Mrs Hornby and all you know about her, I *heard* her, for God's sake, but what's the history? Why does she behave like that? Why do you allow it?'

He was about to say, *because I'm a mother's boy and a hopeless bachelor, easily bullied by women,* thought better of it.

'It's because of Golden Street,' he began. 'Golden Street was once golden,' he said. 'I can never leave it. I was born there. It decayed and it will rise. I have to guard it, you see.'

'Oh,' she said.

'It was once exquisitely bourgeois. I was born there, fifty-five years ago. The truly exquisite period was probably long before that, but it was safe and genteel. We always felt rather superior and privileged in that street, because it was *our* house, my parents and I, and so few people actually owned a house then.'

An only child, Sarah surmised. That might explain a lot. She thought of her own brother and wondered where he was.

'It was a street of respectable hotels, and small institutions. It had the perfect Georgian frontage, but in the 1950s no one cared much about that. Except my mother, who was the sort who scrubbed her front doorstep, painted her railings and furnished us from junk shops, of which there were many. People were keen to throw out the old and bring in the new. Lino, instead of wood floor, Formica instead of wooden tables, electric fires instead of the muck of coal. Plastic and nylon instead of cotton. She wasn't having any of it.'

'She sounds very definite.'

'She set very high standards,' he amended, and sipped his

wine. 'And you may be thinking that a definite, domineering, house-proud mother with rigorous standards and taste could go some way to explaining my bachelor status, and you might be right. My father died when I was young, my mother three years ago. I had left her alone in a street which had become a series of hotels where you let the room for twenty minutes a time. Or, in the seventies, it was students trying dope, cheap rentals and pimps. Not nasty but seedy. With one perfect house. So I came back from where I was to keep the flame alive. To keep it going; to get some continuity into my life. To make up for what I gambled away, and the pain I caused her.'

He stroked the chip in the lip of his crystal glass, enjoying the imperfection. Better a good thing damaged than a piece of cheap completeness. Yes, he was a snob of a kind. He was finding it strange that this current sensation of feeling safe, and even loved, lent greater clarity to his thinking than anything else.

'But it's a house of many rooms. Bigger than it seems, the way those houses are, like warrens. The heart of my house is the raised ground floor, with its three rooms, and the next best thing about it is the kitchen and the garden, downstairs. You might like the garden. Surprisingly big. Anyway, I sort of *lost* the house I had, and then, and then . . . had a career blip . . . or should I say, brainstorm. I mean, a kind of breakdown. Couldn't work any more. I needed the money, so I split the house and sold the top half. To a woman who seemed charming and sympathetic. She got it cheap, three years ago. I kept the heart of it.'

He sighed, then pulled a face at his own sighing. She was still listening, as intently as if she was making notes.

'Always was a fool with money. Should have hung on.

Should never have lost what I had. Now Golden Street is on the turn again. Not turned yet, but on the way. The rail link, another couple of years, the houses will be priceless.'

'Nothing explains why your charming neighbour tyrannises you. Does she want to drive you out?'

He shook his head. 'I don't know,' he said. 'I just don't know. At first I thought she wanted *me*, while I didn't want her, not even as a mother substitute. Otherwise I've no idea why she hates me. But she does, oh she does.'

'How did it start?'

'Lawyers' letters. Saying she could hear me cough, that I must insulate the floor above my head which she refused to carpet. Then another saying *we* must insulate the roof. Then another saying she was entitled to use of the garden for her damn bird. Then another saying I could not have a fire, because the smoke seeped into her room. Then three floods from her bathroom. She taunts me.'

'Lawyers' letters used as weapons,' Sarah observed.

'Yes, it's a hobby of hers.'

'An expensive one,' Sarah said. She rose, gracefully, and drew the curtains. He noticed them for the first time, because they were the colour of thick whipped cream, banded with dull gold ribbon, elaborate by Sarah's standards.

'Nice,' he said.

'I was given them by a neighbour who grew out of them. I specialise in the second hand.'

'Please come back.'

She refilled the crystal glasses, and settled beside him again, as if she had known him for ever. He knew he should go home. He was a coward not to go home, and he had a cat. Sarah tapped an unpolished fingernail on the side of her glass, making a musical *ping*.

'Then there was the noise. I did the roof, implored her to carpet her wooden floors. She said it was her right not to do so. Then, more noise. TV above my bedroom, music booming wherever I was. Then awful cooking smells, incessant onion, then things spilt in the hall, dye on the carpet, then fish left for the cat, it almost died. Then more music, if you could call it that, late at night. I called the police, but all was ever silence when they arrived, so that I looked like the ogre, and she, bewildered.' He paused, ashamed. 'I became afraid. Pathetic, nervous.'

'What's *she* afraid of?' Sarah asked.

'Nothing,' he said. 'She has the malevolence of the entirely self-righteous. Nothing touches her, which is what makes her so frightening.' He paused and sipped. Suddenly it all seemed very petty. Beside him Sarah stirred and then seemed to come to a decision. What she said next was lightly spoken, ridiculous of course, out of the blue like that, but the very idea was monstrously appealing.

'Your mother sounds a lot like mine, only I went in the opposite direction. Listen, dear Henry, it seems to me that we have a lot in common. You seem to have someone who is trying to prise you out of your flat, and I have someone who is trying to scare me about the ownership of mine. No, that's an exaggeration, but the fact is, it might be a good idea for me to be away from home for a little while. Perhaps we should do a swap. I'm OK with cats.'

The thought of going home made him shake. What she suggested, like the rest of her, seemed entirely natural. He longed for that safe room. A few days in that, and he would be brave.

'What about your . . . er . . . business?' he asked.

'My business is mainly conducted in other people's houses.

I only make exceptions on rare occasions, and in emergencies, like yourself, of course.'

'And not for long,' he said, sadly.

'No, not for long. No one stays here for long, and let's face it, Henry, you wouldn't want it for long. A few days? A week or so? What do you think?'

They watched television like an established couple at the end of an era together, ate pizza and went to bed. The complete naturalness of this had ceased to surprise him. The aircast boot stood like a sentinel in the corner, detached for sleep, and the, this time, chaste hugging delighted him. She cared for him, shrouded him with herself, let him breathe the same breath. And it was not enough. Somewhere in the early hours he woke in a hot panic with a buzzing noise in his ears, got up quietly and, driven by an instinct he did not understand, hobbled away from her bedroom and into the end room, with the desk and the single bed. The safe room with the heavy, reinforced, fireproof door, with its fuck-off lock, easing shut behind him, the ultimate security; even with the key on the outside, it felt safe.

Sarah woke and heard, through the ever-open door of her own room, the sound of that soft, heavy door closing on him, and knew immediately what he had done, and thought she knew why. He was a very frightened man. He wanted the safety of locks and solid doors, like a badger going underground. He craved a small space in which to hide and lick his wounds, and he needed that more than he needed company, or any other kind of solace. He would sleep sounder in there than anywhere else. He needed to be able to touch the walls. He wanted to be locked into a small space, in order to be safe.

She paused on the outside, looking at the key in the lock, imagining the handle on the other side, with which he could release himself.

How was she going to explain this to Dulcie? You know your friend? I locked him up and left him there. He really did want to be alone, and that is the only way that some people can cure themselves.

A man traumatised by more than he was ever going to tell. Yet. Embracing alone was not going to cure him, and while that was not particularly flattering, it was also true, and she knew her limitations. Although, of course, there was no way of knowing whether he was telling the truth. You never did know with men.

Eleanor Fuller dreamt of Celia Hornby, and woke from a bad sleep. It was a terrible dream, which she tried to distance by thinking of her, referring to her by title and surname, the way she did with no one else. It was 'Mrs Hornby' on that summons which spiralled Sasha into despair. And in the dream it was Mrs Hornby lying next to Eleanor, as naked as she was, with her pudgy fingers touching Eleanor's spine. She kicked off the duvet and lay in the hot emptiness of her bed until she was cold to her bones and sane enough to get up and make camomile tea. Standing in her kitchenette, waiting for the kettle to boil, she tried to rid herself of the vision of that flesh. Mrs Hornby never drifted off to sleep during her therapy; instead, she talked throughout, in a steady stream of bile, which was never enough to distract Eleanor from the awful texture of her skin.

Mrs Hornby was a slender beast clothed; and unclothed looked like a pig. A plasticine body, stuck together in lumps, with a head on a stick of a neck, like a doughnut on a spike. A terrible rosebud mouth, with permanent red lipstick. Hips encased in spongy mounds of flesh, as if her bottom had shifted to the sides, flabby upper arms which dangled over the narrow table. There was a complete absence of muscle tone anywhere. A lazy, middle-aged body, prematurely old; in short, there was nothing to inspire such revulsion. There were far worse bodies than this: obese men, women at fifteen stone who were also beautiful, stunning in their defiance of gravity or fashion. It was not the flesh itself, or the shape of her; it was not the ridiculous sexy underwear, it was *what*? It was a body which had pampered itself to the point of decay, and it was the smell of moisture milk and ingrained perfumes, a sick, talcumed baby smell. Celia was always washed, but she still smelt. Of medicine and vitamins, of someone who feasted and then starved: amino acid breath, a mustiness, a scent Eleanor associated with mothballs, camphor and old soap. Embalming fluid. Oh, this was nonsense, the stuff of morbid imagination, but it made her want to wash her own hair, over and over, especially when Celia attempted to stroke it. With those strong hands, which grabbed Eleanor by the arm and said, help me up, dear, her red fingernails digging like claws into Eleanor's forearm and remaining there because she could not shake her off. And Mrs Hornby's voice, telling all she had told, and ending with, 'When I've got more space, dear, you can have a room with me. I'll look after you.'

And the look on her doughy face, which was horribly like love.

CHAPTER THREE

Fire kills, slowly, sometimes. This was amateur.

The trick was to get out before it started. Making fires was an art; a delicate process. When he was a naughty small boy, Alan had always wanted to watch the flames. As soon as he had learnt that arson was not only an art, but an art worth payment, he would try to be away long before the smoke, let alone a single tongue of flame. He could not sit in the same room as a fire any more, so nowhere would ever be home.

The smoke, ballooning lazily from the window, had gathered a small group, paralysed with curiosity. Always happened, but any sane person who saw or smelled smoke should run away, the way a dog would, because anything could happen. Animals knew best. Fire did not have a steady, linear progress; it was voracious and unpredictable, demanding evasion and respect. Still, he was only human; waited and watched, for a minute, like all the rest, only with a more professional interest.

The ground floor of the building in Silver Street was a shabby newsagent-and-everything-else shop. The smoke came from the window of the storeroom above. No one seemed particularly alarmed. The shopkeeper and his family stood outside, waiting, and a woman cried, without much conviction. Either they knew they were lucky, or one of them knew they had done more or less what they intended. The clarion call of a fire engine sounded in the distance. Poor sods, he thought: all that adrenalin at this time in the morning, and all for a two-pump call-out, well on time. Alan pulled his scarf over his mouth and moved on.

Maybe the crowd wanted flame, or the sight of gallons of water, shot from a giant hose used like a weapon. A fight with fire. It would not be like that. They would advance slowly, from the inside, with this one, small bursts of water. They would not want to be boiled in steam; they would want to know what was in that smoke.

If smoke and fire competed with each other for the damage they did, smoke would win. Smoke was the sneaky killer. Man and fire: the perfect symbiosis for maximum destruction. Silly sods. You could smell the petrol from here. Must have thought that was all it took, bit of petrol, newspaper, they thought that was it.

The smoke was a soft chocolate brown, changing colour as it dissipated, and when the firemen arrived they would compound the work of destruction, because what they had to do was the equivalent of culling cattle to prevent the spread of infection. Buildings were also culled. He liked the idea of that, since buildings alone did not matter, but he wished it had not crossed his mind to wonder if there was an animal left inside. Alan walked on towards his breakfast, like any other businessman, watching London waking up, but not

49

fully awake yet, imagining himself in a balloon above the city, drifting in the smoke of the fires which would begin and end over any twenty-four hours, and wondering if the geezers in the trucks would think that early morning was not the most popular time for arson. Alan had not set a fire in over a year, far too long. Ever since the one where he had been so cautious that the damage was incomplete, and the man who had paid him in advance took revenge on his face.

Soft hands, cupping his chin, like a vice.

It was still dark when Celia Hornby woke, and lay extremely still before experimenting with a slow easing of limbs, fingers and toes first. Greeting the day without caution had big pain potential, especially soon after a massage, but oh, silly, silly, mustn't complain 'cos of hurting in the mornings, must we? Should be used to it by now, bad back for a year and that neck of hers so stiff she had almost forgotten what it was like to turn her head. Always walked straight ahead, did not see anything coming towards her from round a corner. Story of her life. Should be nimble and mobile at forty-eight, would be again, so much to do. Could not afford to feel one hundred and ten years old at the last count, oh no, and my, aren't we sorry for ourselves this morning? She frowned, remembering how Eleanor had said, *keep movement to a minimum,* and how that was Eleanor changing her tune, the dear, dear girl, since she had always used to say the opposite before, but she knew best. Except when she suggested that Celia might have an inherited disease, at which point Celia closed her ears, every time. She had no such thing. She would not hear of it. Her family had *nothing* like that. They had all died with straight backs and pure hearts, and the idea of inherited disease was entirely unnatural and repellent from a lineage such as hers, simply an excuse for doctors not knowing what to do.

The silence was profound at the back of the house, so complete that she knew the place had been empty for the second night in succession. The thought appalled her, and made the day almost entirely without purpose, leaving her impotent and furious. Supposing he was planning something? Training his cat to kill? Supposing he was trying to *sell*? Oh, no, no, that would not do. It should be hers. *Move . . . slowly.* His absence was an affront, and silence was not good for her. She moved, slowly and cautiously, supporting her neck with her hand until she was upright. She had duties, after all, responsibilities, tasks. Boris the budgerigar was no longer youthful. Outside the constant subject of her dreams, and her dreams for the future, Boris was all she loved. Eleanor would love Boris, when she came to live with them.

Who's a pretty girl, then?

Boris Mark 2 had always been tactile. He had come into her life in Putney when she was clinging to her futile occupation of a matrimonial home, which Boris Mark 1, her husband, had already left. She was fighting divorce and fighting to keep it, and would have considered setting it on fire to spite him, except she was afraid of fire. Boris 2 made her see sense. He had a beak as cruel-looking as Boris 1's nose; she took him home to torture, with a book of instructions.

If a bird is hard to tame or train, or if you wish to restrict its movements, cut the wing feathers. You may cut only one wing, inhibiting flight purely because of the unevenness of the wings, or alternatively cut a few feathers on both wings, leaving the last three feathers. This is aesthetically more pleasing, and allows the bird to fly evenly, although it cannot go far.

She did both wings, and Boris did not seem to mind

remaining beautiful and crippled. She enjoyed the trimming of his claws, and the straightening of his bowed legs, too, and in the days before the final move, when she had at last found what Jane Austen called a good enough address to make it look as if she was not losing everything, she concentrated on starving Boris until he ceased his constant cheerful cheeping. A conscientious starvation, by which she meant she gave the bird daily grooming and everything else it required, a fantastic cage, a wooden perch for the clipped claws, the right diet (crushed cooked scallop shell and charcoal, bone meal and rock salt, greens, seeds and grit), ample for health, only just not enough to keep it from hunger. That was what the real Boris had done to her, after all. Gave her a promise and then took it away. In marrying a builder, she had married beneath the cultural and aesthetic standards of her family, but he had given her another status and a house, and then slapped her down, like everyone else.

In circumstances of perfect hygiene, Budgerigar Boris faded and exhibited the classic symptoms of illness, stopped behaving like a healthy bird and stood with his head tucked under his wing, smooth feathers ruffled in misery. And then produced an egg. Celia Hornby was horrified and remorseful. Boris was a *girl*. She fell into a fever of love, overfeeding and abject apologies, but she never changed the name. It was too late for that.

In the accusatory silence, Boris was the sole reason for living this morning. *Who's a pretty girl, then?* Her gilded cage was pristine; her resistance to speech tuition had been absolute and consistent, and she thrived in her third year. I'll make it up to you, promise, Celia said to her, three times a day, and Boris remained silent. She had told Eleanor this. She told Eleanor everything. Such a wonderful listener.

She needed exercise and handling, Boris; she had to be monitored for health, her cage charged with food and toys. To hold her without harm meant holding her in the palm of the hand, with the thumb and forefinger supporting and enclosing the head, while the other three fingers enclosed the body and left the tail feathers free. She must exercise her feet and her wings by walking and fluttering; she was better at descending from the ceiling than she was at ascending in the first place. She had become to Celia a thing of indescribable beauty, raising her trusting eyes as Celia held her, softly, in the palm of her hand, thumb and forefinger supporting, never squeezing the neck, the way Celia would have loved to have been held herself. Once and for ever.

'Time for our eyedrops, darling,' she murmured. 'And a teeny, weeny clip of that beak. Then,' she added, as she mimicked a kiss, 'lovely breakfast. Not too much. Mustn't get fat, like Mummy.'

She could feel the heartbeat in her hand, beating against a tiny ribcage.

Holding the bird, and taking her towards the window, the silence afflicted her again. A milk float in the street. They woke late here. The insulation between her half of the house and his downstairs was disgraceful at the best of times, but it had been *cheap*, for such a *good* address, with the right post-code and a prettily named street, so no one she had known would guess she had come down in the world. Now there was no one there, she missed the sound of switches, the noise of his radio, everything and anything which gave her a clue to his movements, and her intimate knowledge of them all. She had craved the silence of his absence, and then hated it. Hated silence.

'Speak to me, sweetheart,' she whispered to Boris.

53

Then she heard it: the sound of the front door, opening and closing, reverberating in a house as old as this. She moved to the front door of her own flat, and opened it, carefully, with her left hand, aware that the door too had its own unmistakable sound. The stairwell was black, but she could always hear the exact sound of his key in his lock, imagine the way that he fiddled it, expertly, because it demanded a certain presentation, becoming automatic after a while, but not with this person, this time. A stranger was coming into her house. Standing in her open doorway, her own heart pounding, looking down at the stains and crumbs on the carpet, which came into focus as her eyes adjusted to the light, she suddenly realised that her right hand was squeezing Boris in a cruel and passionate grip, and with a cry of alarm, she let go.

Sarah loved the early part of the day; she often saw it only on her way home, which added to the piquancy of it. She was always moving around London in a different direction to everyone else: going home as they embarked to work, going out in the middle of the day, when everyone else was in, issuing forth at hours when honest workers worked. It was part of the luxury of her existence, being a lady who lunched and took tea, that she could shop when shops were half empty, eat when the hordes had gone, avoid the transport crush. An enormous privilege. Each time she was abroad at the dawn of the day, she promised herself that she would do it deliberately, rather than accidentally, simply to walk and watch and sit, when everything was relatively clean and fresh.

She walked the mile between Buckingham Mansions and Golden Street, wearing the coat. Half-light in winter, the safest time of day, muggers and pickpockets still in bed. The pedestrians were the industrious, the cleaners who caught the first bus, the ambitious racing to work to get ahead of the game while she was at leisure to watch, observe and try and guess what it was each of them did, where they fitted into the pattern, if pattern there was, and how they felt at the onset of the day. Skulking along reluctantly and resentfully, kicking the ground, sorry to have left the place from which they came and not looking forward to the next destination. Walking with braced shoulders and evident relief to have escaped whatever home had been abandoned for the day, full of anticipation. Others, in a numbed daze, moving as if on prearranged signals, controlled from somewhere else, scarcely remembering to look left and right before crossing the road. The traffic moved rowdily. She noticed the misted windows on a bus, silhouettes huddled inside, waiting defensively for the shock of the cold, and she pulled up the collar of her coat. The silk lining felt clean. The damn coat was too new; it needed a little dirtying, so that she could treat it with less respect and make it part of her own, imperfect self, and she had time, so she chose a grubby-looking bench in the square, and sat in contemplation of her surroundings. The buildings frowned down upon her, condemning such idleness as she took off her hat, reminding herself to put it on again soon.

The square she had adopted was still winter bleak, yet full of promise. Green-brown grass, with bare shrubs and trees, and in the flowerbed next to her, the first shoots of early crocus. She used the time to examine the keys to Henry's flat: an old-fashioned thing of massive proportion plus a Yale for the front door; and a five-lever Ingersoll for the inside door. The man cared more about security for his own flat than he did for the house as a whole. She would be able to get in, although all keys developed tricks and habits over time, requiring a knack the owner forgot he had ever acquired. A pigeon limped round her feet, hoping for food. She found a crumbling cereal bar at the bottom of her bag, crumbled it some more and scattered it. A man strolled past with an open cup of coffee in a Styrofoam cup, sipping it. The smell travelled, and tantalised. Mornings made her know she was lucky.

Golden Street was deserted, the tarpaulin on the developing side of the road gleaming with damp. Burgeoning daylight made it new, different and tolerable. Sarah could see that Henry's side of the street was not as neglected as it looked by night. There were at least two freshly painted doors, and several renewed windows. The two grubby guesthouse hotels were actually shut for business, awaiting new occupation, a sight which made her relieved for the guests who had avoided the privilege. Even the houses with boards instead of glass looked solid, so Henry was right: his home street was en route to better times and higher value. The old post-war landlords had died or sold up.

The big key felt warm in her hand, although inserting it into the door she felt like a trespasser, because she knew she looked like one. Bending down, peering at the lock through her spectacles, working out which way the key should go, this way up or that way up, obviously unfamiliar. A feeling of discomfort made her pause and look round to see if she was observed, guilty, as if she had been forbidden to do as she did, instead of permitted. In this interlude before the day began in earnest, there was no one: only a grey light. Sarah hated the necessity for keys, wondered why the world persisted with them. There should always be a button to press, rather than these ever-awkward, ever-ugly implements which belonged in some dark age.

The key required a knack, like all unfamiliar types of keys, and she mastered it soon enough. The door opened on to the turquoise hallway, cheerful and rich and incongruous with everything around it, but shaded, as she shut the door behind her. There was disappointment in finding it so: she remembered the opulent light of the chandelier illuminating colour which had drawn her in the first place. She felt for a switch, must be one somewhere, her fingers grazing the wall fruitlessly. Gradually her eyes adjusted to the dim light arriving via the small curved window above the front door, augmented from the top of the stairs by a dimmer suggestion of light. The key was awkward. Keys were a bane of life. They made a fool of you. The gloom was oppressive.

There was a strange sound, almost like the sensation of someone breathing close by, and then a tiny hand landed on her shoulder. *Something* landed on her shoulder, as silent as a spider. It was a slight and sinister sensation, which made her want to shout; instead, she froze into absolute stillness, her hand extended, the second key in the lock, and the whole of her paralysed. The bird fluttered its wings; she could feel something soft touching her cheek, and she choked on the scream, kept it at the back of her throat, where it died. She wanted to bat the spider away, run away, get it off, it was like fingernails without fingers, but she stood, kept her eyes focused on her hand, turning the key. In the pause of a long second, interrupted by small, breathy sounds, some other sixth sense told her that whatever *it* was, it was less than dangerous, almost weightless, alien, not lethal. She disciplined herself to take a deep breath as the key clicked and she pushed at the door. Get light on this scene; if only her hand would stop shaking. Then someone else was screaming.

'Boris, Boris, Boris!!!! Darling, where are you?'

Sarah thought at first that it was her own voice, shrilling from inside her head, and then the light came on and there were footsteps from above, pounding down. The door into Henry's flat was open. There was more light on the scene; it felt miraculous. Slowly Sarah turned her head and saw the profile of the tiny bird, blurred by proximity. *'Shush, honey, shshh,'* she said. Equally slowly, she placed her right hand on her left shoulder and felt it, clawing painlessly at her fingers. She moved her hand to the front of her body. The bird fluttered for purchase and held on. The yellow feathers were almost fluorescent. Sarah turned round in the direction of the voice and the thundering noise of heavy feet, and when she saw, she recoiled. A small, featureless woman, making all that noise. The place echoed with her.

'Boris . . . oh, thank God.'

She was face to face with a woman, dressed in a dressing gown, clutching the banister with one hand, the other clawing at her own neck. Beneath the light of the chandelier, the doughy skin of her face resembled something half cooked, and she was coughing, making an ugly, phlegm-filled noise, which seemed to calm her. The bird fluttered and held on.

'Oh no,' the woman shrieked again, recovering herself rapidly. 'Oh no, no, *no*, Boris, I thought you'd fallen to your death. Not a good little flyer, are you? Come to Mummy, there's a love.'

She held out her hand, almost touching Sarah's. The gesture was beseeching, strangely pathetic. The bird held on to

Sarah's fingers, then padded across the back of her hand, gingerly, across her wrist and on to the sleeve of her coat. She wanted to lower her arm. It was difficult to hold it as steady as if it was a perch. My, oh my, so this was Mrs Hornby, Henry's nemesis. The one who sabotaged his house, threw dye and litter on his carpet, flooded his rooms, ruined his nights, and wanted him mad or dead. In this light, she did not look very frightening. She looked pitiful, until she spoke, when Sarah noticed her piercing brown eyes, narrowing.

'Give her back!' Mrs Hornby screeched. 'She's mine!'

'I'm trying to,' Sarah said mildly. Then she smiled. It took an effort, but she knew the power of a smile to defuse a situation, and the act of smiling reminded her that this situation was potentially funny, the way so many were, if only she was not the only one who thought so at the time. The budgerigar was not laughing, and Mrs Hornby certainly wasn't. Her eyes were squeezed with fury.

'What the hell are you doing here? You're a burglar. Oh God, get out, oh God. Help!'

The bird hopped and fluttered from Sarah's arm on to the other woman's shoulder as reluctantly as a diplomat shaking hands.

'Did you say *she*?' Sarah said chattily. 'She's very pretty, isn't she? Lovely yellow. How old is she?'

Mrs Hornby's mouth was open to shout. She closed it again and Sarah continued to smile until it began to hurt. Relentless amicability was a useful weapon, especially when she had no other. So much easier than aggression.

'She's seven,' Mrs Hornby said, with a note of pride. 'Well, I'm not sure, really. Possibly seven. She may be as young as three, I don't really know.'

'And she's called Boris?' Sarah asked, almost cooing. 'How

charming. I'm so pleased to have given her a soft landing. It took me by surprise. Is this her daily exercise?'

'No, no, no. I dropped . . . squeezed—' Celia Hornby stopped, aware that she was going to say, *I was crushing her*, but then another instinct came into play. She could never admit fault or mistake about anything; it was weak and foolish to do that.

Mrs Hornby looked at Sarah narrowly, envying that long, swan-like neck turned towards her without effort. The merest suggestion of an answering smile lingered briefly and then disappeared, as if to say, *I know your game*.

'It's your fault. What the hell do you think you're doing, sneaking in like this? You scared us.'

Then the smile widened, unpleasantly. Mrs Hornby stroked the head of the bird with one finger. 'Who's a naughty girl, then?' she asked it gleefully. 'Making a mess on the lady's shoulder. She better get something to wipe that off soon, hadn't she?'

Sarah determined not to look at her coat.

'I'm so sorry if I frightened you,' she said. 'But I wasn't aware I had to inform anyone before checking my friend's flat. He gave me the keys. So I'll just get on with it, shall I? I might be around for a few days. Nice meeting you. And Boris.'

She moved towards the open door of Henry's flat.

'Wait a minute . . .'

'Yes?'

'You can't be his friend.'

'Oh, why not?'

'He hasn't got any friends.'

Sarah smiled at her again and closed the door, quietly. Leant against the wall inside, shocked as she always was by a wasted exhibition of malice – what was the point? – and then

60

took off the coat. Not too much damage. Imagined the bird going back upstairs to be put inside a cage, while all she had to do was let the harmless muck dry and brush it away. She hated the very idea of a bird being caged for any other reason than to save its life.

Absently, she picked up the few letters from the floor. Two days' worth of post. Mrs Hornby was a good enough neighbour to push letters under the door. Circulars, a bill, nothing personal. Who got real letters any more?

Then she explored.

The front two rooms, facing the street, were larger than anyone would ever imagine if looking from the outside in. In the nicest way, it was a deceitful house. The first room looked set for a meeting, distinguished by fine old walnut-veneered furniture, rich plum walls above wood panelling which went from floor to chest height, flanking a fireplace with a surround of carved oak. The floor was mellow old wood, partially obscured by a tapestry carpet extending from beneath the table. The temperature was medium, cooler than she recalled.

Next door, the living room was a poem of paintings against blue walls, another fireplace, in white marble, and the mantelpiece above displaying a small collection of silver jugs. The sofa and two accompanying chairs were not of the same family, but looked happy and companionable together, each old and individual, covered in a fabric of geometric-shaped deep blues, greens and reds, gratefully faded to harmonise with one another and everything else, as if in a kind of liking and acceptance. There were decades involved in such time-worn harmony, complemented by the paintings. She looked at them first. Wherever there were paintings in a room, she always did.

They were watercolours of interiors, vivid paintings of other rooms, each different, with different impact. The first was of the inside of a nineteenth-century inn; in the next, she saw the big, smoke-filled kitchen of a great house, full of industry; and in the next, the boudoir of a woman who sat alone, in front of a window, sewing. There was a painting of a scholar's study, and another of children in a nursery. She found she was looking at other rooms from within this room, and it charmed her. From above she heard footsteps, walking back and forth, purposefully. The ceiling bulged, the way of old age, getting thick in obvious places. Sarah sat; Sarah moved.

She could live here, for a while. Henry's only bedroom was painted in green, light and airy. Downstairs, the kitchen was a comfortable mix of old pine and stainless steel, not entirely marred by the stained ceiling which also afflicted the bathroom, as if some torrent had come through more than once. There was a slight smell of damp and decay, the scent of it kept at bay by an enormous jug of dried lavender which stood in a disused fireplace. Fireplaces everywhere, going back to the time when solid fuel was the only source of heat. Beyond glazed doors, Sarah could see a walled garden, thick with ivy on the back wall. Three terracotta urns stood near the window. She had always craved a garden. The cat wove round her ankles. Yes, she could swap her safe room for Henry's beleaguered place, for a while. Maybe neutralise Mrs Hornby with incessant courtesy and flattery to her yellow budgie, while distracting her own tormentor by the presence of someone else in her own home. Besides, it was time to shake up her life a little, as well as the lives of the clients who took her for granted. It would make precious little difference to the way she lived and conducted business, which was usually away from home, and if it did make an impact, then it might do her regulars good to do without her. Kill two birds with one stone, although that was not an apt phrase for the moment. The cat was not a perfect neighbour for a bird which could scarcely fly. She stifled an irreverent giggle, and returned upstairs. Back in the living room, with the other rooms gazing in on her, she decided it was an inward-looking house. One where all the visual stimulus was internal. A complete creation; a house where you shut the door on yourself and did not look out of the window, rather than a home like her own, which was made by its virtues of street and view, and the pleasure gained from looking out and down, all the time. Her own flat drew her to go out; this house drew one in and invited one to remain. She could hear the sound of Mrs Hornby's footsteps above, with the additional blare of TV so clear she could tell it was the news. Meanness or poverty made her fail to carpet her floors. She wondered if the woman was sad, bad, mad, or dangerous to know, and contemplated how, above what she had done already, she was going to find out.

Better dwell here a little longer, to make sure she was doing the right thing. She sat on the lovely faded chintz of the sofa and phoned her friend Eleanor. Such a network they had. It made London a small world, but then, it already was. She noticed that she was sitting on a funny little chair with charred legs. It looked as it might have been rescued from somewhere else.

A proper breakfast was important. Too bad if your companion did not happen to like it, but if Alan was invited to eat, he bloody well ate, and since there was no such thing as a free meal, he might as well enjoy the food before he understood the price of it. Didn't matter who paid. He bloody loved it, and what was more, he was not going to allow the obvious revulsion of the man who sat opposite to deter him in the least from a slow demolition of eggs, bacon, sausages and glutinously orange baked beans, with two slices of pulpy white toast, burnt brown and yellow with butter. The man opposite drank coffee and smoked. This caff was Alan's favourite place. He had done a job for the owner once; taken out another caff that was not doing so well. Builders, electricians, plumbers came here, as well as contractors and bosses; men in dirty boots and overalls as well as men in suits in pursuit of a good feed, gossip and cash deals. Everyone knew Alan came in at least three times a week, although no one acknowledged him. This was where people who had heard of his skills through the grapevine knew where to come and find him, sit and have a chat, on personal recommendation. Not that they had in many months, or never with any worthwhile proposition, apart from the bloke opposite, who had hovered around for a bit, finally summoned up courage to speak, and then said he would come back. Not exactly promising, since he talked in riddles, but Alan knew he had to listen. It was not like the old days, when he wouldn't have given this one house room.

They did good bacon, and bacon could be terrible. It needed to be meaty and crisp, with no added water. He dipped half a rasher, folded neatly into three, into the second egg yolk, and felt the man flinch as he chewed slowly. It was a rule of his never to speak with his mouth full, unless he really wanted to be misunderstood.

'You'll have to spit it out, JT, whatever your name is. I mean, you have to tell me what you want. And while you're at it, you've also gotta tell me why you think I can do it and who the fuck told you I could. Which isn't saying, by the way, that I can or I will.'

He speared the other half of the rasher on his fork and ate it alone, followed by half the toast, looking at the emptying plate with regret. The thing with this kind of breakfast was that it was absolutely satisfying, gave you fuel without making you bloated, provided you went easy on the toast, and he always felt he could eat it all over again. Protein and fat, worked every time. The best and cheapest way to eat was in caffs like these, especially if you lived in a hotel room. He wiped his mouth with a paper napkin, and let his mind go a bit. It was feast or famine in his line of business; famine at the moment, but he still had to pretend he had choices.

'Also,' Alan added, carefully folding the paper napkin and lining his knife and fork up neatly, pushing the plate to the edge of the table to make it easier for collection, 'there's gotta be a reason. A good reason. More than money. Unless it's *only* money, which is always best. I mean, the purely financial motive I can understand.'

'This is about *justice*,' the young man said, stubbing out his cigarette and reaching for another.

'Oh yeah? Tell me. That was lovely, really lovely,' he said to the fat woman who came to clear the table as soon as a customer put down his fork, the way they did in here. He smiled at her, as he invariably did with women. Loved the very sight of women: big, old, young, thin, loved them. 'And could you make that two more coffees, please?'

'Justice,' the man he knew as JT repeated. JT? I ask you. Silly wanker, does he think I was born yesterday? He leant forward, disturbing in his intensity to anyone other than Alan, who had met other slightly deranged, pretentious dreamers before. Alan stirred his coffee and waited. He had this one slightly on the run and he knew it. For one, the bloke had been disturbed by his clothes and his grooming, since Alan was by far the better dressed of the two: silk tie, silk shirt, dark blue overcoat, and shoes which cost almost as much as the rest put together. Harmony in motion, getting the balance of power right, with his own grey hair thick, straight and cleanly carved into shape. And he knew he smelt sweet, while the man opposite, warming up to talk, wore a suit which had seen better days and although good, once, looked as if he might have slept in it. To be fair, a good suit could take that kind of treatment, but this one was getting near the edge and screaming for an executive dry-clean, like the bloke's brain. City bloke, in search of money to make more money. Or pushing his luck, with that soft, spoilt mouth which a woman would not notice. Mid-thirties, restless, resisting an urge to drum his fingers on the plastic table.

'Justice. My father owned a flat and he left it to a whore. It should have been mine, but it's hers. She has no right to it. I want it back. I've suggested to her that she sells it to me, knock-down price, but she isn't having any. She needs scaring. Make her see sense. Make her see what's right.'

He spoke impatiently, as if it was all perfectly obvious, and Alan accepted a cigarette. Always eased conversation with a smoker if you joined in, but not good for you, though. He was thinking how much he hated the word 'whore', because it was always difficult to say; this man said it like 'hoar', expelling the word like something poisonous out of his mouth along with garlic breath. Didn't think he owed it to anyone to avoid bad breath. Nothing wrong with tarts, Alan wanted to say. Handsome fellow, though. He began to feel a shaft of envy for someone maybe twenty years his junior, with the chiselled face and smooth skin he himself had once had. Man had looks, and enough muscle: what the hell was his problem? Alan drank his coffee, trying to hold on to his contempt.

'So why shouldn't your dad have left his flat to whoever he wanted? Don't know much about that sort of rights myself.'

JT leant back, comfortable in bitterness. 'My *father* was an entrepreneur. He made a lot of money and bought a lot of businesses. He had *me*, by my mother, who was mistress, girlfriend, whatever, and then he ignored me. Oh yeah, gave money for my education and all that, but never came near. I didn't even know when he died. Nor did she, until later. She was afraid to tell me his name.'

'I suppose she gave you everything she had?'

'Yes.'

'Which you lost?'

'No, not all of it.'

'Gambling, was it?'

'Yes.'

'Got a job, have you?'

'Yes, yes, YES. No, I was sacked.'

'And it should have been more? Leave it out, will you?' Alan said, getting ready to leave the table. Dead right there was no such thing as a free meal. Little shit. He could not bear people bellyaching about what they *should* have, *should* have got. You got what you got, was all; no one was entitled to anything. And the man had looks, education; he was lucky.

'My mother died last year,' JT went on. 'And that was when she told me about him. All the money he had. All the companies he defrauded. And how he treated her.'

Alan sat down again. He was a sucker for tales of dead mothers, still mourning his own. He went back to his half-finished coffee. Food here, good; coffee, lousy, but it was warm and bitter, and he had to give JT credit for not flinching at the first sight of his own face, and for having a suit that had been good, once.

'You can't get justice for your mother,' he said. 'Not after she's dead.'

'She was terrified of him. He hurt her badly. And it's not justice for my mother I want, it's justice for *me*.'

This was becoming more familiar. The hand holding the cigarette trembled, a very angry youngish man, who had messed up his own life. Alan didn't go in for anger much himself, not now. Grown out of it.

'So you want someone roughed up, or a house burnt down or something like that. To make you feel better?'

'No. You don't understand . . .'

'Well, I shan't, shall I, unless you fucking tell me.'

JT put his hands flat on the table. Alan looked at his eyes.

'I never met my father, and he never wanted to meet me. Yes, he paid for me, but not enough. Mother never told me he was as rich as Croesus until after he died. And left us *nothing*.' He cleared his throat. 'A couple of years ago, I decided to look into it. Got a copy of his will. Not a will, exactly, the equivalent thing when there hasn't been a will. You just get them out of the Public Record Office. It was executed by a lawyer called Mathewson. Been my father's lawyer for years. Money for my schooling came through him. He administered the will.'

This was too much information. *Administered? Executed?* Words out of books. Should have known this guy sounded like a lawyer, probably drummed out of the camp for putting his fingers in the till. Good enough guess. The more Alan thought about it, the more he thought he could be right.

Having a lawyer for a customer was not new either. He belched, quietly, and listened.

'Turned out most of the real stuff must have been squirrelled away. There wasn't much. And a flat. Which he left to a woman. For no reason. Except she worked at Mathewson's firm. Doesn't that smack of extortion and undue influence?'

Extortion? Undue influence? You could smell them a mile off, worse than smoke. Alan hated himself for being intimidated by mere words, but he was. Unless they were Sarah's.

'I knew someone in the partnership. Turns out this girl was a real looker and a flirt. Probably screwed him. Worked on him, and got what should be *mine*. Should have left it to his only son. I want what's mine.'

'There's a missing bit here, son,' Alan said, putting a shade of insult into the last word. 'Why the fuck should it be yours?'

'He owed it to me, and he left it to her. A tart.'

'Oh yeah, and I suppose this tart doesn't exactly see it from your point of view?'

JT nodded, appreciating Alan's superior understanding. Go with the flow, Alan thought to himself. The bloke's only barking. But angry, and bitter and dangerous, maybe not so harmless at all.

'No. I've written to her, explaining that the flat was only left to her by mistake, and perhaps she'd like to convey it back to me.'

Convey.

'And she's all over you like a rash, I suppose?'

'Not exactly. She doesn't reply. But she knows I'm watching her.'

'. . . And you want her persuading?'

'Either her, or a third party. Someone she loves, maybe. Maybe a place where she goes.'

69

'So how was you *proposing* to pay for this service?'

'I've got cash. You can name your price.'

Alan got up, and shrugged himself into his coat. He left a fiver on the table to cover the tip.

'You can't afford me, sunshine. I'm a specialist. You haven't told me anything worth listening to yet. And you don't *persuade* women. And I don't rough them up. Not at any price.'

'You don't understand. It's fire I want. I could do it myself. I want you to teach me. You're supposed to be the best.'

Alan was halfway down the street when he realised the man was following. He ignored him and strode on. Easy enough to shake him off if he wanted, just find a crowded place and disappear. The man had a mobile number, after all, could always get in touch. Then he realised he hadn't found out who it was who had told JT where to find him; who it was who had talked him up to the man, and that was important, because there could be more work from that direction. Then he was angry, because whoever had put JT in touch clearly thought that he, Alan, was fit for nothing better than having his time wasted by a pathetic little dreamer like this. Then he thought he did not want to know who it was that held him in such high esteem. Alan stopped to stare into a shop window on Lambs Street. The window was full of shoes, and all he could see was the reflection of his own face. Hear his granny's words, *never miss the chance of a trick, especially if they're desperate.* JT almost cannoned into him. Together they looked at the shoes. Christ, the expression on that handsome face in the glass was admiration. It said, *I want to be like you.*

'All right,' Alan said. 'What was it you wanted?'

'A fire,' JT said. 'Just a harmless little fire.'

'There's no such thing,' Alan said. 'There's no such thing as a harmless little fire, you daft fucker.'

'And you a specialist,' JT said.

Alan looked back at him, saw them both reflected in the window, with the shoes at the back, and the truth of the situation hit him. They were two men down on their luck, but the younger one had looks, fire in his mind, and fire in his belly, that was the difference. JT put a hand on the sleeve of Alan's coat. Alan looked at that pale hand and did not move.

Chapter Four

All I want is a room somewhere . . . far away from the cold night air.

Henry found himself singing, or rather humming in a way which suggested happiness, and took a grip on himself. A gentleman had few excuses to be content when he was limping, with one foot in a moon boot, catching on the threads of someone else's carpet, inside a flat high above the world, in a place where he was a stranger, on dubious pretences. Maybe it was contentment to which he aspired, rather than that flash in the pan known as happiness, which was rarely worth a risk. This was a little mild domestic adventure which, if he was honest with himself, he did not quite deserve.

He was pottering in someone else's flat and enjoying every minute. It was the kind of exploration he liked, far preferable to the outside world. He was acting as to the manner born, having explored a huge variety of premises, although they were not usually in this condition. Sifting through debris to see what could be found was how he had once made his living, an expert in his own art.

Most people owned nothing but debris. Or they owned items of little intrinsic value which, when broken down into their base materials, became mere detritus. Rubbish, in other words. Houses were full of crap. What else were all those white goods, cookers and refrigerators, but ugly material turned to useful purpose? What was a telephone but a piece of plastic? What was a shower or a modern fibreglass bath other than something expendable which would melt? He belonged to a more frugal age, when recycling had another meaning; when he had been taught by his mother how to turn something into something else, so as to avoid waste, and to recycle whatever there was. Such as melting old gramophone records in boiling water to render them malleable and turn them into a small lampshade, or some sort of vase. Or making papier-mâché waste bins and pen holders from damp newspaper and flour paste; or turning old bits of material into rag rugs and draught excluders, which took for ever, with unattractive but durable results. Taught him a lot about the obdurate and fragile nature of matter, and later made him despise the disposable age. He sighed with the pleasure of being alone.

There was little of durable value in Sarah's flat either, apart from a painting or two. It was the substance of the place that gave it merit and made it admirable, from his peculiar point of view. It was solid and its accoutrements resolutely old-fashioned to the point of being archaic. State-of-the-art kitchen and bathroom were not her priority. The bath was old cast iron, good; the washbasin, circa 1950, heavyweight porcelain, good; the floor was slightly passé vinyl tiling, also good. The door, like all the other doors, was heavy and panelled on either side. In the kitchen, vinyl tiles again, old wooden units which would be slow to ignite, painted to hide their age, but gloss paint, oh dear, and the minimum of equipment. Shame about the tea towels hanging on the oven door. Yes, it was a safe sort of place from several points of view, but like everywhere, there were still hazards. Such as the fact that some of those heavy doors would not or could not be closed. The door from corridor to kitchen, for instance, could certainly be slammed shut, but that would be a mistake for a person inside wishing to get out, because the inner door handle was missing. As for the door into the living room, it would not shut because as the mark on the carpet showed, it had stood open so long that it was warped beyond closing. Fifty per cent working doors, the rest, not; still, he could fix that in his spare time. From this, and broken window catches, he concluded that the owner was a careless, unsafe person in a relatively safe place. Not a bad combination, as they went, although further deliberation over her personality led him to believe that the current occupant was far too reckless to have installed all the security precautions: the disused burglar alarm with its panel near the door, the smoke alarms so discreetly placed in the ceilings but useless with their dead batteries. Sarah Fortune would not have bothered to reinforce the front door with an extra panel on the inside and bolts into the frame, nor would she have done the same with the door of the safe room, which was propped open with a wedge, although easily closed and self-locking, with the key on the outside. She would never have created a safe room at all, although he had already guessed that. When he had pointed out the locks on the door, she had seemed surprised; she had either taken them for granted, or ceased to notice. People were generally ignorant about their own

74

homes, when it came to the important details. They thought they knew, but forgot. Someone had done all this: her predecessor, maybe. Someone who had been seriously afraid of being invaded, which was a sentiment with which Henry heartily sympathised, with the difference that the invader he feared most of all was not human.

The duvet on the safe-room bed was synthetic. He disliked that, although he submitted to its cosiness. Such things were potentially dangerous. It could bring the whole house down, fireball down that corridor in minutes. He did not wish to think of flashover. The feather duvet on her bed would not light; it would merely smoulder. Such things he had also learnt from his mother. Natural was always best.

Henry knew his conduct was impertinent. He had no right, as a guest of the freest and most generous of hosts, to limp around her place with the eye of a detective, or to find a ladder to examine ceiling cracks and high cupboards, but he reassured himself that his interest was objective, rather than prurient. He was simply assessing the efficiency of her home, for practical purposes. It was not as if he was looking at her love letters, of which he imagined she received many, or examining the household accounts for signs of financial viability, or sussing the place out with a view to stealing from it, which would have been very rude indeed. Nothing personal, Sarah, you lovely, lovely woman, honest it isn't. I am only curious about *where* you live, not *how*; I am simply curious about interiors, rather than interior lives.

He was dithering in the hallway with a cup of tea in one hand, having rather lost his sense of direction after looking in the kitchen drawers for batteries, when the phone rang. It was on the table immediately to his right and proximity made it unnaturally loud. It had sounded in the distance, repeatedly, earlier in the morning, far enough away to be ignored, but the fact that it was now so close, gave the *burr, burr* the power of an order, demanding an automatic response. What had she said, along with her cheerful good-bye kiss, as if from a wife who had known him for ever? I'll be back late this afternoon, she'd said. Make yourself at home, eat what there is and ignore the phone. In the same moment as he remembered the last of these instructions, and considered the etiquette of answering the phone in someone else's house (never, unless requested), he behaved as if he was in his own, lifted the receiver and held it away from his ear.

'Hallo, Sarah dear. How goes it? It's only Dulcie, and I've got to tell you . . .'

A voice like a foghorn. Embarrassment made him lower his own voice into an awkward growl of a mumble which he scarcely recognised himself. He felt silly and awkward, terribly aware of a breach of manners.

'It's not Sarah.'

'So who is it?' The voice was imperiously friendly, as if really wanting to know.

'I'm the plumber.'

'Oh, really. Where's Sarah?'

'She's out. Back later.'

'Well, could you be an angel and tell her Dulcie called, and could she call me back when she's got a moment, no rush. It's Dulcie. D-U-L-C-I-E.' Spelling it out as if he was the imbecile he sounded.

'Right, will do. Thanks.'

He put the receiver down, slowly. Should not have answered. Certainly not to Dulcie, but because it was darling Dulcie, it was probably as well that he had. There was a message he would not relay. She had said no rush. Henry shook his head, cleared his throat, picked up the tea again and limped into the living room to look through the window.

It was strange to gaze down from a non-scary height, and see people and traffic. Watching them scurry by in the grey light made him almost tempted to go out and join in. But if he went out, he might not be able to get back, although Sarah had left him a set of keys. Later, maybe; tomorrow, when the ache in his foot had completely receded, and he had got his balance with the boot, and he had been hugged again. And had a night on his own in the safe room where *it could not get at him*, and knew his own house was safe. All that.

He enjoyed the window, and he knew that wanting to go out meant that he was getting better. Sarah's plan would work. He could be here, and she could be near. The barrier separating their two territories was only Tottenham Court Road: Fitzrovia on this side, his beloved Bloomsbury on the other. Meantime, he would begin to proof her flat against the elements and all intruders, as he would his own, and also attempt to finish the decorative touches which she had merely begun.

Alan always wiped his feet before going in. Set a good example. It was what well-brought-up people did, and he was nothing but. He had his hands in his pockets, nudged the grand revolving door of the hotel with his shoulder and let it take him through with its own gentle movement. A revolving door was a test of confidence, and Alan could lecture on the subject of doors. The revolving door has several purposes, he would say. It is always open on the one side, and always closed on the other, i.e. some part of it is sealed at any time. It therefore excludes draughts, gusts of rain, all sorts of conditions, and makes people get rid of the dirt on their feet before they get as far as the real carpet. It gives the opportunity for making an entrance, for the initiated, *trrah, rah-rah*; exploding on the inside unscathed; catapulted out in high heels without stumbling; or allowing a cool customer to stand there, on the inside, legs spread and hands in pockets, as he did now, looking at all he surveyed like a lord. It was a trial, this fucking door, long since mastered by himself, and he was glad of his own grace in not laughing at others who stumbled through, with all their suitcases and bundles, dazed by the last hazard of a long journey or a long day, trying to look as if they knew what the hell it was they were doing, or why the hell they were there. The door was designed to infuriate.

The revolving door, with its swishing sound, created by the hairy edges of each of its four glass and brass panels, each with a bar to push, was one of the hotel's better security devices. People don't always like it, Sheila said. Should we get rid? You gotta be outta your mind to do that, Alan had told her. Thieves, waifs and strays, anyone you don't want, get caught in doors like this, like moths in a trap. The thing about a revolving door like this is that you can see the person as they try to get in. Judge them. If they don't belong here, or can't pay, they'll come through that door looking like it. Then you watch them. The way Sheila spoke, you'd think it was a place of worship, instead of a five-star hotel, augmenting ordinary business with cut-price weekend deals for tourists and all those conferences.

Although, when he thought of it, the foyer did remind him of a church (he was fond of churches), and the echo was probably because of the flowers. A huge urn full of lilies and foliage stood on a plinth, which could have been a baptismal font. There was something about the allure of flowers which had passed him by, although women loved them. Flowers in abundance suggested luxury, welcome, celebration, money to waste. There had to be a lot of flowers, or they counted for nothing. Give a small bunch to a girl and she only sniffed at them; if you were armed with a bouquet, there was nothing she would not do. He supposed this was the impression the Hotel Belvedere wished to create. Money no object, luxury ever at your service, that kind of thing. It was only like himself, always wearing good clothes to create an impression, before it had become a pleasure and a habit.

Unlike the door, the ten-foot-high flower display was bad for security, he told Sheila. You can't see through flowers; people could sidle round the display and disappear off in all directions, and of course you had to let them, because it was most unwelcoming to say to every single soul who failed to approach the reception desk, *oi, you, where do you think you're going?* You could not stop the stray person who sneaked in simply to use the lavatory, although you could minimise that kind of thing by having the Ladies and Gents in the basement, but that would not be good for the residents and drinkers seduced into the Belvedere Bar and Lounge. If you wanted bums on seats in there, the loo had to be handy. Besides, persons in need of a pee were not really a problem. It was all the others who came in off the street with a whole variety of different agendas who Sheila thought were the problem, long before she thought of the bona fide guests, and the staff. She was always getting problems the wrong way round.

It was just that Sheila, the buxom senior manageress of this eighty-bedroom establishment, had a thing about people getting something for nothing, and didn't like riff-raff. She genuinely thought the place had a reputation to preserve, like the Connaught, or the Ritz, or the Savoy, whereas in Alan's eyes it was just another central London hotel, which would stay in business as long as it competed with its neighbours. It only had to be nice enough and safe enough and warm enough for the punters not to remember it as anything else. But Sheila was ambitious, and wanted it to be something else: a place where customers would want to dwell, think of lovingly, boast about. Given free rein by the corporate owners, who were uninterested in anything but the bottom line on the annual accounts, she was able to put some sort of stamp on it. She kept on initiating changes, which were meant to please whichever nationality of visitor predominated this year, in the hope of persuading them back. Which meant the foyer was a multicultural mess, apart from the flowers. Front of house resembled an airport lounge with a black and red reception desk, to reflect a vaguely oriental theme for the Japanese who predominated at the moment, while at the back, flanking the lifts, there were Egyptian columns, to suggest entry into a temple, and the bar to the left remained like a plush Edwardian gentleman's club, also used as an area for serving tea in the afternoons. Alan was not going to tell her that no one really cared. It was just a base, a place to stay, but her attitude towards it suited him. It gave him a room, and as work went, it was easy money. Pocket money.

There was always a room for him, not always the same room, which suited him even better. Sheila was flustered today. Hard work, being a control freak, trying to create ambience while attempting to cut corners, make that bottom line, and manage a staff of such diversity that few of them had a common language. Some of them were cash-paid illegals, and several had a tendency to fight each other under the

yoke of a hierarchy complicated by race into something pro-
foundly mysterious. Alan admired Sheila; she was definitely
hands-on, although sometimes it would be better if she was
not. Too bloody ambitious and wanting things quick, but she
was family.

'Sorry, Al, gotta change your room today. Can you move
your stuff, or shall I get someone else to do it? Only I would-
n't mind you hanging round here this afternoon.'

She meant the foyer, where they sat, and where she liked
him to sit at key hours of the day, reading a newspaper and
watching. Late at night she would want him to go round
every one of the five floors, and up into the mysterious empty
attics, which he loved, and where she was afraid to go herself.
A man in the basement watched the main areas covered by
video cameras, but Al was the real security. Family.

'I'll move the stuff in a minute. How've you been?'

Sheila was a child of a long-dead older cousin Alan had
scarcely known, which made her family, and that was that.
East End family still mattered. It meant two-way trust. It
meant looking after. You could criticise family, but if any
other bugger tried it, they were dead. Moving his stuff from
the superior room which was needed to the undoubtedly
inferior one was never a problem. He went where there was
space. His wardrobe remained carefully hung on one of the
big brass rails, mounted on wheels, which the porter used for
luggage. His five pairs of shoes were always lined up beneath
the clothes, alongside his capacious washbag, the whole thing
ready to be towed away in one hand, with his suitcase in the
other, the suitcase never quite unpacked.

'Oh, you know. Usual problems. Two short on Reception,
cook got mugged on the way home, flood in sixty-five, three
double bookings. Nice jacket, Al, is it new?'

Part of his value depended on looking like the better kind of guest. Being accepted as appropriate to the scenery by staff and guests alike; not being noticed at all, unless he made himself noticed. Being agreeable, until he absolutely had to be disagreeable, which was often done by simply staring, from close quarters. He would keep his own hours, lean on people rather than bite; diplomatic violence, containment of a problem. As in the smooth way he had of intercepting the more than occasional girl who ignored Reception and made for the stairs. 'Excuse me, madam, can I help you? Oh, you're going to see your friend in room fifty-five? Well, I'll just phone him to let him know . . .' Only the cheaper end of the sex trade did that. The more expensive ones carried briefcases and were indistinguishable from the working colleagues they purported to be. It wasn't them who needed protection. Sheila did not think it was part of his role to look after tarts. He did.

'And we're not quite making targets this month,' she said. 'Don't know what to do about that.'

Targets for food and drink profits, targets for room service, targets for overall turnover, customer satisfaction. Alan knew she sat in her office and personally completed the satisfaction questionnaires left for guests and largely ignored, did at least fifty of those a month, using different pens and degrees of accuracy, so that some said 'Good' and some said 'Very Good', but she could not massage the financial figures in the same way. Make targets, keep job. She was working up to something: he knew it, and he thought he knew what it was.

'Well, that's not going to happen, not at this time of year, is it?'

'Must,' she said, mouth in a straight line of determination.

He kept silent. Sheila's yellow uniform blouse strained across her bosom, and her straight skirt rode up over plump, shiny knees. The hotel bar consumed a minimum of twenty kilos of peanuts a week; Sheila did her share.

'Oh yeah. Someone in room fifty-five complained they could hear someone above. She couldn't have done, but you will go up there, won't you?'

He nodded. She shivered. She always wanted him to go up there.

'Yeah, doll. After I've moved my stuff. Quiet, isn't it?'

'Too quiet.'

They'd do better on that bottom line if they could control theft from the kitchens and the bar, tolerable until it exceeded a certain per cent. Sheila thought problems came from outside, thus her paranoia about intruders, but the real trouble was within. Impossible to run a hotel without letting a certain amount go. He made for the lift. Used his universal key card to go into his bland twin-bedded room at the front, collect the gear and trundle quietly along the endless corridor to an equally anonymous, darker single room which faced over the back. Each had the same limpid landscape on the wall. A bed was a bed and a room was a room. He changed his shirt and tie, resumed his coat, and went further upstairs.

The Belvedere was old, built, like others, as part of a late-Victorian boom to house the visiting bourgeoisie intent on culture at the British Museum, West End theatre, insurance brokerage and medical treatment. Alan knew all that, but the bit of history he noticed most was the attic floor, and what it was for. Rooms for the tribe of servants who lived in situ, beneath the roof, in a straight line of fifteen, each judged big enough to house two or three, but too small for conversion now into anything but the meanest bedroom, unless they were doubled up and made en suite, for which the plumbing would be difficult. One water closet for them all, a hundred years ago, inferior timber on the floor, the smallest windows, all facing back, the wood planks rising with the heat from below; garrets unfit for habitation, subject to one conversion scheme after another, and gradually forgotten. Servants were called staff now; they no longer lived in. The attic floor spooked Sheila. She wanted someone to set fire to it, because the only way it could make revenue was as an insurance scam, and it was also the only way to kill the fucking ghosts.

It was reached by a back staircase, no longer in use, and also accessed through the main stairwells and the lift to the floor below, which was as high as the lift went, and after that through the FIRE DOOR ONLY, which, if the bar was pushed with full, panic-stricken bodyweight, would lead upstairs towards the mandatory fire escape. Safety regulations, obeyed more in spirit than practice. There was access to the fire escape on every floor, smoke alarms everywhere; there was no reason to go up, but rules were rules, and the door had to exist. This wasted attic floor continued as it was, redundant, in need of money. That bloody woman in 55, the last room of the last habitable corridor, may have heard her own footsteps, or the creaks of the attic floorboards, or the ghosts Sheila feared up here.

The first thing he could see when he opened the door was sunlight coming through open doors, while the first thing he could hear was the cooing of pigeons. Rats on wings, sometimes sweet-sounding scavengers, living on city rubbish, adept at nesting and reproduction in precarious places. The back window ledges of the hotel were covered with net to prevent their landing and habitation, except for up here, which did not count, and where they thrived and multiplied. There was a muted chorus of *cooo coo, cooo* greeting him, not a bad sound in the middle of the day. He liked that, too.

It was either godforsakenly cold up here in the buffer zone between the habitable floors and the insulated roof, or suffocatingly hot. Alan was not concentrating. His stomach had finally digested breakfast, but not his experience of JT or the chat after, or the next meeting, to which he had agreed, disliking himself for feeling cornered. *Just a little fire.* His left eye watered in response to the chill, a shock after the warmth below. Sheila would want *just a little fire* up here; just a large insurance claim, but it was not a good place for that small, containable fire, the like of which he had told JT did not exist, and there it was, nagging him again, a challenge. And he was going to have to do it, before he lost his nerve, and it was a novel request, when he came to think about it. Usually he was asked for the other kind, big, gutting and thorough. He liked it up here. A secret wilderness. He liked the fact that everyone else was scared of it.

No mice at this level. Only in the basement, where the population varied. He had always liked secret places and rubbish dumps, like all hotels had, and this was both, full of dust. He brushed his coat sleeve, fastidiously, thinking, *couldn't do a fire up here, Sheila.* Too much to burn, look at it, mattresses, broken furniture, old suitcases, you name it. Way too much to burn; you'd have to move it all first, and that'd be a giveaway. And then, oh shit.

He stopped, halfway between rooms, sniffing something new here, something not quite right. A different, warmer smell than dust and rubbish. A ghost. He walked forward slowly. A floorboard creaked.

In the last garret on the right there was a boy with a dog, sound asleep. A lanky youth, rather than a boy, spark out on three piled mattresses, with his big feet dangling over the edge and his arms crossed across his chest, protectively, next to the dog, which began a soft, slow growl. Oh sod. Alan tried to assess the height and fighting weight of the youth and what he was going to be like when he was rudely awoken – was it better to belt him first, or have a fucking dialogue? – and as he thought about the alternatives, his stubby fingers delved into an inside pocket, to where he kept his flick knife tidied away beside his heart, all the time keeping his eyes on the dog. Which stopped its useless growling and stared back for a long few seconds. Alan's eye watered; he stood as still as a monument, and felt an unaccountable urge to cry.

That bloody dog, the graven image of the other dog, black and mustard, ugly as all get-out, with great big boxer eyes. And the boy, with dirty yellow hair and big feet, the graven image of himself.

'You *what?*' Eleanor said. 'You're out of your mind. You let some strange man into your place and invite him to stay there? Christ, I've heard of risk-taking, but this is the ticket. Sleeping with the bastard's one thing. Let one of them have the run of your house? You must be mad.'

'He comes with the highest recommendation,' Sarah explained. 'And judging from the condition of his own flat, which is near perfect when it comes to housekeeping and cleaning, at least, he'll show the greatest respect for mine. In fact he'll probably improve it. And besides, if I'm staying overnight in his, I've got him over a barrel, haven't I? Why should he abuse my flat, if I can abuse his? He just wants a break. So do I, as it happens.'

'More of the letters, is that it?'

'You've got it.'

'What are you going to do about them?'

'I don't know. Nothing.'

'Apart from slumming it in Bloomsbury? Don't tell me, Sarah, I don't want to know. You won't like it for long. It's a village. Same people go round and round to the same places. Everything connects here.'

Eleanor pushed off from the end of the pool, and cut her way through the water in an aggressive crawl to the opposite end, then turned underwater and swam back. Sarah followed with a slower breast-stroke, looking as if she was being considerate with the water, parting it with her arms carefully, to create an elegant wake, rather than a splash, as if afraid to disturb it. She loved the pool when it was calm, was always amazed at how long it took to resume a smooth surface even after the disturbance of a single body. Equally startled at how the ripples stretched out and lapped against the edges, and the whole surface danced, long after any intrusion had ceased. The health club pool was an undiscovered treasure, scarcely used in the early afternoon. They swam together on Wednesdays; otherwise, separately, whenever they could. Eleanor had a different approach to water, so that when the pool was empty and still, she ran towards it, jumped, clasped her knees and bombed herself into it for maximum impact, as if it was a glass surface which had to be cracked. She liked to make the water explode, and if someone else swam alongside her she had to swim faster, even though Wednesdays were for dawdling and talking at the shallow end. The gentle slap of water loosened the tongues of two close but reticent friends, who confided in each other within limits. Easier to talk when the eyes were unfocused and the body swayed, moving weightlessly; where voices echoed, unintelligibly, so that they could shout and not be heard.

Sarah pushed off, gently, side-stroke this time. Leisurely, scarcely disturbing the choppy water. Turning on her back to look at the ceiling, deciding not, since it was the same azure blue as last time and the lights unrestful. Two slow lengths to Eleanor's rumbustious four. Thinking time. Suspended responsibility, a version of freedom. Blissful security, hanging on to the edge, lighter than a feather, made safe by water. The minute she learnt to swim was one of the very best moments of her life. Eleanor was angry today, but then she often was.

'How's business?' Sarah asked.

Eleanor rolled her eyes and pressed her fingers against her nose. 'Still going. Still got a few regulars. Got one who's as regular as clockwork, pays my rent. And she really, really likes me. Could be my big chance, but I hate her.'

'Hate? That's a shame. Why?'

Hatred bewildered Sarah. Hatred involved wishing someone ill. Or dead.

'Oh, she's spiteful and moans all the time. That would be bad enough, but I *hate* her. I think, never mind what else she is, I hate the *texture* of her.'

Sarah could understand that. She sank up to her chin, warm below the water, stretched her arms. Herself and Eleanor had much in common. They both dealt with bodies. Texture mattered. She shook her head.

'I'd get rid of her soonest, if I were you. Just get rid. Hatred's bad for you.'

Eleanor shrugged, dark shoulders slick with water. 'Can't. Duty first. Couldn't give up on her. Guilt second. The guilt you have over someone who revolts you. Am I condemning

her for being ugly? How dare I be so unprofessionally
squeamish? Are the ugly to be barred from everything? Am
I in practice only to treat the acceptable of the species? Oh,
and three, I need her money.'

She shook her wet hair and pulled it back with both hands.
Her hair was like the plumage of a blackbird.

'Four more lengths and then I'm done,' Eleanor said.

'I'm done already.'

Eleanor hesitated. The other end of the pool seemed a
long way off. 'You know? I think I hate her most because she
fancies me.'

'Ah.'

Sarah watched the wake left by Eleanor's long body. Hmm,
yes; another person's desire could certainly add a whole new
dimension to native dislike and put them way beyond the
pale of logical consideration. If the other wanted to possess
your body, wanted to claw at you and touch you, and you
found it unimaginable, then you hated them for embarrassing you. For putting you in the position of having to explain,
evade, shrink away, justify self, avoid giving offence. It made
you question yourself and squirm. No dislike as intense as
physical dislike, no threat as great as that of intimacy, or so
easily distorted. Unreciprocated lust was tyranny. Enough to
put the yearning lover beyond the realms of all normal consideration, therefore to be treated as despicable, scorned like
a dirty, infectious animal, instead of simply another merely
mistaken, merely unpleasant, lonely, insensitive, daft, besot-
ted human. Yes. Lust could create hate and quite
unreasonable fear. She should know. That was how she had
felt, long ago, about Charles Tysall, a client of Ernest
Mathewson.

Standing beneath the shower, shampooing her hair, in

advance of Eleanor, whose four lengths had turned into a furious six, Sarah was counting her blessings. It was a blessing and a privilege to have survived so far and not to be ugly. Look at Eleanor and herself. So well favoured, the pair of them. Big-boned Eleanor, with her strong body and endless legs, broad shoulders to power her through water, beautiful face like a Nefertiti, inhibited only by what she had lost and could not recover. And Sarah herself, rubbing a soft towel across the small scars on her back and belly, which she had once thought were a total disfigurement, while they were nothing but the subject of mild curiosity from an unusually observant lover, even after all that blood. By any version of a God, they were lucky.

Ernest's client had pressed her back into broken glass, made her feel uglier than sin and debased by hatred, because he had wanted her, been disappointed in her, until, finally, she had disgusted him. Sarah could think of it quite objectively now. It would have been quite different if the scars had not healed, or if she had provoked him by anything other than trying to evade him. She had healed herself, but what if she had not? It had been easier to pity him in the end, when it was he who was old and sick.

Enough. Exercise of any kind made her feel virtuous. They were in the coffee queue, damp-haired and salivating at the smell. Eleanor was a caffeine junkie, which could explain the irritation, as well as the rapid speech.

'You know this client I was talking about? Another reason I can't stand her is because she's in denial, all the time. She's got arthritis, only she won't believe it. Can't be, she says, 'cos she comes from a good family, she says, which in her book means a family free of any genetic disorder. She's that stupid.'

'I think I get the picture that you're not very keen on her,' Sarah said.

Same old anger, which she did not understand, only because her own never lasted long, as if she could not quite maintain it unless it nourished her, which it never did for longer than a day.

'Well, congratulations to you for going on dealing with her without paralysing her,' Sarah added. 'Which you probably could, like you told me. Good on you. Can't function, myself, unless I like something about them, including the texture.'

'You don't need to,' Eleanor said quietly. 'Anyway, I'll get my revenge. Don't need to hurt her, she'll do that herself, way she goes on. Sorry I've been so waspish, it's that time of the month. What's next for you today?'

She was changing the subject, reminding Sarah how they never named names, and only went so far in what they told each other, which was a hell of a lot further than either admitted.

'I shall check out my guest. Change my clothes, come back to Bloomsbury, see who I can entice,' Sarah said lightly. 'As for my house guest, honestly, he's an ideal client for you. Got shoulders stiffer than a board, recovering broken bone which will screw up his posture if he isn't careful, and what he wants is massage in a small room. Much more than sex.'

'Thanks a lot,' Eleanor said. 'Send him along some time. I think, maybe, I prefer men after all as clients. And as for what you are about to do next, Sarah, don't tell me you're not blushing. Wednesday-afternoon regular. You really like him, don't you?'

'Only problem with the house guest, though,' Sarah continued, outside, as if Eleanor had not alluded to either her

91

blush or anything else, 'I like the texture and temperament, but *I don't know who he is.*'

Dulcie tried the phone again. For Christ's sake, she only wanted to know about the coat, and to tell her, don't bother with Henry. He phoned and he's fine and he's moved.

And the other little thing, which was beginning to nag her, because of that other foul letter she had received and not torn apart with her bare hands. It went against all instinct to shred paper.

Perhaps it was time Sarah knew the truth about that flat of hers. High time, but it could wait.

CHAPTER FIVE

He had a good job here. Worked his own hours, kept out the riff-raff, had a room and cash, and a mobile phone. No one gave a fuck what he did for £200 a week and a room. A cushy job for a hard man.

Who couldn't stop crying, no, wanting to cry. The boy was only a skinny kid, little bastard, still spark out, and that dog, somewhere in between a miniature mastiff and a nothing, with its squashed-in face which looked like someone had taken the palm of a hand to it and punched it, right back level with its own skull. Just like that other dog. Fucking useless, that other dog. It had licked his hand and let him lock it in. Dogs run from fire, see? They run like hell, it's nature, innit? Dead giveaway, if you take that dog home with you. It looks more natural to leave it locked in.

He had backed out of the room.

He was not crying, only the bad eye, watering, as he went back through the door, down, down, down, still in his coat, still fingering the knife. Oh, this was a bad one, this was, and then he was down in the kitchen, asking for a couple of sandwiches, please, whatever you've got. They didn't like him much, who the hell did, and who gave a shit if they did or didn't, as long as they gave him bread and lots of water, please. He never asked for the rib-eye steak, or the fucking champagne, or any extravagant freebies, and got some brownie points for that. He passed Sheila in the foyer, looking round that bunch of flowers, gave her a thumbs-up sign, still looking good in his coat, and then back upstairs in the lift and through the door marked FIRE DOOR ONLY.

The boy was still asleep with his pretty face upturned to the ceiling, and Alan could have kicked him. Instead, he left the food.

'I've lost it,' Alan told Sarah. 'Fucking lost it. Lost my fucking bottle. Should have hauled him out of there by the scruff of his neck, and chucked his bloody dog out the window, but I couldn't.'

'Where is he now?'

'Still up there. Told him I'd be back later to get him down. He couldn't even remember how he got there. Said he just needed to sleep.'

'You don't want you to lose your job, Alan.'

'Look, girl, I shan't care about my poxy job if I've lost my bottle for the real stuff.'

'What's the real stuff? No, don't tell me. You'll only regret it. And so might I.'

'You're a good girl, Sarah.'

'No I'm not.'

'There used to be a saying, "There's nice girls and good girls." A nice girl then.'

'Not nice and not a girl.'

'Why can't you women ever take a compliment? Why do we have to dress it up? All right, you're a bloody marvellous fuck.'

'Now you're talking,' she said. 'That I understand. And so are you.'

He felt like it. He could feel the tension ebb away, and he didn't care if she lied, although he didn't think she did. She'd been his first after what felt like years, at a time when he thought it would never happen again. Lost his looks, hadn't he? And every ounce of the confidence given by looks. Took to walking, more than ever, but aimlessly in parks and squares during the day. They both liked to walk. He could remember the park bench where she had found him, or he had found her. Started talking, just like that. Lost your looks? Sarah said. Christ, you must have been terrifying before. You're a bit of all right now. Can't do it any more, he said. Just let's give it a go, she said, after they'd covered a mile. Bloody hell, that had been a good afternoon. One when he went out punching the air. Like he did every week, now. Only he stayed longer these days, and they went out walking all over. Nothing special, just walking.

'You know what your trick is, Sarah? I've been trying to work it out. You teach your blokes how to please in bed, as well as get their end away. You know nothing makes a man feel better. I mean, there's no comparison in the sense of achievement. And we've messed up this bloke's bed good and proper.'

'Give us a kiss.'

They were lying on Henry's bed, comfortably starkers;

didn't matter where he was, he was temporarily happy, and it didn't matter if it was temporary. He could tell anything to Sarah; no, correction, not everything, because he never told anyone anything much, but a bloody sight more than he told anyone else, such as doubts and shameful things, and about his dad, without ever getting specific about what he did for the real money. She knew him somehow. She was a lady who swore like a trooper and didn't care about her own saggy bits any more than she cared about his. No furtive shagging here; she wrapped herself all around and she liked being stroked as much as she liked stroking. 'Scuse me, a double entendre. He stroked her back. She encouraged him to talk and tell and warned him when to stop. She would take him wholesale, for whatever it was; she saw some worth in him, but she did not want his fucking soul. And she knew when not to waste time talking. They had scarcely made it to this strange bed and he had never even really found out about the change of address. Well, a bed was a bed and a room was a room. He stretched his arms above his head, looked down at his own body and her brown thigh chucked over his thigh as if it was spare, and thought, I can't be all that bad.

'He's a poofter, this bloke who lives here, right? Frilly curtains.'

'No, a purist, a bachelor, a collector. Sexually timid heterosexual who's put all that on the back burner. Not a passionate man. Neurotic, maybe.'

He turned and settled himself against her, loved this. Her bum in his groin, his hands round her body, closed on her bosom, you didn't get anything closer to trust than this. Made him wary and garrulous, a contrast to all the other times, when he was simply the listener, and people told him stuff. She knew all the big words, never talked down.

Sometimes she sounded like a fucking book, and he liked that, too.

'Was it the dog or the boy?' she said.

He pressed his cheek into her back, and stroked her shoulder, with its small erotic scars, scattered like confetti.

'Who did this, Sarah?'

'Who scarred your lovely face? Better mind your own business, my sweet. Boy or dog?'

He hesitated.

'The dog, if you must know. It was just like a dog I killed once. Always haunted me, that bloody dog.'

'Why did you have to kill it?'

Not why did you kill it? Why did you have *to kill it?*

'The fire killed it. I had to leave it locked in a place. The place burned down. It howled.'

'Not your fault then.'

He was going to say, *oh yes it was. I had to leave it locked in that back room so the fire would look like an accident. I left the dog on the chain, to die in terror*, but he did not say that. The dog had known what was going to happen; that was why it had howled. A nice, useless watchdog which had licked his hand, stupid brute.

'Hmm, yes, I can understand you being sympathetic to the dog, but why the boy? This is London. We trip over homeless youths every day of the week and cease to notice, even when they look at death's door. We treat them like pigeons, give them a crumb and shoo them off.'

'Yeah, doll, I know. Step around them in the underpass. Can't stand their headless bodies in sleeping bags. Like I said, I'm going soft. It was the dog I was sorry for.'

'And you're paid to keep people out.'

'Someone had duffed him up,' Alan said. 'And he looked

just like me at his age after a couple of rounds with my dad. Only he didn't look old enough to hit back.'

'What are you going to do?'

'Let him stay a while. Get him some gear, and walk his fucking dog before it stinks the place out. Have to do that late at night.'

'Risk your job.'

Again he opened his mouth to say something more, such as it wasn't his real job, but she knew that already. She knew that the ready money and the clothes did not all come from being hotel security, but she didn't know where it did come from. She knew about family; they talked about families. Must have known he was some kind of thief, some kind of buyer and seller, something not quite right, and didn't ask or judge. 'You're a kind man,' was all she said. He had a sudden desire to be normal; to have a house and an identity, like other people, so that he could say, come on, Sarah, come home with me, and this was very dangerous thinking. He was as homeless as that boy, with the difference that he had three bank accounts with next to no money in them and he needed a real job. *Just a small fire.*

'What do you do about paying taxes, Sarah?'

'A creative accountant.' He could feel her smiling. 'What do you do?'

'Like I told you, I don't exist,' Alan said. 'Never paid a penny in tax, never claimed one, either. Only time I was ever registered for anything was when I was born, and when I went to prison. Only time I ever saw a doctor without giving over cash was then, until I got burned. Old age isn't a great prospect for someone like me.'

'I'll look after you,' she said.

And there was that gobsmacking moment when he

believed her. Before a certain sort of insult set in. Him? Needing looking after? By a woman? No way. Him? Wanting to be looked after, feeling weak like this, even less way. Really had lost his bottle, made him restless.

'D'you mean that?'

'Like family, Alan. Yup, I mean it. I don't love everyone, but I've got a lot of time for you.'

He looked at his watch, feeling the restlessness even more, and yet not wanting to move.

'Got it all planned, Alan,' she was saying, drowsily. 'We get a massage parlour going in the attic floor of the hotel, the bit you're always talking about in your sleep. I'll be madam, we'll get a team of gorgeous girls, and you can be the butler. You got the figure for it. And then when our own hair goes, we'll get wigs.'

And he started laughing then, and the dangerous moment passed when he never wanted to leave and he knew she wanted him to stay.

'Quiet here,' he said. 'What the hell are you doing here anyway? I like your gaff better. Even though this is closer to mine.'

She had turned over, holding his head in her hands and kissing his brow. The small scars were prevalent on her left shoulder, and that was how he distracted himself.

'I'm house-sitting. It's nice to have a change. I'm doing a swap with the man who lives here. He's in mine, and I'm in his. He hurt his foot, you see, and he needs a break from the neighbour upstairs while he gets his strength back. She seems to have driven him mad.'

He looked at his watch again. Relaxed now. Plenty of time. Time went fast with Sarah, and yet seemed endless.

'She's the neighbour from hell,' Sarah continued. 'The poor

man told me he even considered setting her upstairs flat on fire, if only he could do it without causing any damage to his.'

Alan thought of the way in, and the way out, that narrow corridor and the stairs leading up to the top flat, and in order to control the spasm of jealousy which flared and died at the mention of any other man, engaged his brain with the problem.

'You could do it, you know. Tall house like this. Get up there first, open the windows, make a draught. Put the flame through the letter box; I mean, a nice fat petrol-soaked cushion, something that would burn a bit, and the whole thing would likely bowl upstairs, missing this floor completely. Something for it to take hold of at the top, an open door, and Bob's your uncle. It tends to go up, for oxygen and fuel, know what I mean?'

She put a finger on his lips; her eyes seemed to melt into her face and she was laughing, gently.

'She can't be all bad. She's got a budgie.'

And his heart sank, and he was out of the bed and looking for clothes, because the moment of weakness, when she looked at him like that, was as soft and unnerving as the temptation to talk about what he was good at. Shouldn't give himself away like that, and still wanted to say, I can read, you know, I can work it out, I've studied for what I do, and she wasn't having any, and she was right. The temptation was awful. He wanted to tell her everything because she had the sense not to ask. He wanted to tell her and he wanted to *know*. And after a year, he loved her as much as he had ever loved anyone, and that wasn't right either. Made him vulnerable, but two of a kind, peas in a fucking pod, they were, and all the time she knew so little of him, except his heart. Trust was oh so lovely, and dangerous. He had never known such sound sleep.

'Tell us how you got those scars, Sarah, please. Never seen anything like them.'

He was asking for her trust, he who asked for nothing. They were getting dressed. He wished they were going out for dinner, like a couple.

He watched, out of the corner of his eye, as she pulled a black sweater over her head. Nice soft wool. Her face emerged from the polo neck with her hair rumpled, smiling at him. After all, he'd told *her* that he let himself be scarred by a man with manicured hands.

'Was it a client?'

She shook her head and the curls fell into place. 'You don't want to know.'

'I do.'

She sat on the edge of the bed to pull on her boots. He liked her own flat much better than this. Just far too many colours and ornaments in this. Old lace curtains, behind old velvet curtains, and a shelf full of porcelain; who needed that in a bedroom?

'It was a client,' she said. 'In the early days when I was planning how to get out of a legal career and into something far better suited to my temperament.'

She said this with an exaggerated primness, which made him laugh.

'I was a lousy lawyer, but awfully good at seducing the clients,' she went on. 'It seemed a far more effective way of making them settle their differences. The equivalent of knocking their heads together. However, there was one I kept away from. He got into my flat, smashed a mirror, and pushed me into the fragments. I was rescued by a dog, so I see what you mean about being haunted by dogs.'

She paused in brushing her hair. 'He tried to cut the dog's

throat with a piece of glass,' she added. 'But it survived, so you see, everything was all right in the end. Would you like a drink? Henry has some very nice wines.'

'Cup of tea would be nice,' he said, faintly.

Christ, and he thought he was hard. She was making him soft. He must *not* love her.

'No, second thoughts, I'd better be off.'

'Wait, I'll come with you. I can walk you home. Got to check my own homestead.'

'That's a very nice coat, lover. You look good in that.'

It was good to be walking out with her. He liked that best. Walking down the street he resisted the urge to take her hand. Thought, instead, of the boy. It was cold, and it was a terrible weakness to want something you could call your own. Debilitating to want to protect her, because she, in her way, protected him. He wished he had a talisman of hers to carry with him.

Golden Street was still ungolden in the early-evening light, with a comfortable lack of polish. Still the same litter, the same carelessness, the sense of being a backstreet which had lost its importance, even as a thoroughfare. This time, she noticed how the street curved, slightly, so that she could not quite see the whole of it, and from the middle it seemed as if she could not quite see either end, both of which sloped away tantalisingly. It was in better nick than nearby Silver Street, where Eleanor had her room in student bedsit land, but it was still similar: a place where people began and never stayed long enough. Or ended up, washed up. Both streets led into Hotel Row and the grand square. Sarah was beginning to see how a small, quiet, dirty and anonymous old street was preferable to many alternatives; how it was a place of refuge and passage. She liked the crooked railings, the lack of uniformity, the colour of old brick, and understood how the people who had lived there first might well have considered themselves superior to the relatively vulgar who could afford a coach and horse, which might have been stabled in this street. There was no envy in Golden Street. She linked her arm through his, and felt him stiffen. Perhaps he suspected how fond of him she had become. She withdrew her arm and flicked imaginary dust from the shoulder of his coat. He missed the feeling of her hand in the crook of his elbow. A sharp breeze stirred the litter; the tarpaulin on the other side of the road snapped, as if angry. He stopped and turned up the collar of the coat, wishing he had worn his good grey Liberty scarf, and knowing, in a quick, irrelevant thought, that he was going to have to give it to that boy.

'Why was it called Golden Street, Alan? And why Silver?'

'Something to do with silver or gold, I expect. Trade. Not far from Clerkenwell and all those watchmakers. Some kind of trade. Usually is, isn't it?'

'Like Gutter Street, in the City?'

'No, that's for guttersnipes.' He stopped near the junction, where the traffic grew louder. 'They should burn it all down and start again. Bet that's what they did with the other side. Who wants buildings so old that they're listed and protected, so you can't demolish the sods even if they're neglected? Not property developers, unless they can wait for as long as it takes.'

He picked up her hand and tucked it into the pocket of her coat, with his own. On the corner it was as if they met a wind tunnel, and it was unexpectedly, viciously cold. He wanted something of hers to keep with him. Even inside that coat with every button fastened right up to the high neck she felt thin. Oh *fuck* this. He needed to feel protective like he needed a hole in the head, and if this street wanted burning down he was probably the best man in London for the job, provided they got the people out first, and the dogs. Christ, he was losing it. He pulled her into the doorway of the first shop on the main street, kissed her hard, holding on to her by her ears, let go abruptly, sighed.

'Wish you didn't earn a living this way, Sarah. I really wish you didn't.'

She kissed him gently, standing on tiptoe in those high-heeled boots to do so, holding his head, as he had hers, by his cold ears.

'Why? Does it make me deaf? Does it make me blind? Does it stop me knowing a good man when I see one? Does it stop me being a friend? No, no, no. And,' she rubbed his nose gently with the knuckle of her forefinger, 'just in case you ever wondered, you'd be surprised at how little *sex* it actually involves. Look at how much time we spend walking. And now, lover, you go that way, and I go this. Phone on the mobile, or I'll phone you. Don't quite know where I'm going to be, but you'll always find me. I'm not hiding, and I want to know about the boy and the dog.'

He grabbed her by the shoulders this time, and kissed her again. Still too thin. Then he walked back towards the hotel in the rising wind, with the traffic roaring around him in the road and the people cluttering the pavements, without turning back.

Time to find another fuck. All very well having your manhood proved, but not if it made you incapable of thinking of anything else. Christ, it was difficult, being a man.

★

Beyond the revolving doors, the heat inside the Hotel Belvedere had the same effect as a blanket over the head. Warmth was an essential welcome, like it was in a hospital, but enough was enough and even those damn lilies were wilting. Sheila was behind the desk, nodded recognition of the fact that he was back for the last part of Happy Hour in the Belvedere Bar, busiest time of the day, and around for the night; never counted his hours, bless her. Looking as if she wanted a word, later. He waved himself through, nearly colliding with Mario, the barman, loaded with a tray of drinks and smiling on the way to the posse of guests who needed a drink in the foyer lounge before they even checked into their rooms. Must belong to a conference, and Mario was up to something. Double gins would be single and the rest sold out the back door. Sheila looked like a peanut, taut and round.

Up again, still in the coat, push open the fire door, and back, via the stairs, to the now refreshing cold. If the foyer was warmer than a hospital ward, the upper floors were just as bad, until he was up here, where he felt he could breathe. The pigeons were silent and the place was dark now, until he turned on the switch. The single hundred-watt bulb lit the whole corridor, and showed the way to the lav and washbasin at the far end, which would be enough for the boy to clean up, surely. Could get his clothes cleaned, easy, and his dog walked, easy. Only thing he couldn't do was own up to him. Report him to the police? You joke.

Then he smelt it, cinder in the air, didn't know if he smelt or heard it as a distant, ominous sound, like someone crunching cellophane paper carefully. He knew what it was, picked up one of the old extinguishers, hoping to God it would work, and ran. There were no smoke alarms in here, everywhere else but here, no point. Suddenly the place was larger than he remembered, the distances greater, the doors more numerous. The boy had been in the third room down there on the right, and it was from that room that he stumbled, with the crackle of flame behind him, stood, for a moment, dazed, dithering, disorientated. Alan pushed him in the direction of the fire door and yelled, *'Run, you fucker, run!'*

He was trying to remember what else was in that room. The mattresses, the duvet taken from somewhere else which he had used to cover the boy, the dog, not much else. A window which was stuck open at the top: that would draw the flame. The door was ajar and the dog would have gone. Let this fucking extinguisher work, *now*. It would be that duvet that had gone up. Boy wakes up, tries to light a fag with a match maybe, fumbles and drops one, or maybe two, the way you do, half awake with a body full of dope.

From the door he could see the duvet was in flames, big high flames, reaching hungrily for the ceiling, as yet uncertain where to go, beginning to bowl towards the back of the room, the smoke rising and moving, a fresh, virgin fire. Release clip, depress trigger, pray: foam spewed into the room and on to the flames like a great whispering enemy; Christ, the colour was strange, the heat dire, and the amount of foam ever surprising. He felt as if he was peeing on this fire, he hated it enough to shit on it, and amazingly it worked, the adrenalin and the foam and his shouted curses. It all felt like for ever, but it might have been a minute before the fresh flames suffocated in foam and died without dignity. He thought he could hear the fire sigh, as if to say, *I had only just started and you killed me*. Just a small fire. The room was black and acrid. He used a second extinguisher to be sure. Maybe some water on the mattress, in a minute, but that had scarcely taken hold.

He was trembling with triumph. God was good; it must have just begun. You could stop a fire if you got it soonest, before the minute when it reached the ceiling, burned the light fixture, dropped molten gunk and paint on the floor and the mattresses. Flashover, and then, and then . . . Get it in the first minutes and there was only mess. A lot.

He shut the door on the room full of smoke and foam, moved down the corridor, choking and clearing his throat, shaking with relief and a familiar sense of achievement. The fire door behind him stood open, the boy long gone.

In the last room he found the brindled, squashed-face dog, hidden behind a stack of chairs in the corner, detected by the smell of crap. He bent down near it, and went, c'mon, boy, c'mon, clicking his fingers, trying to be persuasive, c'mon, boy, life's not great, but at least you're alive. He tried to reach behind the chairs to grab it by the scruff of the neck, avoiding the crap on the floor, noticing that his coat was already filthy. The dog bit him on the arm. Held on like a limpet, not getting much purchase over the thick wool of the coat, but giving it a bloody good try. He grabbed the rope round its neck, yanked it towards him; it held on to his sleeve. Letting go of the collar he hit it sharply on the back of the neck; it let go of the sleeve and he dragged it out. Christ, it stank.

'Good boy,' he said. 'Good boy. Just what you ought to do. Why the fuck should you love me?'

If there was one thing he hated, it was snivelling gratitude. He dragged the dog by the rope collar into the lavatory at the end, flushed the chain to clear the brackish water in the pan.

'Here, you daft mutt, drink.' Shut the door on it.

He was struggling with the end window, to open it and clear the thin pall of smoke which hung in the corridor. Smoke got everywhere, get rid of it, but the window was not going to budge, so he fetched one of the chairs and smashed it. No balconies at the back; let the glass fall in the back road. Breaking glass was a satisfying sound.

Then he heard Sheila calling, in a high, frightened voice.

Sheila, flanked by the other security man who watched videos in the basement. 'Al? What you doing up here, Al? What's going on? Shit, it smells bad.'

She moved a couple of steps towards him, not wanting to lose the security of the exit door behind her. Her face looked green in the light of the single bulb which waved in the draught from the broken window. Alan wiped his hands and shoved them in the pockets of his coat, came to meet her halfway.

Behind him, the dog began to scratch at the door. She noticed the filth of his coat.

'What the hell are you doing, Al? Thought you'd be down for a drink, was waiting for you. Then this kid came running through the lounge like a bat out of hell, knocked Mario over. Stan got hold of him, and he said, there's a fire up there, and he wriggled away, which was just as well, stinking little brute, with vomit on him. I've run up through all the floors. No smoke alarms . . . Are you all right? That smell makes me sick.'

'It's only smoke, Sheila. Kid got up here, don't know how. Either through the back or came in with a crowd. Set light to a duvet in there.' He nodded vaguely towards the room. 'He ran; I put it out.'

She was recovering, rubbing her arms with her hands over the sleeves of her blouse. Despite the fire it was cold, and the acrid smell of smoke made it seem colder.

'What's that noise?'

'His dog. In the lav. It ran in there.'

'Ran away? What kind of dog is that?' Stan said.

'Normal kind,' Alan said, suddenly irritated.

Sheila turned to Stan. 'You better get back down and watch those cameras. Case he comes back for his dog.'

Stan was happy with that.

'Show me.'

The third room on the right was brown and black, the walls streaked with molten soot, as if some mad surrealistic designer had been let loose with a series of monochrome colours and the mandate to make it look sinister.

'All that, in a couple of minutes?'

'Yeah, that's the way it goes.'

'And you put it out, just like that?'

'Yes, easy.'

She missed the sarcasm in his voice. Nothing with fire was easy, and he could tell that she was suddenly pretty pleased and even excited, patting him on the shoulder.

'No wrecks, no alarms and nobody drowned,' she said. 'No fire brigade, no complaints, and someone else to blame. It's perfect, Al. Come on, admit it, this was a dummy run. You were just trying it on, weren't you, and it would work, wouldn't it?'

She walked down the corridor, talking over her shoulder. 'We could torch the whole of this floor, or at least a couple more rooms, get rid of this crap, say it was a trespasser. We'd just have to be sure there was someone around to put it out.'

'Just like that,' he said, this time with the sarcasm loaded. She did not notice. She belonged with the majority who thought fire was a comfort and a tool. Such innocence infuriated him.

'Might even get the kid back to do it.'

The papery skin on his cheek throbbed; he could feel his

eye twitch. He wanted to touch it, but knew his hands were soot- and dog-dirty, something he remembered while being amazed that she was actually almightily pleased with him. The dog's scratching at the back of the lav door was now accompanied by low whining.

'I'd better do something about the dog. Call the RSPCA or something.'

She looked at him. 'I don't think so, Al. Forms to fill in, they want to know where you found it . . . Remember when we found that pet snake? Nightmare. Put the mutt out in the street. Then come and have a drink, when you've cleaned up. Never thought I'd see you as mucky as this, Al, I really didn't.'

It was later when he went through the revolving door, leading the dog, which consented to be led and no longer snapped at him. He slipped off the towel he had used as a makeshift lead and let it go. Traffic was still heavy on the main street in front, slushing through the rain which came as a surprise. He nudged the dog with one foot, a reminder, not a kick. It felt like the middle of the night, rather than time for dinner.

The dog ran. He watched it with regret. Christ, he was getting soft.

The sofa was soft, with far too many cushions in a riot of colours, which proved useful for the elevation of a foot. Henry was using the whole of it, lying like a pasha, listening to music though the earphones of Sarah's old but adequate CD player, and conducting an imaginary orchestra with one hand, so absorbed he did not notice her come in. To say he was a different man from the one she had left in the morning was not quite an exaggeration, but he was improved.

Cheerful and contented would describe it, although a little guilty to be so. She could almost imagine he had gained a little weight during the day. He swung his feet off the sofa, as if caught in some illicit act, and then fell back.

'Sarah! I'm so sorry for putting my feet up, so rude on someone else's furniture, I do apologise. How are you? I thought you'd be here sooner. Did you have a very busy day? Do you know, your phone never stops ringing? Could I get you a drink? Something? Are you staying long?'

There had been another letter on the desk downstairs. She had paused to read it. It was brief and nasty, enough to distract her, make her want to go away again, and actually feel relieved that this man was here; that *someone* was here. She was so grateful for that, that any irritation she might otherwise have felt about Henry's evident colonisation of her home disappeared before the feeling had any chance to arrive. She scarcely noticed that he treated her as a guest in her own place, and had she considered it, would have remembered that she had taken considerable liberties with his flat, after all. She sniffed the air. There was the sweet smell of polish. She put down the groceries. Bread, cheese, vegetables, milk, none of it very imaginative, and expensive, like everything in the open-all-hours shop which had been on her route.

If you do not agree to meet and discuss the disposal of your flat, I regret I shall have to take unilateral action to persuade you. If I cannot have what is rightfully mine, I shall not hesitate to destroy it. It is not yours.

On the way upstairs it had struck her as ironic that in these days of technological communications, the only way to deliver a message entirely anonymously was by the old-fashioned medium of a handwritten letter without even a postmark. True, he had given an email address for her response in the very first letter, but that could be from any-where. She looked round the room. Henry had drawn the grand curtains she had been given by the wife upstairs before they moved; not only drawn them, but arranged them so the folds fell neatly into a cascade on the floor. She had never drawn them as artfully as that. The table near the sofa was fingerprint-free and shiny; the mantelpiece bare of dust, and the two framed watercolours near the door had clean glass. It felt strange, but then, latterly, ever since the letters, it had always felt strange coming home.

'I hope you don't mind the rearrangements,' Henry said apologetically.

Who are you? she wondered, but could not bring herself to suspect a man so thoroughly domesticated. She thought of the nature of their meeting, which could not have been con-trived, or planned, even by a genius.

'Wine, I think,' Sarah said. 'And I shan't stay long.'

A cleaner kitchen greeted her, with tea towels folded over the back of a chair, rather than hanging over the oven, which seemed odd. The plants had been watered and their leaves washed. It was beginning to be funny, slightly ridiculous to be coming home to a guest who liked it better without her there, and seemed intent on rewarding his solitude with small improvements. Let Henry be just what he seemed. That would do, for now.

She carried the wine back in the same chipped glasses as before. He was smiling at her as if hoping for approval, anx-ious to please and yet wondering if he had gone too far, endearing, in a way, and she had never been able to resist a man in need. There was still that haunted look at the back of his eyes. Men needed approval to make them brave.

'I have to report that your own flat is sound and ship-shape, Henry,' she said. 'And so is the cat. No trouble from Mrs Hornby, but I shall see what she's like overnight, if you still want to go on with this arrangement, that is.'

He nodded, gratefully. 'The safe room,' he murmured. 'A couple more nights in the safe room, with no sounds around me. No footsteps. Then I'll be fine.'

'And I shall be better for a few nights away from here,' she said brightly. 'As well as perhaps being able to form a strategy to deal with Mrs Hornby. But don't let in strangers.'

He looked shocked.

'I wouldn't dream of it.'

CHAPTER SIX

Dulcie Mathewson was a morning person and a fatalist, which seemed to go together, somehow. It meant, in other words, never thinking of anything important late at night, and the development of a knack which enabled her to clear her mind before she went to bed in exactly the same time it took to wash her face. The washing of her face had nothing to do with water, but the careful application of prohibitively expensive liquid cleansers of two different varieties, one for the eye area, one for the rest, followed by two different toners in delightful shades of turquoise and blue, reflecting the colour of the bathroom tiles. The salesgirl had even tried to extend her pitch to preach the necessity of a separate item specifically for the neck, but that had been pink and it would not go with the scheme. No fool like an old one, Dulcie told her, the loudness of her voice proving a point. And don't you think I'm buying this for vanity, you nice little stick insect; I'm buying it because we widows need a ritual, a lovely period of calm and self-indulgence in a bathroom that someone else used to turn into a mess, in order to persuade ourselves that bereavement has some compensations, whereas, really, there are very few.

She squinted in the mirror in the morning and shoved on a bit of the old cold cream she really liked best, scrubbed her teeth and began to do battle with her daily list. Her silk dressing gown, patterned with a feast of birds and tropical vegetation, lined with the softest towelling, was held at the waist with a double-knotted emerald-green sash. Only with the last gasp of the old coffee percolator, which spoke to her with its wheezing protests and final, spluttering sigh, would she allow herself to contemplate the challenges of the day. She was a firm believer in sleeping *on* a problem rather than *with* it. Ernest had had the reverse approach.

Spectacles in place, squeaky clean, caffeine-refreshed, then she could think. There were more colourful birds on the curtains, humming around in the same landscape as the material of her easy chair, and roughly the same as her favourite dressing gown. Dear Ernest had said it was like the Garden of Eden in here. Give me anything but bland, she told him; it's the white walls of your office and the faceless men in there that give you heart attacks.

Thus to the business of the day, beginning with the letter of the day before, upon which she had slept, although not under the pillow. It was not that kind of letter.

Dear Mrs M,

   To reiterate what I have said before.

   My father was Charles Tysall, A VERY IMPORTANT client of your late husband's legal firm.

(She did so hate people who were so deficient that they had to resort to the use of capital letters to make themselves noticed in writing. SO childish.)

> *It has come to my notice that his estate was dealt with by Mr Mathewson, and his will apparently altered to divert a valuable property which should have been bequeathed to me to a tart who worked for your late husband and his firm at the time. She may have been a family friend, but she slept with my father and also with your husband. I am sorry to tell you this, but THIS IS TRUE.*

Dulcie shook her head, pleased with yesterday's hairstyle, which was so much less fussy than the old . . . Must ask Sarah. She took up a pen to write a brief note in the margin. *No.* Sat back for a full minute.

No, you clot: it isn't true. She did *not* sleep with my husband. She slept with my *son*, and rescued him from perdition, but not my husband. She simply cared for my husband: there's a difference, you know. And she didn't sleep with your father, either. That was the problem. Mind you, she slept with quite a few of the clients, and their enemies, with amazing results. She was an absolute natural at settling litigation, but that's her business.

> *My father abandoned my mother and myself. When he died, he left us nothing. Instead, he left a flat he owned and once occupied for a while to that tart, SF. I wonder why? Was she blackmailing your husband? Was she blackmailing my father? Not that it matters which way she got hold of what's now half a mil-*

116

lion's worth of property. It is not hers; it's mine, and
your husband, one way and another, helped cheat
me out of it. I want it. I have made overtures to the
woman in question, with offers of compensation, but
regrettably, she does not reply. Please talk to her,
before anything else untoward about your husband
comes to light.

Julian Tysall

She did not need her specs to read this print. And she
knew who he was, the whinging little git. A bastard of
Charles Tysall, my my, also inheriting a wicked gene or three
from his father, who had left many victims, mainly of the
financial kind. And he was *wrong*, because Tysall had *not* left
a will, simply a comprehensive power of attorney, plus surprising instructions, for a psychopath, to compensate one of
the victims. The worst one: the one who got away and
haunted him; the one he debased and scarred, Sarah
Fortune.

Dulcie put her feet up, considered the view of her hummingbird room, with the noises outside of Kensington
Gardens South, coming alive. Of course, Ernest was capable
of manipulating anything, including his own conscience, but
never for long, although he sailed close to the wind sometimes and had an awful habit of not paying people. He was
not, let's face it, a frightfully good lawyer. *They*, namely
Dulcie and himself, did most of the legal business for the
more dubious of his private clients on this very sofa, of an
evening. There was no money in it for the firm, anyway. She
patted the upholstery, not for comfort, but in sheer impatience. So much twaddle talked about the law. It was mostly
common sense.

117

Charles was a psychopathic misogynist, charming, handsome and once a rich business tycoon, unleashed by Ernest towards Sarah, who knew better than to touch him, with the result that he became obsessed with her indifference, and her resemblance to his dead wife, tried to rape her and scarred her for life. That blasted flat was the least he owed her, especially when it was she who found him at the end of his wicked life, she who forgave him, and got him the last rites. This little bastard should know this. It was not some bloody grope Charles Tysall got from Sarah Fortune. It was his last embrace.

Dulcie liked her coffee when it was half warm, despite her own excitement at the progress of the percolator with the frayed lead towards its sighing orgasm and the promise of boiling hot liquid. Half warm or half cold aided reflection.

Must buy fresh flowers. Must find an electrician to fix the lights.

Maybe they had been wrong, though, to interpret the wishes of the late Charles into what they should have been. They had been, at least, a little creative with his letter of intent, but no one else was claiming at the time. He was a widower, never mentioned an heir, although Dulcie suspected a score of bastards from such a good-looking man. It had all been done when Charles had been missing, presumed dead. And it had been a teeny bit inventive to tell Sarah that her flat was left to her by that other client of the firm, that sweet, clumsy judge, who stuttered, whom she had entertained, on weekday mornings only, for a long time. The one who arrived with his wig box at dawn, and from whom she had never expected a single thing, apart from very modest contributions towards her savings every now and then. Her first punter. Dulcie and Ernest did the pro-

118

bate for the judge, too, sitting on this sofa and thinking how sad it was that wills and testamentary dispositions so rarely acknowledged good friends, but the judge couldn't, could he? What with wife and kids. But he *might* have done something of the kind, so, Ernest dear, just get her Charles's flat and say it was Smith. All perfectly legal, within the ambit of the powers of an administrator, although a bit tricky. The flat had never been owned in Charles's own name anyway, nothing ever was. Some company or other. The rest of his dough, severely diminished by the time he died, went to charity, again at his request. Dulcie was sure this request was not philanthropic, simply an attempt to stop it going anywhere else.

She looked at the letter again. Silly man. Why didn't he email, like everyone else? So much quicker: this had taken days to arrive. Dulcie tried to picture the face behind the letter.

A bastard of Charles's would be in his thirties by now, at least. Charles was five years dead. Why, if the son thought he had a claim, did he not make it properly? She checked off the reasons on plump fingers, admiring her rings as she did so. The sapphire needed cleaning. Reasons: he has no money for a lawyer, or cannot find one to act for him. He knows he has no hope of substantiating this claim, either because he is not really Tysall's bastard son, or because he knows that children have no rights of inheritance. Your parent does not have to leave you a euro, legitimate or not. Or he is one of those who cannot set about getting what they want in a non-devious way, but must do it by the short cut and the crooked route. It was the favoured method of those with a warped sense of entitlement and a bad mind. Some people, like Charles, could not operate any other way.

The coffee had reached the point when it was no longer half warm, but downright chilly, and Dulcie always aspired to have planned her day by the time the coffee was cold, leaving the arrangements to be refined over the cup of tea which would follow.

So, either way this was an empty threat. A cheap try-out, especially with that crack about Sarah sleeping with Ernest. Based on misleading, half-baked tittle-tattle from someone who knew someone, which took away the impact and made it all no more than hot air. She supposed she should give him the courtesy of another reply to the given address in King's Cross, dreadful place, but the last had only encouraged his attention-seeking, so it too could wait a few days. Indifference was best for now.

And Sarah was busy with her plumber, whoever he was. No need to bother her.

A few days, then. It was less than a week since she had seen Sarah, and maybe another three before she would see her again. It could probably wait until then. No, she had better reply. This young man probably only sent letters because he thought she couldn't use email. The cheek. She had written enough letters for a lifetime.

> Dear Julian Tysall,
>   Bugger off. Again.
>   You have no entitlements. If you harm a hair of
> SF's darling head, I'll be round to cut your balls
> off . . . She's been better than a daughter to me.

Not quite the right note, but never mind. Two committee meetings today. Henry coming to supper in the evening, with his friend. The light was too bright in here. Resplendent on the mantelpiece was the invitation to the Buckingham Palace garden party, later in the year. She really would have to buy a hat. They gave one such authority.

Celia Hornby had arrived in Eleanor's room wearing a woolly bobble hat of jaunty yellow, which she kept on her head while she managed the tortuously slow taking off of most of her clothes. Never all of them, thank God. She brought winter into the warm room with her, although in the last few days the world had felt more like spring. The sheer ridiculousness of Celia Hornby wearing her black lacy underwear and a yellow bobble hat had enchanted Eleanor to the point where she remembered the spring buds in the square through which she walked in the morning, and practically crowed with triumph. A black lace Wonderbra, emphasising nothing, black lace panties with a red bow to the side, and a yellow bobble hat. *Yes.*

'Hold it there a minute, Celia, there's a love,' she said in her soft professional voice, with just that small hint of affection and respect in it. 'Think we'll just take a picture for the files. Not cold, are you? Won't take a sec.'

'Do we have to?' Celia asked in her little-girl voice.

'Pretty please. You're looking so sweet today, and I told you, we have to have the photos to record progress. Just raise your arms above your head . . . Show me your back . . . then turn. Give us a smile, lovely, there, all done.'

Several clicks on her digital camera, while Celia forgot about the hat, and Eleanor felt a sense of unholy triumph not yet compounded by shame. Lovely shots. It had been so easy to get her to agree to this, easier than taking candy off a baby. She had taken photographs of other clients, although never with the intention of making fools of them, because it worked. Gave them evidence of progress. The ones who lost weight during a course of therapy liked it best. Hell, she had a snapshot display on the wall to prove to everyone it was OK, and definitely not mandatory. The ones in the photo-montage were flattering. Celia's would be insulting. Light in here was good for skin tone and the camera was brilliant. Celia took off the hat, absent-mindedly, releasing the iron-grey hair, adopted her usual method of getting on the couch. Grasped it first with both hands, shook it, to make sure it was secure, then rested one hip against it, sat, gingerly, and slowly rolled herself on to the Naugahyde surface. Eleanor knew she would have liked to be helped. It was definitely getting worse, even in a week.

Celia always began the conversation almost as soon as she entered the room, as if it had never ended and Eleanor had thought of little else. Eleanor cranked up the couch to working height. Celia adjusted herself, face down, care-fully placing her head into the padded ring hole at the end of the couch designed for the purpose. Some clients did not like it, preferred to lie with their face turned left or right. The ring hole was better for massage and breathing, ultimately more relaxing for the shoulders, if you could bear to have your face pointing to the floor. Celia found it comfortable, and it reduced her wheedling voice to some-thing which seemed to come from the near distance, rather than being close. Eleanor selected the oils, knowing that as soon as she touched the flesh she would find it slightly damp and sticky in the areas Celia could reach with her moisturisers.

'I wrote to Boris,' Celia Hornby said. 'I always think letters are more effective than anything else, don't you?'

Eleanor began with Celia's left ankle. The massage always had to be comprehensive, touch every inch of this repulsive body. How the hell the woman managed to take care of her feet was a mystery, when her ability to bend was so limited. If she sat in a chair and bent sideways, maybe; she wasn't so bad with a sideways bend, although straightening up might be a problem. Red nail varnish on her pinkies was standard, but it was a little chipped. Could have been there a long time.

'I forget,' Eleanor said, softly. 'You were writing to Boris a while since, weren't you? About the maintenance and all? Was this something different?'

Celia sighed.

'A variation. He won't give me any more, and I haven't got enough, so what am I supposed to do?'

'It's tough,' Eleanor agreed, kneading the toes and moving on to the ankle, which was definitely puffier than three days ago. Was there a purpose in this money talk? They had negotiated a discounted rate for massage long ago. Celia had money: from her husband, from her litigation; she had enough. What she lacked was the status she felt was her due. Eleanor could feel the old, cold hatred, temporarily dispelled by the hat, return with the force of a hot flush. Celia was covered with warm towels, to be removed section by bodily section, but her thick white neck was exposed, as if to the executioner. Eleanor knew she could immobilise her, cause her pain. She knew how, but she did not do it.

'Did I say I wrote to Boris?' the voice went on. 'What I meant to say is, I wrote to Boris's wife. She's called Jasmine. Such a pretty name, makes me think of flowers. I told her I'd seen Boris in one of those hotels down the road,' Celia said, as majestically as possible in her mumble. 'Slipped in there for a drink at the bar, non-alcoholic, mind, I never do, but if you want the loo you have to buy something, don't you? I wouldn't dare otherwise. Told her I'd seen him there, wrapped round another woman, and thought she needed to know.'

'Oh,' Eleanor said. 'And was he?'

Celia shuffled. It was always her hips got uncomfortable before long. Her pudgy fingers, with the same red varnish, rested snugly on the edge of the couch. She giggled.

'Oh, he *might* have been. He's a building engineer, you see, and his company often use that place for conferences and training stuff. There's a notice inside the door telling you which company is there, and it was. It would be just like him. He met *her* on a conference. Just to think, I go in to use the lav and see it! I'm so clever!'

Poor old Boris, Eleanor thought. Central London, that good old melting pot. Sit in one of those big hotels for a week or more, and you had a good chance of coming across half of the people you had ever known, just like big train stations.

'Any response?'

'I didn't want a response,' Celia murmured. 'I just wanted her to get the letter. Mid-week, when he's usually away. He works so hard, poor lamb. Something to worry her and the baby.'

Eleanor was moving up to the left hip, gently, gently, dreading getting there. Those pudgy hips, which looked like removable lumps of suet, ridiculously delineated with black lace. And she was supposed to put her hands under the lace, push it up, work round it, then pull it back, go on.

'I'm sure it did,' she murmured, to quell her rage. There was no response. Suddenly and miraculously, Celia was asleep. Eleanor got up and took another couple of pictures of her like that. Enough. There was a cartoon on the wall which Celia had never noticed, a faint, reproduced thing which Eleanor adored, depicting a frantic masseuse pushing up on the shoulders of a supine body so hard that the ribcage was torn free of flesh, and neither of them noticed. Impossible but tempting. She wanted a cigarette, paused in her labours, glad of the rest.

There was never any positive response from Celia. Certainly Celia *thanked* Eleanor; expressed pleasure and relief in the attention her body received, fulsomely telling Eleanor how marvellous she was, embarrassing and black-mailing her with praise. It was just that her corpse did not reflect what she said. There was no physical response in this body; it gave nothing in return; it simply *took*. Other bodies resonated, quivered in response to touch, gave themselves up to the massaging hands and encouraged them to work. It was difficult to explain to anyone who did not already know what she meant. Most bodies, even sleepy bodies, made small, uncontrollable gestures of encouragement, tiny reactions of awareness, a slight shuffle, a sigh, a twitch, a curling of fingers and toes, even increased floppiness, to indicate they were alive, while working with Celia Hornby was like working with thick, damp, unmouldable clay. No, worse than that, because clay could be fashioned into something, whereas there was not a chance of that here. This body, sucked up energy, like static fungus. Falling asleep was the most positive reaction yet and Eleanor did not imagine it would last. Celia Hornby's body might be a resistant piece of clay, but she would know when she was not the full focus of attention.

A mere minute's thinking time, then, to consider what she

was doing. This woman had excuses for her hatefulness, such as pain. She had chronic inflammation of the joints, and accompanying arthralgia, nasty pain, and this could only get worse. Eleanor would not necessarily have known this diagnosis, but for the referral from the rheumatologist who had sent Celia along out of despair, the way her doctor contacts so often did. Celia would not accept his diagnosis and advice, although she had accepted the prescribed drugs. She had argued, demanded more tests with the aim of getting another diagnosis of a condition less invasive, and she would not do anything to help herself. She was deeply suspicious of doctors, and what with her litigious history, they were suspicious of her.

The doctor must have figured that massage could do no harm. Let her spend the money she had got on harmless pampering which might do some good.

He was right: it could do no harm. Eleanor could not reach the damaged cartilage and make it worse. Nor could she make it better. A pair of strong hands could only do so much with a willing body, to stimulate muscle, improve circulation, keep what was in order in order and inhibit the progress of disease. Advise the patient on the right kind of positive conduct to improve their chances. The opportunity for harm was offered by Celia Hornby's blind faith, the hypnotic nature of this room, and the power of suggestion.

No, of course that doctor was wrong, Celia. Silly man. What you need is rest. Try to get ten hours' sleep a day and keep all movements to a minimum. Wait for the selenium to work.

Yes, Eleanor dear, anything you say. When I get better, will you come and live with me?

Yes, I'll think about it. And in the mean time I'll just give you a little rub all over and watch your muscles atrophy.

It really was as simple as that, and it was also a shock for Eleanor to realise she had been doing it for weeks. The best thing Celia Hornby could do was what her rheumatologist had ordered. Exercise. Keep moving. Walk, swim. Keep it at bay.

Yes, but it was only now, following the frankly wrong advice to stay still and seize up, that Celia was definitely worse. Eleanor was surprised to find that there was very little satisfaction in that. She conjured up the memory of Sasha's abject misery, the sense of disgrace which had sent her spiralling into depression and the final running away from all who loved her, and stifled the treacherous thought that Sasha would have gone even without the intervention of Mrs Hornby. She skipped the hips and began to massage Celia's pale spine. Celia stirred, and continued to talk as if she had never stopped.

'Stupid little bitch,' she said. 'Why ever would she think that Boris would be faithful to her? Why should she be secure, after what he did to me? And as for him, let him suffer.'

Eleanor paused, went on. The smell of lavender and camomile, masking Celia's other, milky smell.

'How's life at home?' Eleanor asked, wanting to change the subject from the all-too-frequent topic of ex-husband Boris, and Celia's attempts to make his life a misery. Why can't she just let go? She's got enough money, she's never had to work, why can't she count her blessings and just let go? *I can't let go.*

'It's very quiet at home,' Celia said. 'I wish he would come back, that man.'

This time Alan had eaten the breakfast, and paid for it, before JT arrived at the Marchmont caff. He was nursing the same filthy coffee, wearing the same blue coat, and burping gently. Was it his imagination, or did JT look really good today? Or was it the fact that his own coat smelt chemically clean? He loved this coat, but after the hotel's disastrous dry-clean to rid it of the smell of smoke, it did not feel quite the same. It had lost its soft feel and was slightly itchy, but maybe that was his skin. He was listening to his own voice phoning Sarah, not once but *twice*, to tell her about the boy and the dog. Phoned her to tell her what happened, then phoned her when the dog reappeared. It was sitting outside this caff, unnerving him, more than his dependence on Sarah did. Now where had that come from?

And JT really did look good and vigorous. It was as if he'd taken an example. Brilliant white shirt, pressed trousers, quality jacket. As if he had actually grown inside good clothes. His presence made a mark. He wasn't pleading any more; he was demanding. He was angry, but it was under control, and he made Alan feel small.

He needed a job, and he needed one soon. Even from a man like this. There was not enough money in the kitty to buy a new coat.

'I'm sick of the hypocrites,' JT was saying. 'These women looking like professional, middle-class ladies, and just *bitches*. I write to the tart who stole my property; she doesn't reply at all. I write to the widow of the bastard lawyer who cheated me, and she does, with insults. Seems to me in this rotten society there's no justice, no bloody way to get anyone to notice . . .'

'Except by screwing them down,' Alan finished, as the man's sentence died away. It was no good. His hands were shaking and he had to keep them hidden under the table. JT's hands were on the table. Christ, he had had himself another manicure. The nails were clipped and polished, the fingers drumming rhythmically. Alan gazed at the hands.

'That's what lawyers do, isn't it?' he made himself continue. 'So why don't you get one, and do it that way? If you really think this tart's flat is yours.'

JT snorted and flung his arm across the back of his chair. Alan noticed there was a thinning patch on the inside knee of his own once-good suit. JT was angrier, more self-righteous than before. Alan was trying to tell himself it was what people became when they felt they had no status, grabbing at the moral high ground because they had nothing else. It had been wrong to underestimate him, treat him like a boy. Once JT succumbed to the violent temptations which beset him, it would not be pretty. He was not fraying at the edges any more; he was strong. Blokes did that: turned old overnight, vicious in a day. They did it more often than they turned from sour to sweet. But there it was, Alan needed this man. Needed the money, needed the challenge to get back into practice.

'So, like I said, a small fire. I say and I pay.'

'Doesn't come less than two and a half grand in cash, for starters. And a lot of information.'

'So you said. It's all here.' He slid a fat brown envelope on to the slightly sticky table. Alan believed that it contained notes, and was surprised that JT was so willing to put money where, so far, only his mouth had been, while being, at the same time, faintly insulted and amused by the fact that the envelope was old and scuffed. The man couldn't even find a new envelope. All the same, the presence of money was impressive. It seemed to burn a hole in the top of the table. Alan could imagine the feel of it in his own inside pocket, shook his head.

'I don't think we can be in business. You want a small, containable fire to be started in a flat while it's empty, to send out a threat and do no real harm. Without the fucking thing going over, as they do. And you want it to look accidental.'

He thought of the fire in the hotel attic, contained only by luck. The money on the table was making him engage himself with the problem, against his better judgement, trying to look as if he didn't want the job when he did.

'I don't want it to do serious damage, it's *my* property after all. That's what we're talking about. *Mine*. And it would be better if it looked accidental, so that she couldn't complain about it, even though she'd know it wasn't. She'd know it was me, but she wouldn't be able to prove it.'

Alan wished the she was a he. Far less responsibility. It was a relief that so far JT did not want anyone to be hurt. Yet. He would soon. They did, men like that with hands like that.

'I still don't get why you think this flat is yours,' Alan said. 'Why did your dad owe you anything?'

JT said nothing.

Alan touched the scar on his own face. Fathers, God bless fathers. How he had despised his own.

'Listen, mate, when someone starts a fire deliberately, it's usually fucking obvious, unless they've done a really thorough job and reduced the place to ashes, which is what I'm usually asked to do. Even that's difficult. Fire's quirky: you never quite know what it might destroy and what it might bypass, and absolute total fucking destruction's as rare as hen's teeth, unless you're out in the wilderness and it can go for hours without anyone noticing. Central London, forget it. The fire service is brilliant. There's all these clowns who think fire would get rid of a body, for instance. Once in a fucking blue moon. You need a bomb for that.'

He realised he was repeating what he had said to Sheila the other night, after the attic fire. She had listened to him far too closely, just like Sarah did.

'You know what gives it away as arson? Just about everything. Pouring your accelerant on to something where it soaks in as well as burns, leaves plenty of traces. Setting the fire in two different places, just to be sure. An accidental fire has one source, not two or three. Lighting up the wrong material, imagining that books and wood will go up, just like that, when you're much better off with fabric. You've got to know what you're doing.'

The other man lit a cigarette, also listening far too closely. Alan couldn't help but take a pride in his subject. Odd, that it was easier to talk in a crowded place. He looked around the caff. Full of meltable plastic. Remembered what he had said to Sheila. The best way to make it look like an accident is to have someone to blame it on. Wait until there's contractors, electricians, a plumber on the premises. They're always good to blame. Or wait until you've got a politician in the building, then you can blame terrorists, only terrorists won't target unimportant hotels and VIPs come with security.

JT leant forward, the money still between them. He looked amused. 'All right, then, how do most *accidental* fires start?'

'By accident. Machinery, blow lamps, welding stuff. In the house, chip pans, cigarettes. An overheating lamp with the wrong-wattage bulb, inside a melting shade, next to the curtains . . . that was Windsor Castle. Candles, of course. Don't people love candles these days? Only don't know how to take care of them, the way people did when they were the only source of light. Those little nightlights left on top of the TV, melt through. Candles and plastic count for a lot.'

'I know all that,' JT said. 'I can read, you know. I can apply science as well as the next man. I could do it. I could get someone else to do it.'

Alan knew he was talking too much. Yeah, perhaps you could learn it from books. Perhaps all there had ever been to it was the ability to run away, fast. He was longing for the good old days of straightforward instructions, *just torch it, Al*. The warehouse where they couldn't pay for the ordered goods; the shop where they wouldn't pay for the goods; the taking out of someone else's business for the good of the competition; the amusement arcade worth more in insurance than profit; the building where the developer couldn't get planning permission and was stuck with a preservation order; a couple of churches, for the same reason. Buildings and stock worth more on paper than they were ever going to make. It was only money. Get in there, get out, remember not to let the petrol get on your clothes. Do it at the time of day when the fire service was busiest. Phone them up with the wrong address, to buy time. It was all a bloody sight easier in the good old days before smoke alarms and video cameras. He was getting old. Like he had told himself before, he needed a different challenge. Small and domestic, like this. A taster. There must be a market for stuff like this.

'I've got the florist watching. I go by this flat every day, once or twice,' JT said. 'And she's not there. There's someone staying there at the moment. Old bloke, like you. A cripple. Comes out of the place with a stick and a big boot on his foot, never goes far. We could blame it on him.'

'Give me the address and I'll scope it out,' Alan said. 'And the name of the tart.'

He was still hypnotised by those revolting hands.

'Sarah Fortune, Buckingham Mansions. Off Welbeck.'

Alan pretended to cough, deflecting the smoke from the man's cigarette smouldering in the ashtray with a wave of his hand, to hide his confusion. Confusion? It was more like a punch in the gut. Oh Jesus God, bloody hell, no. JT was searching through his pockets, failing to notice how Alan's jaw had dropped off his face. That gave him a second or two.

'Look,' Alan said. 'Why do you have to go for the tart at all, if you want the flat kept safe? Why don't you go for the lawyer who fucked you over in the first place? Make him put it right?'

'The widow, you mean? That's a good idea. Look what the bitch wrote to me first.' He pushed a single crumpled sheet of headed paper across the table.

It contained a scrawl, beginning with, *Bugger off . . . Push off, pipsqueak. Dulcie Mathewson.*

Alan noticed the highlights, wanted to laugh he felt so fucking hysterical, but thought it would not be a good idea. *Dulcie.* The only person Sarah had ever mentioned when he asked about family. The wife of an old boss. The world was suddenly, crashingly smaller than the single room of this caff.

'She could be next,' JT said. 'I'd like to have a crack at her myself. How dare she write to me like that? She's just as much to blame as Sarah Fortune, and she loves the tart.'

So do I.

Alan put his hand over the letter and the money envelope, drew them towards him slowly, as if making up his mind. The money seemed to glow through the envelope, which was warm to the touch. So would the thirty pieces of silver received by Judas Iscariot. He could not quite believe what he was doing.

133

'Are you going to tell me your proper name, and address?'

'Julian Tysall, Flat 2, 14 Leegard Road, N1,' JT answered, promptly. It might have been true. It probably was.

'And yours is the Belvedere,' he added. 'Where you work, illegally, for cash.'

How did he know that? He knew everything.

Then JT smiled, and that was the worst thing of all. His smile made Alan shiver. A man with looks and money. And second sight. It was as if he knew that Alan had the keys to the place all along. Keys he had found in the pocket of that lovely soft grey coat, closed his hands around, and kept. For access to her; out of a desire to protect her, he didn't know. Wanting something of hers. A talisman. Ashamed of it, later.

He stuffed the scruffy envelope and the letter in his inside pocket, near the knife, rose to go. The balance of power between them had completely changed. It was palpable. Alan saw himself all too clearly: a man in a stiff coat, getting old, with a scar on his face and with only a borrowed dog waiting for him, caught in the confident smile of a good-looking man with twenty more years' worth of choices.

'Give us a couple of days to think it out.'

'It's either you, Al, or someone else.'

'You're paying *me*. What do you mean, somebody else? Somebody else like you, you mean? You really think you can learn how, that quick?'

JT dipped his head in mock salute. Good thick, healthy hair.

'I don't see why not,' he said, smiling again, pushing the hair back off his forehead with that elegant hand. 'You've just given me the basics, and it does sound fun. Another time, maybe. I'd be good at it.'

He left with a spring in his step, a man with places to go and people to see, leaving Alan with a racing heart and the pallor of wretchedness. This could not be for real. There was money in the dirty envelope warming the lining of his coat, and he wanted to weep.

CHAPTER SEVEN

'I hope this isn't going to be permanent,' William said. 'I don't like to see my lovely jubbly jellybean getting bogged down in domesticity. The scale is simply too small for her.'

William the dentist was a fond and regular lover, one day a week, subject to other obligations. Lunch was followed by what were known as siestas at his place, after which he would sometimes, gallantly, insist on seeing her home, as he had today, although today it was partially out of his incessant curiosity to see the inside of another house. If William was invited to dinner, he would stand at the door with a bottle of wine in hand, unless he had dropped or lost it en route, with his eyes already wandering over the head of whoever greeted him, his whole presence begging for a guided tour of every room. An insistence on examining the details of the furniture and the crockery could cause offence.

In between their irregular interludes, William would send Sarah notes by post, using the headed notepaper from his surgery, so that the sentimental twaddle contained within in his sprawly hand contrasted nicely with the stiffly embossed address. *William would like to inform Miss Fortune that, regrettably, another appointment is necessary,* he would write, *and that he looks forward to it, very much.* Long accepting of his foibles, Sarah guessed that his sometime habit of referring to her, and others, in the third person, even when they were present, evolved from the manner in which he spoke to his patients. *There, there, there,* refusing to make eye contact unless they were children, otherwise talking about them as if they were in another room, so that he could forget they were really there. He was at home with teeth, but not with the individuals who owned them. In a similar way, he preferred relationships at a distance, on well-defined lines, although this did not stop his long-term thing with Sarah being love of a kind. Daily intimacy would have driven him mad, but he knew where he was with Sarah, because they had made a bargain to meet as they did and otherwise stay apart, though all the same he liked to know where she was at any given time, and imagine the colour of the walls.

'Well, I don't understand what on earth you're doing here,' he said, reverting to normal on his way out after a quick, admiring exploration of the rooms, tut-tutting as he went. 'Experimenting with life as usual. Which is a jellybean's privilege. What a pity you don't have the whole house. Can I look upstairs?'

'No, nothing to see anyway. Stairs blocked off, another flat . . . William, do come back.'

He had charged up the stairs leading to the upper regions; she followed, admiring his complete indifference to trespassing and emboldened by it, waiting all the same for the sound of Celia Hornby's key in the front door.

'You're right,' he said. 'Nothing but a nice window.'

There were gritty crumbs of something on the floor beneath their feet. He had gone further than she ever had in a few days, and it was awkward, standing in the small lobby facing the door to the second flat, surprised by the sight of the window, hidden from below, round the bend of the blocked-off, rerouted stairs. When the house was one, it would have been a feature, with its curved Georgian shape, meant to be seen and admired en route upstairs. Mrs Hornby's own front door was contrastingly plain, cheap wood with a glazed panel, against which William put his nose so close he could have been sniffing at it. She could feel a draught from the edges of the door, pulling her in.

'Come away, Will, do. There's nothing to see, and you may disturb her budgie,' but he was already on his way back down, feet thumping on stairs as he went. 'What a messy woman,' he was muttering as they reached the hall. 'But that might be why.'

'What might be why?' Sarah asked, relieved that he was on his way out. If Celia Hornby returned to find a tall, permanently stooped dentist lurking in her entrance hall, it was hardly likely to improve the neutral state of pretended indifference which had persisted between them so far. William had noticed the marks on the carpet, as William would. It looked, in daylight, as if someone had dropped splodges of a different-coloured dye on the pale green, or ground something into the wool with a grubby heel. There were also more of the crumbs, like spilled gravel beneath the feet.

'All these marks on the good carpet,' William began.

The necessity to keep a pristine waiting room and a sterile surgery had somehow made William a natural domestic detective, and his unduly sensitive sense of smell was an asset as well as an affliction.

'Bleach,' he went on triumphantly, 'I smell bleach. A budgerigar, you said? Well, I bet the thing got out and pooped on the carpet. What a silly fool to use bleach on it. Takes out the colour. Should have used shampoo. Is she ill? Does she drop things? Looks like bird food. Oh dear, I must rush. Thank you, dear bean. I think it's time I went. I wish you'd stay at home.'

She closed the front door behind him, paused to hear him whistle down the street, wishing she could have walked with him, but William would not have liked that. He liked to stride out alone, retrieving his isolation. She looked at the carpet again. What he said made sense, as it often did with William.

Henry had told her that the marks on the front-hall carpet were Celia Hornby's deliberate sabotage, but if the same crude damage occurred on the landing outside Celia's own front door, that theory did not make sense. She might, out of spite, shit on their communal territory purely to annoy him, as he was convinced she did, but it hardly explained why she should sully her own. Henry referred to a campaign of terror; William referred to accidents with the yellow budgerigar, which would foolishly try to escape if ever the opportunity was granted, followed by misguided, clumsy attempts to clear up after it, using whatever means came to hand. Then there were the crumbs of anonymous stuff inside the front door, and outside Celia's own, which Henry described as a deliberate scattering of litter, but which Sarah could see now might be the bird food she dropped as she entered, fumbling with her key. Gritty substances carried in and out. It was all about that damn bird, which hated her.

Two mornings before, waking early, Sarah had heard Celia singing to the bird, a tuneless noise with an oddly penetrating quality, an endearing attempt to capture the attention of something on which she lavished care and affection in the absence of anything else. William's insight also explained the constant burble of radio and TV noise: she left one or other turned on to provide dear Boris with company, perhaps. The effect in a poorly insulated conversion was irritating, but it surely did not make her as malicious as Henry described.

Sarah went down to the kitchen and out into the garden. It was essentially a paved, walled courtyard, reached by three steps down from the French doors, with ivy growing on the back wall. The east and west walls were covered with winter-dead clematis and jasmine, clinging to brick and holding its breath until April or May. She knew enough to know it would be quietly spectacular then, and it was not what she had stepped out to see. Looking up, she could see that Celia's sash windows were open a few inches, which must make it cold up there, but maybe that, too, was for Boris. Maybe her failure to carpet her floor was also on account of the bird. Or an allergy. There were other theories than Henry's.

It was growing dark in the garden, although it was becoming apparent that the afternoons were longer, as daylight increased its mean daily ration, and suddenly she wanted to be out into the wider world, before it faded away. Living in a house which was not her own was subtly exhausting, even if, for the last seven days, she had returned to her own home every day in the early evening, before coming back. The swap appeared to have achieved its purpose only too well. It was as if the presence of a *man*, actually in residence at her place, as opposed to visiting, made the vital difference. The letters had stopped landing in the foyer of her block of flats, and Henry, whoever he was, was insanely cheerful, while she was sick of being cautious around the possessions of another. Despite its damaged state, with stained carpets outside and ravaged kitchen ceiling within, Henry's place was just *too* pretty. Like a model with all the accoutrements, easy to admire, not that easy to touch, and with far too many bits of spiky jewellery for intimacy.

Everything that Henry possessed was of fine quality, from the last silver knife, fork and spoon to the first delicate china cup, which obliged her to be uncharacteristically careful. The CD player was complicated, the bed sheets fine linen, the covers on the dining chairs were silk, and everything she touched or sat upon had value. There were fresh candles in every room, each on an elegant stand, as if he had a fetish with candles. It was a haven because it was not hers, and uncomfortable for the same reason. She liked quality, but was coming to realise that she disliked it if it was fragile. She needed things around her which could be dropped, or torn, or lost without it really mattering. Henry, on the other hand, need have no reservations about what belonged to her.

Out in the street, it was easy to know that nothing was hers. The cold had relented; in the last reaches of afternoon, the daylight was becoming a visible promise of colour, and in the square she now regarded as her own, spring had really begun with a sly, obdurate hope. The crocus shoots were an inch above ground, and the buds on the barren shrubs began to compete with the solid evergreens. There was a low-level fountain in the square, more on than off, surrounded by the benches where it was too cold to sit for the hour she might have sat, but warm enough already to linger for minutes, enjoying the stubbornness of spring. The scars on her back itched less; she could understand the temptation to talk to plants, because spring was relentless in its determination. The rest of the world can go to hell, she told the crocuses; you have to grow.

And so must I, even if it means going backwards.

She shrugged deeper into her coat, with the thought that philosophical considerations, however deep or shallow, did not become her any more than they did the progress of nature. A plant did not, after all, consider its situation, since the situation was something it had arrived at.

She sat, snug in her coat, and raised her eyes to the sky, watching the light struggling behind the prohibitive cloud of darkness, bidding it good night and goodbye for the evening, with that hint of cunning which was already saying, I shall be back in the morning and I shall win. A boy sped by on a skateboard, totally absorbed in the effort to balance, completely impervious to anything else. She glanced at him, wistfully, because she had always wanted to be able to do that.

She was deft and quick in her movements, she would run rather than walk, she could still turn cartwheels, but she could not really move very fast.

Hands in her pockets, with her bag carried across the front of herself, she saluted the skateboarder as she sauntered out of the square and began the walk home. London was small, after all. She was wearing her favourite handbag, rust-coloured to match the petal scarf, shaped like a soft, square envelope, with a broad strap which hung across the coat like a sash. A handbag was to be worn, rather than carried. She had found it in a second-hand shop with Dulcie, long ago. At the bottom of the bag was the spare set of keys to her flat, which she always carried in addition to the one she usually kept in her pocket but had lost, somewhere in Henry's house, she supposed. Walking from one home to another was like being in limbo. Limbo, what a word. She knew it as the state between heaven and hell to which a soul was relegated when it deserved neither happiness nor punishment, and awaited redemption. Others without her convent education knew it as an exotic body-distorting dance. She must learn to concentrate.

She walked through one square into another, from Russell to Bedford, arrived within the vicinity of her own flat, and did not want to go in. She had been running away this last week, and it was time to stop.

No, not running away, buying time. Securing space for herself and for someone else who might not deserve the privilege. Not that being deserving was a qualification for Sarah's attention. On balance, she preferred her men to lack conventional virtues, but she did require them to be truthful, even economically. She did not care who Henry was; she had seen a man in dire need of affection, who might also respond to it, and that was enough to begin with, but she was starting to think that whatever it was that had reduced him to the state where he longed to lock himself into a small room with an impregnable door was not simply the antisocial behaviour of a neighbour, but something else entirely. A previous trauma which made him prone to terror, creating a persecution complex. Maybe he had acquired one of those simply by guarding the inheritance he had created; maybe it also drove him mad to be surrounded by precious things, with the constant fear that someone would discover them and take them away. My, my, she chided herself, you'll get a degree in psychology next. Doesn't matter what makes Henry suffer, except that it might be the clue how to make it better.

At the same time she was trying to work out how she had lost those damn keys from out of her pocket. It was easier trying to understand other people than it was to understand herself.

★

Henry hugged her enthusiastically when she let herself in, as if hugging was all he ever wanted. He was assuming the occupation of her flat ever more naturally, and since she had brought him back shoes and clothes from his own place, and he had begun to go out and about, seemed even more in command. Henry was creative in his self-management and now wore a hiking boot on his left foot, to counterbalance the added height given by the aircast boot on his right, so that he could move about, nimbly and evenly balanced, which he obviously did, because the place was spotless and he had the energy of a flea. She could not have appointed a better care-taker, either for love or money: he saw her place as something to be improved. He persisted in the habit of rearranging things and conducted a jealous mission against dust. He was *awfully* pleased to see her, which she sensed had little enough to do with her herself. It was the pleasure of a man showing off what he had done, like a proud interior designer who had not quite cottoned on that his own ideas and those of his client were not exactly coinciding. The old brass planter which had lingered in a kitchen cupboard because of a miss-ing leg did indeed look marvellous, filled with flowers on the living-room table, which, polished to a shine, looked unfa-miliar. The lights in the corridor looked better for the removal and washing of their glass shades; the place had lost the Stygian gloom of winter. There were candles, strategic-ally placed on surfaces, as if he wished to mimic a detail from his own house. Worst of all was a mantelpiece full of ornaments, culled from God knows where. It was imperti-nent of him, and he said so, but he simply could not resist it. It was as if he was treating her flat like a wardrobe which required revamping without the budget to acquire anything new. She liked it, and yet she did not like it all. On the last two evenings when she had checked in, he had greeted her even more as if she was a guest. She could not bring herself to object. It would not be the first time she had relinquished control, and Henry being so pleased with himself was infectious.

'I went out today. Got those flowers. Found the deli, so you will stay to supper? No? What a shame. Quite a picnic I have.'

'And the foot?' she asked, with the politeness of a guest.

'My dear, I'm David Beckham. Not a twinge in the old metatarsal, nothing but a fading bruise and the tingling which accompanies healing. I venture forth on it, and the people in the vicinity are so kind. The florist understands, the bank allows me access to money, the wine shop permits me to purchase, so I have a sufficiency of everything the human soul requires, while the vile boot is a subject for conversation, so I have that, also. Life is a breeze, I feel full of energy . . . oh dear, I've gone too far, haven't I?'

He followed the direction of her gaze, watched as she registered the fact that the old battered tray she had had for a hundred years was covered in a lace cloth. Where he had found such a thing she could not imagine, since lace did not currently feature in her lifestyle, any more than candles. It must have been some relic Dulcie had donated, during the brief spell when Sarah had cohabited with her son, rescued from wherever similar items resided. Sarah had never been good at throwing any gift away.

'You're looking well, Henry, must be the prospect of spring,' she said. 'And maybe it's time you went home, or I did, or we both did. And anyway, you should be resting your foot, sitting down with your leg raised above hip height. And doing your static exercises, like a good boy.'

'Oh, I do that too,' Henry said. 'Indeed I do, for most of the day.' An armchair and footstool had been dragged to the window. 'I've sat so long that I've found the outside world irresistible, and five days ago I'd never have thought it, when not tinkering around indoors, of course. And I do apologise for my impertinence. I wanted to be useful. It's a poor return for a place of safety.'

Sarah said nothing, which she did when she had nothing to say, took the glass of wine, as if it was she who was the perfect guest. She wanted to be home, in a half-hearted way; she wanted to tell him about Mrs Hornby and the budgie, of which he was ignorant, but she could see the thought of going back to Golden Street was not on his agenda. Not yet. He had not even asked about the cat.

'Of course I'll go back,' Henry said, a trifle forlornly. 'But am I not useful here?' He leant forward. 'Someone watches the place, you know. Or they have done, today and yesterday. I saw, from the window.'

'Watches?'

'I've seen a man,' Henry said. 'He stands on the other side of the road. Smoking a cigarette, rather elegantly as it happens, outside those offices opposite. And I know he's watching you, because although he looks as if he has an appointment at said offices, he looks up, directly here, every now and then. *You,* or this flat, or *us,* are clearly the focus of his attention. Or he is clearly fixated by the windows, which are the object of his scrutiny. I've cleaned on the inside, by the way. It makes a small difference.'

'What does he look like?'

'Young. Good-looking. He may only be flirting with the florist, or she with him.'

'Do you wave at him?' she asked, flippantly, aware of her own quickening pulse, which the wine would not cure.

'Oh, dear me, no. Sorry, yes, I do, although I'm peeking

from round the perimeter, so to speak, so I doubt he notices. I think he did, once, and then he went away.'

He might have been making it up. He wanted to stay here, and he had a persecution complex.

'Anything other than handsome?'

'Oh, he's just a man in a suit. With a scarf. Looks like the better kind of estate agent. Don't ask me to tell you about his facial features. From this height, how would I know? Regular, businesslike.'

A fiction, then. He had begun to shake. He was a nice man, and she could not bear it. He cradled himself into her arms on the sofa, hauling his foot alongside, in its crazy boot. When he was warmer, he stopped shaking.

'What did you do the rest of the day, Henry? I hate to tell you, but you've only accounted for about three hours.'

His face was buried in her shoulder, his voice a mumble.

'I go into the safe room,' he said. 'I like it there.'

She did not have the heart to cross-examine him. She would continue to rely on instinct until he was ready. Ah well, it could all wait.

She did not like to tell him that his own place was watched. Not watched as such, simply visited from time to time.

By a big man, wearing a suit.

'I've told you, Al, you can't bring that dog in here. The only dogs I'll let in are poodles with diamond collars belonging to millionairesses. And that dog isn't that kind. That's a homeless dog, that is.'

'They let dogs everywhere in Paris, so I'm told. I hear people go shopping and eating in all the best places in Paris with mongrels.'

'This isn't bloody Paris. It's bloody London.'

You could bring a dog into the foyer of this hotel on a lead, sit with the brute and have a drink, but that was it, and nobody ever did it anyway. Basically, there was one set of rules for the ordinary clientele, infinitely variable for anyone rich or important enough to insist. Sheila would have organised caviar for a pampered poodle belonging to the kind of famous model who never came to a joint like this, but was not inclined to give house room to a cross-eyed mutt, just because it had attached itself to her security man. Even if he was family. She was irritated with him for other reasons. Mainly because he was avoiding her, just when she had something very important to discuss with him, such as how to torch the redundant top floor, the idea of which had turned from mere wish to obsession ever since she had seen how easy it would be to do. And because he was distracted, not concentrating. Alan was thinking of the message on his mobile from JT. *Do you know what, Al? Had another letter. Seems the widow thinks the tart is her daughter. Have we got this the wrong way round? Don't forget I paid you.*

As if he could. It tormented him.

'Keep your hair on, Sheila. He's been useful, this dog. Show a dog to a drunk, and the drunk quietens down ever so quick. Even a drunk knows not to try and punch a dog. Got a lovely growl, this dog.'

'Get rid of it, Al.'

'Tomorrow, OK? It's been sleeping at the back of the kitchen. Doesn't go up to the rooms. And I keep trying to get rid of it, but it just keeps coming back.'

'Have you tried kicking it? You're just not concentrating, Al.'

She was right about that. He was plain miserable. Money

in his pocket, along with the obligation to earn it by shitting on the person he liked or loved best, fuck it. He tried to tell himself it was Sarah's fault, but that did not work. Couldn't see a way out of it, whichever way he turned it. Heaven-sent, in one way, because he had the fucking key, and she was not there, and if he didn't do it someone else would. Carelessly, savagely, even. If he didn't do it, he would unleash JT on Sarah, and JT would want his money back. It went round and round, the whole horrible guilt thing, making his head spin and without producing a single idea of *how.* How to do something without hurting anyone, how for her not to know it was him, how to take the money and run, except he wanted to see her. Be a man. He had even thought of sitting down and talking it through with her, but that was a stretch too far. No woman would understand if you said, *look, I've just got to set fire to your place, but don't worry about it, can we still be lovers?* Not even lovers, no way.

Sheila and he were sitting in the alarmingly empty foyer, irritated with one another and pretending they were not. Sheila opened her mouth to speak, but her mobile phone rang. She listened to it, in that rapt way people did with their phones, as if hearing a message from God, giving it far more concentration than they did the person they were speaking to at the time, then said, 'I'll send him,' turned to Alan with a loud sigh, and said, 'Room forty. Some silly cow's got a problem with her bathroom. Says she wants Security. The handsome one, she says. Got to be you.'

Not his kind of job, really, but she was punishing him. The dog knew the score and crawled behind the fat armchair, out of sight. Business was bad today, and all this week. There was no one to notice and be offended. Business was bad and Sheila was twitchy.

149

Alan knew the type, as soon as she opened the door. A lone traveller, American, in search of learning rather than adventure. You could tell by the awful clothes. She had wild grey hair and wore a leisure suit of the kind loved by the serious-minded tourist. Two things struck him first, apart from his guess at her identity: one, she was drunk, and two, there was that oh so familiar smell of smoke. Dead smoke, he called it; smoke that had been, rather than smoke which was being made. Alan inclined his head towards her, as if to say, your servant, ma'am. Always best to begin that way. She recoiled, slightly, but he was used to that. His eyes took in the contours and arrangements of the small room, registered the existence of the smoke alarm, fixed to the centre of the ceiling like a limpet. Standard issue for every room and all the corridors. The sash window was slightly open. Her forehead was beaded with perspiration, she was embarrassed, but drink had taken the edge off. She would have purchased her own supplies; no money for the minibar.

'It's in the bathroom.'

'What would that be, madam?'

She giggled. 'The towel I burned. No, it burned. I didn't burn it. Did it all by itself.'

The door to the small en suite bathroom was firmly shut. There were no smoke alarms in the bathrooms. It took three steps to reach it, open the door to the acrid smell of burned cloth. The washbasin was full of charred bath towel. He picked up an edge of damp cotton, dropped it back.

'I put my little water heater thing in my mug, this thing here, and plugged it into the shaver point. It's a good little thing, easy to pack and everything. I guess they don't sell 'em any more. The thing boils up a mug of water in no time, then you make your coffee for a lot cheaper than room service.

150

Only you gotta remember to unplug it, otherwise it just goes on heating up whatever is around, and I laid it down on the towel, see, and came back in here to drink my . . . coffee.'

He did see. He picked up the heating device and looked at it. It was a type he had not seen in a long time, consisting of a coiled element, like the kind on the inside of a small kettle, attached to a handle, a plastic-covered wire and a shaver plug. Simple: no switches, no safety features and no longer available. If you left it plugged in after using it, it would get red hot. Touch the coil when it was like that, very burned finger. He turned it over in his hand, affectionately; such a dangerous travelling convenience, loved it. He could make one himself, dead easy, with a kettle element, old knife handle, wire and plug, but he preferred hers. He looked at the bathroom, too, laughed out loud, then turned to her. She was nervous and ill at ease, not a natural for a five-star hotel, a Midwestern culture vulture on an out-of-season bargain break who could not afford the trimmings and was used to obeying rules. Kind he liked best. I know what I'm going to do now, he told himself; God bless you for showing me a way to a neat little fire.

'Am I going to be charged for burning down the bath-room?'

He patted her plump shoulder. 'No, madam, you get given a prize. You did ever so well to catch it. How long did it take to set the towel alight?'

'Oh, a good few minutes. Then I saw the flame . . .' She shuddered.

'No problem, really. Only I've got to take away your coffee-maker. It's a bit iffy, if you see what I mean.'

She did, sagging against the bathroom door, nodding in agreement.

151

'So I won't be charged for the towel? Only I feel so bad . . .'

'No need, madam. And I do take your point. Room service is way too expensive. So what can I get you, on the house, of course? Tea, coffee, a sandwich, a drink from the bar? New towels will be with you in a minute.'

She looked at him, squinty-eyed, as if she had been absolved of all sin and a fire in her bathroom was commonplace. The look said, *stay with me,* and the next, as she sobered by the second, said, *why is this guy being so nice?,* while the third look took in the dangerous face. She retreated towards the door of the room and opened it.

'Why, a steak sandwich and a half-bottle of red would be just fine.'

She ushered him out, and when he had gone wished she had asked for more.

He knew what he was going to do, and knew he must do it now, while she wasn't there and the idea was hot. *Small, containable fire, ideal space, bathroom.* Especially hers. Great clunking cast-iron bath. A big wooden window, solid old door, not much plastic. A shaver point. Fine. Didn't even need the accelerant. He thought of JT and his promise. *It's either you, Al, or someone else.*

The foyer was empty and the flowers dying when he slipped out with his haversack. The dog followed.

Alan particularly liked walking at night. He had walked every inch of central London and the map of it was in his head. He cut through the squares, walking in the middle of the empty side roads as if he owned them, making a noise with his steps because it was never good to be furtive. Usually he felt king of the place, but now he was anxious and dogged by guilt. He avoided the top bit of Oxford Street: he hated to see the homeless bodies huddled in doorways, looking like dead people in body bags, because one of them could be him, any time now. No identity: he wouldn't even be able to collect the dole. As long as he walked with a purpose, no copper would stop him, and if they did, all he had on him was a thing for heating water. The bloke who was staying at Sarah's would have to take his chances. It had to be now.

The plate-glass door to Buckingham Mansions always looked intimidating, but hey, he was used to a big fuck of a revolving hotel door, and he knew how to approach a door with confidence, even if he had never used the key before. Easy. He had been here often enough to know the way, followed her in, admiring her legs as she went up the stairs before him. Oh, Sarah, Sarah, what am I doing?

Third floor, mercifully carpeted stairs. Another smooth lock. She had a burglar alarm, but didn't use it. He was willing to place a bet that the smoke alarms would not be functioning either, not her style. She didn't even know they were there and she was always burning food.

The long corridor stretched before him, smelling clean. Alan took off his shoes and tiptoed down it, realising that he did not know it all that well. Knew the bathroom and the bedroom, had other things on his mind when he came here. Would she understand, if ever she knew, that he was doing this for her own good, as well as his? Perhaps not. He was going to do it anyway.

The corridor led to two rooms at the end. One with the door firmly shut; the other, her room, with an open door. Nothing, not a sniff of occupation. If there was a man staying, like she said, he was out, or dead to the world. Everything so clean and tidy, emphasising the emptiness.

Couldn't remember what was behind that other door with the lock, didn't matter, no one here. Looked like the cleaners had been in.

But his memory was right. The bathroom was ideal for a small, containable fire. There was that tough old vinyl floor, not easy to set alight, unless something really molten hot dropped on it. Naff plastic lampshade fitted like a globe around the central light, would melt and drop if the flames went over, but there probably wasn't enough of it to burn for long. Plastic casing round the lights and all the doodahs above the washbasin would also melt and drop into the porcelain. Towel rail was metal, good; walls, tiled from floor to ceiling, good; shower machinery, plastic and metal, would drop into the bath. The lav was next door, the way they did in these old places, so that was all right. There were all those mysterious bottles of stuff arranged on the ledge above the basin, plastic too, but full of inhibiting liquid. The inside of the solid wood door would be slow to take, and it fitted snugly. He checked the window. Old, solid, firmly shut against winter. Rule one for limiting a fire: limit air supply and fuel. He looked at the shower curtain. Thin stuff, more for effect than anything. Useless for the purpose of containing water, it would burn itself out. Fuel for a fire, but not much.

It was a small, almost severely practical bathroom. No fuss about Sarah.

He took all the towels he could find, one bath sheet and two smaller, and put them in the washbasin. The largest towel was slightly damp: good. Then he plugged the coffee-making thingy into the shaver point, and left it resting on top of the towels. Would have been better if the wire was long enough to reach into the bath, but it wasn't. He caught hold of the diaphanous shower curtain and draped it round the edge of the basin.

Then he left, as silently as he had arrived. Kept his hands in the pockets of the itchy coat, and felt like desperate hell. Tried to tell himself it was always bad news to get close to a woman, and walked on, faster and faster. The money had grown cold, and felt like a wedge of ice. He did not feel like a man; he felt like the sort of cheap thief in the night he despised.

Henry woke, in the middle of a nightmare which he thought the safe room had cured. It was all eerily silent, like the silence before a storm. He was hot and he needed water. Tut, tut, fancy forgetting to bring in water. It was very hot, but that was the dream, of his house being on fire, like all those other houses he had seen, afterwards. No grief like the grief of fire. He opened the door of the safe room by pulling the handle, looked down the corridor, felt heat and saw the light of flame licking from the inside of the bathroom door, like a hungry tongue. He began to scream, NO, NO, NO, NOT AGAIN.

Then the smoke alarm went off. He stood, mesmerised by the line of scarlet and gold at the bottom of the bathroom door. He hobbled towards it, wanting to run, wanting to retreat at the same time.

Went back into the safe room and closed the door.

Chapter Eight

No, no, no, Eleanor said to herself. I cannot face Mrs Celia Hornby three times this week because I do not like either myself or what I'm doing, and if I was a kind person I would pity her, rather than loathe her. And now she wants to come every day. She is convinced that massage and lying down is making her better, and that at any moment she will rise from this couch, or her own bed, or from a seat in the big department store coffee shops and hotels where she sits all day, as lithe as a young girl.

I should like to be like Sarah, immune from hatred, but I am not. I should like to be able to see the good in people who are weak, silly and greedy, as she does and I can't. It would be nice to want to understand them, but it isn't worth the effort. Look at her. Mrs Celia Hornby deserves neither analysis nor pity. She is as nasty a piece of work as anyone can imagine. Listen to her now. Look at the malice in that face. Someone like Sarah would think that having reasons for being nasty is the same thing as having excuses. It isn't. This woman may have been corrupted by youthful expectations; she may be in mental and physical torment. I don't care. All I know is that she is simply a vicious old cow.

The massage room looked tawdry in the morning. Eleanor had hastened to close the curtains after she cleaned and dusted, but she noticed it. Spring would make it worse. At this hour of the day, her surgery looked less like the slightly theatrical oasis of calm and peace she had struggled to create with paint, paper and fabric, and more like a temporary stage set, held together with staples, all of it peeling at the edges. Cheap effects, cheap practice running out of steam, sick and tired, like Eleanor was herself. The lump on the couch spoke.

'Do you know, that woman, his wife, wrote back to me today. Got the letter before I came out. She said thank you for telling her, but she still loved him.'

'Love conquers all, doesn't it?' Eleanor murmured.

She was being a little rough around the back of the doughy knees. Mrs Hornby giggled, like a child, tickled.

'What exactly had you told her this time?'

'Told her Boris couldn't be trusted with children. He fantasised about little girls. Girls with no knickers. He liked that kind of porn. Maybe she better look out for her daughter.'

'Was that true?'

Celia giggled again. It was the most depressing sound in her repertoire.

'It might have been. And she might not believe me, but it will make her watch him, and he hates that. A baby daughter, at his age. It's ridiculous.'

'Why didn't you have babies?'

She asked the question she knew it was always wrong to ask a childless woman. There were so many reasons why not.

'Couldn't. Didn't want. Relief to find I never could've, anyway. Ovaries wrong. Would ruin my figure.'

Eleanor paused, monumentally. If Celia Hornby could never have had children, *didn't want them,* then what was her suing Sasha over the removal of a redundant ovary all about? She wanted to scream at her, what is your justification for being a kept woman all your life? Why should a man keep you if you won't have his children and you really prefer women? Celia's sense of bloody entitlement enraged her. And the wilful fantasy of being a wronged virgin. She suppressed a shudder. The photographs were in the bag. Not yet.

'And how's the flat? Everything warm and comfy in this cold weather?'

Celia's voice was petulant. 'That man downstairs is still away. He should let me know what he's doing, really he should. All the same, I hope he stays away longer. It'll give me a chance to do something about the cat. I worry about Boris. That cat has to go.'

For a moment Eleanor was confused, before she remembered Boris the budgerigar, rather than Boris the husband.

'It's a greedy thing, that cat,' Celia said. 'It'll eat anything.'

A crack of sunlight intruded round the velvet curtains, illuminating the back of Celia's neck. She could scarcely move it at all now.

'Anyway, this *friend* of his tries to be neighbourly, offered to help me with the shopping yesterday, but I'm not having it. Keeps ungodly hours, this so-called friend. Do you know, I heard the door slam at five o'clock this morning? Gave me a fright, I can tell you.'

'I hope it didn't make you jump. I told you about moving as little as possible.'

Celia Hornby moved her hand awkwardly, and touched Eleanor on the arm with a soft stroking of fingers.

'I don't know what I'd do without you,' she said.

If only the next client was someone Eleanor liked, to restore the balance, but there were no more today. It was as if they knew she no longer cared. The rest of the week, the rest of life, resembled a deep pit and she could feel herself teetering on the edge of it.

Hatred was seductive. A woman could get to depend on it. Perhaps what Celia Hornby felt for her was not love, but simply an enjoyment of her power. Whatever it was, she was winning the game, because Eleanor felt wretched and small, like the room she occupied. For what she was about to do, if not now, next time.

The phone in Sarah's alternative home had bleeped by the alien bed with its stiff linen sheets, waking her into confusion, because she had never used that phone and did not know quite where it was, and when she found it, it was cold to the touch. Henry's hesitant voice, saying, you've got to come back, come back, then, no you don't. Sarah found the single taxi cruising round the square at the top of Golden Street, like a lonely moth circling round light. She had slammed the door and buttoned her coat as she ran up the street. A nocturnal animal, who knew she belonged in the middle of the night, in the darkest hours before dawn, she had nevertheless needed this sleep, and the sleep had been deep if not tranquil. She looked at her watch, as if time was relevant to emergencies, and registered the hour of five a.m. without much surprise. Henry was the kind of person who would always choose the worst time. She felt for the keys at the bottom of the bag, any activity to take the edge off anxiety, concentrating on the thought that if Henry could speak, and there was someone official-sounding on the premises, then this was accident rather than tragedy, theft rather than injury, and she refused to be anxious about mere things, any more than she could be particularly proprietorial about a flat which had an uneasy history; there was nothing about possessions worth a panic attack, except perhaps a single picture. She had the same attitude to her body as she did to property, as if once scarred and used, it deserved respect, but not any degree of veneration. Let it not be fire, though. Fire had been a dread ever since she read fairy stories about pigs living in houses built of straw.

Once inside, there where two men in uniform, running out of patience with Henry, even though Henry was restored to a certain, hysterical calm, like someone who had recovered from a fit. It was the smell which was appalling as she walked through the open door of home. It was the stench of grief, acrid, lung-shrivelling. There was also candlelight, conversation which appeared to come from another planet, a body which brushed past hers, too close. Her throat was dry, her tongue stuck to the roof of her mouth.

A uniformed policeman, in the full light of his torch, saw a small woman, hair pinned above her head in a barrette, specs on silver chain, good coat and boots, and ignorant of the nightclothes beneath, found her presence reassuring. She looked like a respectable schoolmarm, disturbed from reading.

'Do you own this flat?'

'Yes.'

'Does this man reside here with your permission?'

'Yes.'

'Only he only seems to have set fire to your bathroom. The window went out like a bomb, that's why we came . . . all quiet now, though.'

'Oh dear, I'm sure it was an accident.' She injected warmth into her voice. 'I'm so sorry.'

'Probably a candle in the bathroom. You got candles everywhere.'

She nodded, automatically taking the blame. The only flame she could see was the candle on the telephone table; she wanted them gone as much as they wanted to go.

'Only the bathroom?'

'Yes,' Henry said.

The bathroom, by torchlight, resembled a surreal cave, with a jagged hole in the window, letting in dim light from the well of the building. It seemed miraculous that the breaking glass had not woken the world, and that those around still slept, indifferently. The hall carpet was squelching wet, like a rain-soaked lawn. The room was hot, but cooling, almost steaming, and the smell was abominable. It was a spiteful smell of frustration, toxic and animal, as if something had been slaughtered. The walls were every shade of black, from dark soot, fading out to sepia, in swirling patterns which looked artfully, deliberately contrived. The vinyl floor was pitted and crusted, the ceiling light was a molten lump of plastic, in the bath, surrounded by greasy soot. The mirror above the washbasin was crazed with cracks, but held to the wall, while the light fitting above it was a melted, unrecognisable shape, frozen into drips. Below that, in the basin, there was a multicoloured mess of different colours, the remains of her plastic bottles of shampoo, conditioner, cleansers which lived innocently on the shelf, transformed into a slurry of hardening material from which wafted a different, pungent smell. Turning, she saw the remnants of the rail from which the shower curtain had hung, and the teardrop of the shower fixture, distorted beyond shape. Sarah had an overpowering desire to cry; distracted herself by marvelling how the slightest undertone of Penhaligon's perfume could survive this, and invite not pleasure, but nausea. The men melted away, as if leaving her to mourn. There seemed very little to say except to wonder out loud if it was possible to turn on the lights. Not yet, someone said.

Henry and Sarah sat in the living room, illuminated by the streetlight from the window and the light of a candle on the table. He had become strangely solicitous, fetching a blanket to place round her shoulders, even though she had not yet taken off the coat, which she wore like a protective skin. It was cold without heating. She longed for dawn; it would make all the difference. Henry's calm was faintly offensive. After the men had gone, he spent some time in the bathroom, while she patrolled her territory, establishing that, apart from that dreadful, pervasive smell, everything was the same, and yet everything subtly different. Fire altered everything, even where it had not touched. It was contamination. Henry was fiddling with a metal coil, as he might have done with worry beads. He had the slightly triumphant air of a survivor.

'It wasn't a candle in the bathroom, was it?' she said. 'Not even you—'

Henry was indignant. 'Myself least of all. Yes, I know I have them all over the place, and I assure you, my dear, not merely for decoration. They have such nice proportions, candles, but they're only there for emergencies such as this.

Power cuts, terrorist attacks and suchlike. I hate the dark, hate the idea of the lights going out, leaving nothing to see by. I mean, nothing with which to facilitate observation. Oh, I do feel better.'

He clutched her hands in his and chafed them warm.

'You . . . feel . . . better,' she said slowly.

He continued chafing her hands, and she thought she would like to slap him. He was nodding at the phenomenon of himself feeling better and in control.

'Yes, because I went to pieces, and then I pulled myself together again. I was asleep in the safe room, you see. I heard it, felt it rather, the fire, and I'm ashamed to say I crept back and locked the door. Couldn't bear it, you see. I just screamed and screamed to myself. It was like the last time.'

'What last time, Henry?'

'Before I came back to Mother's house,' he said, a touch impatiently, as if she should have known. 'The house I lived in was gutted by fire. I woke up to find it, and could do nothing but blunder about in the dark, and run. I lost every single thing. And my sanity, for a while. Bit of a nervous breakdown, actually. The thing is, after it happens, you keep expecting it to happen again. Everything's threatening.'

The room was growing lighter. It felt, for a moment, as if the mists were clearing. Henry resumed with confidence,

'But anyway, the fact is that this time, I *stopped* screaming. Not like all the other nightmares; this was *real*, and I stopped. I got up and put on the boot and went and looked. It was raging behind the bathroom door. I got water in a bucket from the kitchen and slung it at the outside of the door. Just to keep it damp. Three, four bucketloads. It hissed a bit, but I could see, feel rather, that the fire was going down. I knew that the worst thing I could do was try to open the door and

let it out. Better to keep it inside, let it go for the window . . .
Perhaps I was only being brave because I knew it was dying
down . . .'

'How would you know?'

Henry paused. 'I don't know. I've lived it in my mind.
Same way you might know that a man isn't dangerous, even
if he looks it. There's a certain sensation, of a fury spending
itself,' he said, dreamily. 'Of a roaring beast going away in
search of other food. And that was possible, of course. Fire's
a monstrous predator, you know. It knows it has eternal life,
has no need to linger where it won't be fed, and is very discriminating as to diet. I had the sense it didn't like what it was
eating, and found it, in any event, insufficient. Your bathroom served a temporary purpose. A tasteless canapé, no
more.'

She had always been fond of talkers. Nonsense talkers,
dreamers, makers of similes, ponderous speakers, writers of
obituaries and lengthy epitaphs. If only men knew that it was
their voices which seduced. It was always the voice which
calmed, even when it spoke with Henry's expansive precision.
She did not interrupt.

'I just kept throwing water at the door, but I can't take
credit for that, or not, at least, for containing the fire. The fire
contained itself. The point was, I felt brilliant. I was no longer
afraid. I'd lost my paralysis, and I really doubted I'd ever do
that. It was *only* a fire. I had hidden and ceased to hide, so
thank you for that. I'm sorry about your bathroom. Now do
tell me, dear Sarah, who has keys to your place, and who was
it who started it?'

She came to life, startled by the pressure on her hand. He
was suddenly inquisitorial.

'I hoped it was an accident, caused by you.'

164

He shook his head. 'Oh lordy, Sarah, would I ever do that? Simple little fire neurotic like myself? And do you know what? I've felt useless for years, and now I can be useful. Because the one thing I can tell you is that whoever started that fire was a specialist. And he did it in such a way that he had a ninety per cent chance of it going the way it did. Which means, if I can reassure you, he did not intend you harm.'

She digested this, thought of the letters and the threats. Disagreed. 'Don't be silly, Henry. If I'd been here, rather than you, I'd have gone down that corridor and opened the door. Got a face full of flame.'

'He must have known you weren't here.'

She had a sudden vision of Alan's scarred face, speaking in sleep. The winter dawn began to seep into the room through the window. The candle flickered. She got up and went across to look out. The road outside was still grey, but lit with returning life. Over the road, the florist took deliveries. Sarah came back and snuggled close to him, still in the coat. They warmed each other. He sighed, and adjusted the blanket over their knees.

'The thing about fire is that it reduces you to nothing. Any illusion you ever had about being in control goes. You cannot do anything, you can only analyse. That fire was both deliberate and contained. Mind you, he took a risk, but a controlled risk. As much as he could control it.'

He felt strong and assured, a new Henry. She wanted to go to sleep, at the same time as wanting to listen.

'If you want to contain a fire,' Henry went on in his measured tones, 'there are two rules. Limit the food, and the oxygen. He did that, whoever he was. Your bathroom was good for that. Enough to cause a flashover after a slow-burning towel caught light, but little enough to burn for long.

165

Nothing as vulgar as petrol accelerant. Someone would have smelt that. Used a little element, mostly melted, quite likely to be missed. Gave him time. I have to admire him, really.'

She sighed, her throat still drier than dust, and aching.

'What was it you used to do, Henry, before the breakdown? Or should I still call you Henry?'

'If you would, I think it rather suits me.' He took a deep breath. 'But I'm not Henry Brett, friend of Dulcie's, whoever she is. He lived two doors down, or may have done, I think.'

'And not the art expert?'

'Yes, in a way, but not the way you mean. Much more boring. Insurance was my line. I investigated fires, until I lost my nerve. My own fire shot me to hell, it shouldn't have happened to me, and after that I couldn't go near the scene of a fire. The smell, the grief, oh dear, no.'

They were silent for a full minute, until Henry coughed nervously.

'Am I forgiven for becoming acquainted with you on entirely false premises?' he asked.

Sarah stirred.

'I knew you weren't Henry Brett, ever since I looked at your books and collected your post.'

'Oh. So it doesn't matter who I am?'

The light was brighter.

'Not particularly, although it's usually better to be who you are, but I suppose we all have to go around being someone else. Otherwise we'd be savages. And now, I owe you. I put you in danger. I didn't mean to.'

'And made a man of me,' he said. 'Touched me. We might be quits.'

The light intruded further, and the traffic grew louder, like the comforting growl in the throat of a harmless dog.

'Could I just ask you one thing, Henry . . . Why didn't you call the fire brigade?'

He sprang away, aghast.

'My dear girl, I couldn't possibly. Have you seen the damage they do? *Everything* would have been ruined.'

Alan decided he would go round to the Kensington address as soon as decent. After two hours of self-hating, turning it all over and bringing back to mind every single thing JT had ever said, he could not think what else to do. Had to behave like a man. Couldn't undo what was done, but he could stop it going further. Had to see Mrs Dulcie Mathewson. She was family. He expected her to shut the door on him, but he had to try. The dog, which he had collected from the back kitchen door of the hotel, plodded behind him. He had a vague idea of trying to lose it somewhere in a park, where someone who already loved dogs would take it home. Or maybe he needed the company.

Only three miles to Kensington, would do him and the dog a power of good. Part of it on the bus, and with a bit of luck they'd refuse to take the dog, and he'd lose it, but they didn't, they fucking welcomed it and made a fuss. He rode past Sarah's without looking up, thinking of the little matter of how JT would be able to confirm the fact of his small, containable fire, beyond the message he would leave on his phone, and then telling himself that wasn't a problem. JT had his spies, and no one ever kept fire a secret. There was always evidence of the clean-up, the talk, no worries about that. JT would know, and if not, he'd better believe.

The address on the letter was a tree-lined street, with plenty of evergreens, the sort of street which had always been up, and never down. Everyone had a different version of where the real heart of London was. He knew it was off the Commercial Road and Arbour Square in the East End, and those who lived here knew it was really here. Each to his own.

Alan had been here before. He had been everywhere in London before, on foot, day and night, night and day, walked it inch by inch, yard by yard, mile by mile, had it mapped in his head, with the favourite bits surrounded in an aura of knowledge. Fucking loved it. And if this bit looked safe and settled and better established than any other, well, that was just another lie, because it wasn't always like that, and might not be again. Safe? Look at all those fuck-off burglar alarms. They were as safe here as anyone who expected to be robbed on a daily basis, as soon as they got out of their locked cars, taking a quick look around for the Rolex mugger, or the car stealer, or the child kidnapper, or the straightforward envious nutter with a gun. The people who lived here were living proof about how affording a million-quid house was not the same as feeling safe, and he loved them for the simple fact that he didn't envy them a single brick, and would be suffocated by their responsibilities.

It was handsome, though, this avenue of old trees and deep-veined houses, where, with all its solidity and air of permanence, no one lived for ever either. The houses were simply units of capital, like stocks and shares, or money in the bank. He knew how the old generation had bought for investment, the new with the same attitude, and nobody owned anything, because you couldn't keep it for ever and always had to sell in the end, which was why he had never seen the point himself. The house of Mrs Dulcie Mathewson was typical old Edwardian, with wooden shutters, look at it, purchased for the good address and convenience and the right kind of neighbours. Probably. There was a brief moment when he knew he was suicidal to be doing this, but he was not going to be able to live with himself if he did not.

He went up imposing steps to the front door, rang an anti-quated bell, and began to get the picture. No burglar alarm, no modernisation noticeable from the outside, window frames gasping for paint, and an occupant who did not give a shit. She answered the door herself, a big giveaway. Answering it in a dressing gown with a toothbrush still in her mouth even more so. It was all so sudden and unexpected, after the anticipation that a street like this created, that he almost fell down the steps, mesmerised as she stuffed the toothbrush into the pocket of the gown and smiled. It was a pleasant smile, he noticed, but she still kept hold of the door, with him a step lower, as ready to slam it shut as she was to give him the benefit of the doubt.

'Oh, I thought you were the postman. Sorry about the teeth. Can I help you?'

He was immediately taken with her, and mesmerised by the gown. Took a brave woman to face those colours first thing in the morning. Her eyes went to the dog, panting and lingering two more steps below him. He was also confused, because she had answered the summons of the bell so promptly, and in a street like this he had expected a Filipino maid, or a nanny, or at least a chain on the door. There was scarcely time to draw breath.

'I'm a friend of Sarah Fortune's. I want to talk to you about someone called Julian Tysall. If you don't mind.'

She stared at him, looked him up and down. In other cir-cumstances, the scrutiny would have been downright rude, but in these, he could hardly blame her. He was dressed in his grey suit, with a sober tie visible beneath the newly brushed coat, and his shoes were polished. There was no recoil. Then she looked closely at the dog, and made up her mind. What a fool to have brought the dog.

'Oh for God's sake, come in, come in. And bring that animal. Looks as if it'll die without water.'

Perhaps not such a fool. He sensed a woman who was a sucker for a dog. Mind, there was something appealing about this silly trusting bitch, which the kitchen staff had nicknamed Bimbo on account of the soulful eyes and the general ugliness. Alan stepped inside, and wiped his feet on the doormat, anxious to continue the good impression, and wondering at the same time if he was about to make everything worse. Dulcie's letter crackled in his pocket as he followed her into the kitchen at the back of the house. It took him by surprise. In a house like this, he expected a posh kitchen; this was decades old. A pine table, venerable units, ancient gas cooker, and perhaps the oldest coffee-maker he had ever seen. She fetched a bowl, filled it with water for the dog, set it on the floor, and waved Alan to a chair. There was silence for a minute, apart from the sound of the dog drinking noisily, and Dulcie tearing open a packet of coffee.

'I suppose the brute's house-trained,' she said. It was all so incongruous, he could not help laughing.

'What? The dog or me? Yes, she's house-trained. Amazingly so, since she's homeless. Not sure about myself.'

'If you're a friend of Sarah's, it's extremely unlikely,' she said, spooning coffee. 'What do you mean, the dog's homeless? Isn't it yours?'

'She's off the street; she adopted me.'

'You must be all right then.'

Judgements had been made. Silence fell again. The coffee

arrived, so thick and strong that the first, scalding sip took his breath away. Quite a contrast to the Marchmont caff. He kept looking at the ancient hob, which took him back a bit: she saw him looking.

'I never see the point of replacing things which still work,' she said. 'Money's for spending, not for wasting. Now, talk to me.'

He had been unsure of his purpose. Up until the moment he turned into her street, he had not known what, if anything, he wanted to achieve. It was, in part, the expiation of guilt, because he felt like shit, and the two and a half grand distributed round his pockets burned a series of holes. It was also the knowledge, which had come to him as he tried in vain to sleep, that this would not, of course, be the end of it, because JT was mad, and once he found out that his small, containable fire was going to make no fucking difference, he would do something worse. To Sarah, to her flat, and possibly to this woman here. He could see the man's handsome face, even now, coupled with the shameful realisation of how he, Alan, had set that fire for money, and *because he was afraid of him*, and that was the most excoriating admission of all. JT was a man who would not stop, because he had no other life. A man who had Alan by the balls, and could blow him out of the water, any time. All right, so he felt guilty enough to try to head off what was coming, and the thought of anyone hurting Sarah felt like a body blow, but before he could do anything he had to know what the fuck was going on. He took the letter out of his top pocket, where it nestled among a bunch of money. He had made the unspoken decision to trust her completely, even before he set out.

'You wrote this to Julian Tysall, who is a bitter and twisted shit of the first order. And that's all I know about him. He wants to force Sarah out of the flat she lives in, because he says it should be his. He thinks he can make her transfer it to him, and he may be right. If he can't, he'll probably blow it up, on the basis that if he can't have it, no one can. Or he may try getting at her through you. Can you fill in the gaps for me, please?'

Dulcie was fondling the ears of the dog, which was looking at her like a woman he had once seen in a church, praying to a statue of a saint, in an idiotic trance.

'How did you get that burn to your face?' Dulcie asked.

'A man I did a job for didn't like the result, so he got me in a corner and put a cigarette lighter to my face,' Alan said. 'Put me off smoking, I can tell you.'

She nodded sympathetically, offering no comment.

'Are you a hit man, then?'

'No, I do strictly damage only. And I don't do women. What I want to know is where this JT's coming from. If he's got any right on his side at all. Because he thinks he has, and it makes him dangerous.'

'What does he look like?'

'Dark hair, good-looking. Very.'

'Sounds like a genuine Tysall son, then. Shall we go through?'

He followed her again, into the living room, where the volume and the busyness of the upholstery and curtains assaulted his eyes. There were lace curtains screening the huge window and its drawn-back shutters, offsetting the draping folds of jungle print to either side. There was a gas fire of the kind long deemed unsafe, but highly effective, old standard lamps like his mother had, furniture not quite antique but serviceable, and little lace cloths on the coffee table. He took her example and set his cup down carefully. It was a grandmother's room, apart from the colours, a place which had adamantly renounced change, a million miles from bland hotel taste, and he found it immensely comforting. There was an untidy file of papers on the floor.

'It's a timely visit, Mr . . .'

'Alan.'

'. . . because although I thought it best to ignore Mr Tysall, I found I couldn't, so I was looking through some old stuff relating to his father. My husband acted for Charles Tysall, and also employed my very dear Sarah.' She picked up a pair of reading spectacles and jammed them on her nose. 'My husband acted for some very dubious people in his time, which perhaps explains why I don't find you at all alarming. Or Tysall junior, either.'

She paused to sip her coffee.

'Charles Tysall was a psychopath, who drove his own wife to suicide many years before we met him. He became obsessed with Sarah, apparently because of her resemblance to the dead wife, but who knows? She didn't reciprocate his foul attentions – she knows a bad one when she sees one, but she's better at spotting a good 'un.' She shot him a piercing glance over the spectacles. 'He didn't like that at all. He attacked her, tried to disfigure her—'

'Those scars,' he said.

Another piercing glance.

'Exactly. Those scars at the end of a hellish experience. The upshot was that Ernest and I, having the management of Charles's affairs when he disappeared for two years, and subsequently died, were able to juggle things, quite legally, so that he left Sarah a certain *bequest*, if you see what I mean. The flat she has now, in other words. He had indicated he wanted to make some reparation. Only she thinks it was left to her by someone else. She wouldn't have taken it, otherwise, and I was determined she should. I did not know that Tysall had a son. There was no one else he wanted to have anything. If he knew his son, he didn't like him.'

'Paid for his education, he said.'

'Well, what more was he entitled to?'

'Recognition.'

'Bollocks. We used Charles's money to compensate the people he'd ruined.'

'Doesn't sound like the kind of bloke who would have been worried about that,' Alan observed, noticing how the dog had taken up residence next to Dulcie's armchair, in which she sat, bolt upright.

She shrugged. 'Perhaps not, but what's a few forged signatures between friends when you're trying to do the right thing?'

He could not have agreed more, but there was something about her native authority, her certainty about being right, which made him want to argue with her. His gut churned and the dog crowded closer to her legs.

'Yes, but. You can see why he might be bitter. JT. Abandoned, forgotten, all that. Might he not have a point?'

'Crap. He wasn't abandoned, he was brought up by his mother, apparently at Charles's expense. What he made of his life's his own concern. I looked him up, of course. He's another bloody lawyer, and as much of a thief as his father since he fiddled the client account and was struck off. He had all the chances and blew them.'

'I know about people who do that,' Alan said. 'There's nothing worse than a man who needs someone to blame. And I know what it does to you. Makes you mad as a snake. Which he is, promise.'

He did not mention the giveaway symptom of manicured hands.

She rose, with great grace for her bulk, turned down the tap of the sputtering, too-hot gas fire with its wooden surround, and plucked a cigarette from a silver case. The colourful dressing gown brushed the gas-fire flames with impunity, and he thought, irrelevantly, that the place was a tinder box. She hefted the file of papers from off the floor on to the lace-laden coffee table. Dust flew across the light from the windows.

'Sarah's name is on the title deeds of that flat, and that's it. Leasehold of a hundred and twenty years, should be enough. How it came to be there doesn't matter. Your man will have a devil of a job proving any kind of ownership; well, really, no chance at all. The only remote chance is if he can show he was dependent on his father when his father died. He wasn't. That's why he fights dirty. Burning this paperwork would dry up the tracks a bit, but worst is if Sarah finds out. Great moral rectitude, Sarah. Never wants anything she feels she's not entitled to. Big mistake. Moral blackmail would work very well with Sarah.'

She puffed at the cigarette and put it out, leaving it smouldering in an ashtray so large it seemed to commemorate something, and resembled a murder weapon. He was half in love with Dulcie, and for the dog which was not his, the process of comfortable infatuation was complete. Bimbo lay, belly in the air, in front of the fire. Alan shrugged, giving up.

'So, what do we do?'

'There's no "we" about it, young man. There's what you do, and what I do. If this fellow has a go at me, I'll see him off. And what do I care anyway? I'm a widow, and I've had the best of life. Wasted a lot of it, mind. Who doesn't? You

175

spend all that time working out who you love best, and it isn't always your own family. It's the few who really connect with the little black heart of you, the two or three you might want to see at your deathbed. There's precious little rationale to it, but Sarah's one. Do you know, I quite forgot to ask precisely why you were here.'

'Because I think the same about her.'

'Maybe you do, but for God's sake never tell her. That really would be the kiss of death. I think breakfast would be a good idea. I was going to have bacon and eggs, and I'm sure there's enough. I find it difficult to get out of the habit of buying for two.'

He said yes please, sat back where he was, staying as still as he was instructed to stay, and noticing that the brindle bitch went with her. Cupboard love, discrimination; all bitches left in the end. He must remember he was not allowed to love them, or not in a way which made him depend, and then he thought, it's too late for that. He sank back into the comfort of the armchair, which enveloped him in its colourful embrace, and felt safe enough to snooze. Obedience was not natural to him, and he enjoyed it. This room, my God this room: everything in it would burn. The smell of bacon woke him, then her imperious voice, beckoning him.

'Kitchens,' she was saying, 'are the best room in the house.'

He was hungry, couldn't remember the last time he ate, but when he was faced with it, he paused. Then looked down at the plate. The sausage was chorizo, the bacon was lean and the eggs had welcoming eyes. Overlaying it was the scent of coffee, from the ancient contraption burping in a corner.

They ate in companionable silence, applying the industry of persons who loved cholesterol so much above all things, it required no comment.

'So,' Dulcie said, as she buttered a slice of toast and gave it to the dog, 'I'm charmed to meet you both, but at the risk of repetition, what made you come?'

He had known as soon as she opened the door that there was no point hiding anything. No other way but telling the truth.

'I got paid to set her bathroom on fire,' he said. 'Which I did, as safely as I could, when I knew she wasn't there. I did it for the money, and because I had something to prove. And because I didn't want anyone else to do it.'

She leant forward to give a cold rasher of bacon to Bimbo.

'And I'm sorry for it. Because he isn't going to stop there, like I said. He frightens me. He didn't, at first, but now he does. Frightens me to death. Hates women, see, even if he wants them.'

Dulcie reached for the marmalade and handed it to him. In her experience, people talked better as they ate.

'That bathroom needed renovation,' she said, equably. 'And Sarah's not going to leap into cooperating to give up her security because of a silly old fire. Especially if she thinks it was an accident. Depends what she knows.'

'That's what I thought. She'll just carry on regardless, because that's what she does. And it'll make him madder, so that when he doesn't get some kind of response, he might go for someone else. Someone connected. And you've given the game away, just a bit.'

'Me? How?'

'Writing back to him. Big mistake. He thinks you rigged the whole inheritance thing and cheated him. And because you've made it so clear that you aren't going to call his bluff and go to the cops. He might ask himself why not. You sort of prove his point. And you've made it clear that you and

177

Sarah love each other, so he could get at her through you. He hates you.'

Dulcie got up to fetch another heavy ashtray.

'Shit. I should never write letters first thing in the morning,' she said. 'Ernest used to be so frightfully bright and cheerful in the morning, and it's when I'm loneliest. Judgement goes to pot.'

'Bad, is it?' he asked.

'Awful, sometimes, but there are worse things. Look, I'll have to think about this. At least she's got someone with her at the moment. I've been meaning to tell her about the flat for the last year, while hoping I would never have to do it. She hates being helped. I've got to think what to do.'

He rose, reluctantly. Replete with breakfast, relief and this uncanny, unfamiliar feeling of being liked, respected, trusted. For sure, this woman could have been Sarah's mother. Or a sister under the skin, with a common ability to fall into liking and abide by it. He didn't know quite what it was, but it felt like coming home. These two women loved men the way he loved women. The dog sat still, watching.

'Can I do anything?' he asked, gesturing to the pile of used plates she had dumped in the sink. He meant the washing-up. She misunderstood.

'You can try and keep tabs on Tysall junior. *Ask* him if there's any more you can do for him. And keep in touch with me, while I think. And . . .' She hesitated, suddenly shy.

'Anything, madam,' he said, wanting to hug her. 'Anything for either of you, you and Sarah.'

'There is one thing . . . If she's really going spare, I don't suppose you could possibly leave me the dog, could you?'

CHAPTER NINE

The day had passed. In the afternoon, as Alan walked home, and Henry organised, and Sarah took orders, as Dulcie went to a committee meeting and JT heard news, the rain came down in sheets, as if attempting to obliterate all traces of civilisation. That night, it was Sarah who slept in the safe room. Henry insisted. She hated it.

On the next day, it rained again, and Henry was in charge, with a list and questions. She wondered how she could ever have thought he was anything other than a technical scientist.

New locks, tick, already done.

Ablutions perfectly easy at the washbasin in the lavatory.

Electricity restored, yesterday.

The burglar alarm to be restored to functioning mode, later.

Cleaners, en route.

Get out, Sarah, you're in the way. She was desperate to get out.

Are you going to tell the police what's behind this, Sarah?

It's out of the question.

I think you should.

No.

By mid-afternoon there was nothing else to do but go swimming.

Don't ever attempt to clear up fire damage yourself, Henry said. It breaks your heart and your back. What you do is inform your insurance company and try and turn it to your own advantage. You'll get a new bathroom out of it, as long as you explain how you came to demolish the old. You get professionals to clean up and mend, and I know who they are. Leave it to me. He was in his element.

'Let's just go on as before,' he suggested. 'You go back and look after my house, and I'll look after yours.'

'Won't you be afraid to be here by yourself?' she asked him.

'With a safe room? With the new locks? And an alarm? Are you joking? Of course not.'

'I've had another letter, Henry. It says, *You should not ignore me; think again.*'

'Well, do it. Think again. Tell the police.'

No.

'My dear, you are quite ungainly with self-recrimination. And perfectly useless here. Do get out of the way.'

She felt redundant, with the humiliating knowledge that by now she owed him far more than he owed her. Sarah did not like to feel in debt. She went to the pool because the pool, of all places, was surely immune from fire. She needed to submerge, consider the effects of her own cowardice. Her conscience was heavy and irksome; she could smell nothing but the acrid stench of smoke and guilt.

Sarah's conscience was something she occasionally tried to

visualise. It was a thing trapped in a lift, an animal on the run, a man in a street, her brother, a bird in flight, a great big cloud on a breezy summer day. It took on shapes and smells, and was sometimes simply a mist which obscured vision, like cataracts over the eyes. There was no room for it. It did not affect her on a daily basis as long as she considered herself good value for money, but if afflicted her with varieties of pain whenever she knew she had departed from her own peculiar standards. She had her rules. Such as, be loyal and kind as far as possible, refrain from laziness, adopt generosity in all things, give of oneself, and try to avoid being a coward. It was not the positive things she had done wrong which affected her, not the mistakes, but the omissions, the failures to engage, the tendency to postpone decisions which forced her to swim as if training for a marathon, up and down, down and up, like an automated bathroom toy.

She had ignored those letters, and that was wilful cowardice. She pounded out another two lengths of the pool, colliding once with the single other person, who swam with slow deliberation. She had put Henry at risk. She had attracted harm, somehow, by her own fault. She should have confronted Dulcie about the flat as soon as doubts were raised. Cowardice. Another three lengths.

Conscience was supposed to be the spur; conscience was designed to point the way to the virtuous course of action, but to Sarah it involved a temporary paralysis. Guilt was not useful to begin with. It had to be mollified into something less acute before it became constructive. So she swam. It had a cleansing effect. The man got out of the pool and padded away. She swayed in the shallow end, the better to think, pinched her nose, and began again, slower. Other people thought best when still. She had to move. Expending energy

181

created more. Sitting and thinking did not go together. Analysis and movement were natural partners.

A man wanted her flat, considered he had a right to it. She had ignored him, and his letters, no time for anyone who would not give a name. That had been lazy, although not necessarily foolish, since there was a lot to be said for procrastination, but it had attracted danger, not to herself, but to someone else she had put in the way of it. That was the stuff of guilt, to put it mildly. That was the worst. Three more lengths.

If she had redeemed herself by really doing something for Henry, such as sorting out his neighbour, and ensuring future harmony in that house, she would not feel as bad. What vanity she had had, to imagine that she would actually be able to do such a thing, and in a short time too, simply because she was usually adept at pouring oil on troubled waters. Fool that she was, she had seen herself befriending Mrs Hornby, or at least working out what it was that made her so difficult, giving Henry a lever, an understanding, something. And she was not helping other friends, such as Eleanor in her state of misery, either. In fact, she was not helping anyone at all, which was a state of affairs she detested, because that was what justified her otherwise entirely frivolous existence. Except Henry: Henry was a new man this morning, but that was because he had been brave and helped himself. Sarah could take no credit for that.

She would have to give serious thought to her home and how she came to own it, but this was old ground. She had thought of it, often and with bewilderment, because it was a stroke of luck, to benefit from death, which made it in itself a matter for conscience, and because she was under no illusion that it was hers of right, or that she had deserved it. It had been a gift which freed her from the drudgery of mortgages and rentals, allowed her freedom and gave her the duty to pass it on. That was what you did with good fortune. She had stopped thinking about it, ceased questioning Dulcie about it, long before the letters arrived, because it was easier to reconcile herself to luck than it was to dwell on it, but she had always believed luck was either pre- or post-paid, and had a sting in the tale. Someone would always want to take it back. She had been sincerely fond of her old judge, and Dulcie had reassured her that his bequest robbed no one in his family. The London flat had been his own well-kept secret, bequeathed to him in the first place, no doubt, Dulcie said. On the fifteenth length, Sarah remembered how fluently Dulcie could lie when she had the best intentions. And then she wondered why her predecessor in title in the flat had fortified it and created a safe room.

Sarah hated asking for help and having to accept it. Independence had always been her ambition. Financial, emotional independence. She needed to be the giver, not the taker. And now she would have to call in help to find the man who wrote the letters and what exactly he wanted, preferably without involving Dulcie, who for all her buoyancy was still dealing with grief. The only person she could think of who could help was Alan, because he knew more about life than anyone else. But then, she had realised on the twentieth length that Alan was the only one who could have taken her keys. She could feel his hand in her pocket, covering hers, searching, and she could not imagine anyone else, apart, perhaps, from Henry himself, who had the skills for such a neat little fire.

I am telling you, again, whoever started this fire did not intend to hurt you. If he had wanted that, he would have done it very differently.

Henry's words. Comforting and discomforting. She supposed that if it was Alan, he would not have had much choice about setting the fire. She knew what he did, because he talked in his sleep, let slip far more than he realised when he was awake. She would like him to know it was already forgiven. It was a pity, though, because of all the men, she was closest to loving him. He was an aristocrat of a sort, and they were two of a kind. He was the one she had come to miss; he was the one she would have turned to first; might, would turn towards yet, because she knew how dangerously close he was to understanding her, and she him, something neither could afford, which might explain, perversely, why he might have done what he might have done, and why, if it was he, she found it so very easy to condone it. Everyone had to earn a living somehow. He had to exploit his talents, as she did hers. No one really owned anything, anyway; it was vain to think otherwise. Sarah consulted her own knowledge of him, her instinct to trust him, and rather to her surprise, found it was still sound.

First things first. She had to do something in the interim; there was nothing she could do about the man with the letters until either he, or further contemplation of the subject, or the operation of instinct again, told her what to do. She first had to deal with debt and the weight of this oppressive conscience. Conscience was only cured by positive action, doing what she *could* do, or might be able to do, rather than dwelling on what she could not. After the swim, with her hair washed and dried to an outstanding volume of coppery curls, face lightly painted to hide the fatigue, high-heeled boots polished to a shine, and a different coat, severely black, enhanced by a fur collar of a similar colour to her hair, so the predominant image was rust red and black, with a hint of aggression, she sallied forth. To Golden Street, to begin to pay her debts to Henry. Otherwise, he might never go home.

On an impulse, and because her own reflection pleased her, she detoured to the Belvedere Hotel. If she saw Alan in the lobby, where she had met him once or twice before, fine. If she didn't, she would phone when she had the courage. He might have left a message: in the normal run of events, he would have done so by now, but her mobile was on the bedside table in Golden Street. Fluffing up the fur collar, which merged with her hair, she rolled through the big doors into the foyer, brandishing her half-closed, dripping umbrella. The foyer was crowded with people making decisions and avoiding the rain. From behind the safety of the huge urn of greenery, she peeked into the bar. There was Alan, clearly identifiable from the back of his head, facing another man, bent forward towards him, as if cowed. A wave of affection and indignation made her shake the umbrella. From behind it, she looked at the other, younger man, who seemed to tower over him. She examined his features, recoiled in shock. Then Sarah Fortune turned away with her umbrella, which bore a depiction of the umbrellas of Cherbourg, and went off, back through the doors, into the dark.

It was one of Sheila's ideas that the Belvedere Hotel should become a notable venue for Tea, with a capital T. Americans had this image of the Brits being devoted drinkers of tea at all hours, with a traditional penchant for the stuff in the middle of the afternoon, accompanied by small sandwiches, et cetera, and Sheila thought she might capitalise on the myth. It did not work very well unless it was raining and the tourists were trapped into haunting the foyer while waiting for it to stop, and eating something out of boredom. Nor was it as elegant as Sheila hoped, since it was difficult to give the dark bar the appropriate atmosphere by the simple addition of white tablecloths and small sprigs of flowers culled from the arrangement in the foyer. Still, with sufficient imagination one could consider oneself out to tea, as at the Ritz, or the Savoy, and disregard the fact that cappuccino was the national drink.

Alan sat in there, facing JT over an eggcup full of wilting greenery, hating him with every bone in his fingers. Sure, he had left him a message on his mobile, early yesterday, relied on him to find out the rest. It did not follow that the man should come to find him here. He should simply have phoned back, should have left home territory alone. Instead, Alan had come down, on his way out, to find JT sitting in the bar/tearoom, flirting with Sheila. Just her kind. Got looks. Sheila's track record with men was bad and naïve, so he knew she would go for something with looks, it ran in the family. And JT did look good today, as good as a gangster looks in a clean suit, with a fresh shave and sitting with his legs wide apart. There you are, Sheila said, as if he was a kid late for school. Been phoning you for ages to say that Mr Tysall was here to see you. No longer anonymous JT. Mr Tysall, sir.

Truth was that Julian Tysall was the kind of man who knew how to fool most of the people most of the time, in a whole variety of ways, just as he had fooled Alan in the first place. And he brushed up nicely. He could fool you by looking desperate and seedy; he could fool you by bleating; he could fool you by being mad; but give this one an ounce of confidence, and a setting, he was worse. The only thing comforting Alan was the fact that JT seemed to think this hotel had class, and drinking tea in it gave *him* class. Not quite a creature of the

greater world, then. It was small reassurance. He was still powerful and growing more so with his own version of success,
and Alan could feel himself shrivel as the insidious fear of JT
took hold again. He should never have listened to anyone moti-
vated by hatred, rather than the relatively pure motivation of
greed, and he should have known because that was how he had
got the burn on his face. Hatred made them madder than des-
peration. Self-righteousness took away all inhibition, and the
stupid were far more dangerous than the wise.

'So you did all right then,' Mr Tysall, *sir*, said.

'I did what you wanted. Found a way to do it. Gutted the
bathroom, nothing else.'

'Clever old man. Not lost your touch. There's been a
parade of cleaners and fixers in and out since then, or so I'm
told. But it didn't work, did it?'

It was when he leant close and tore the piece of greenery in
the tiny vase that Alan could smell him. Sweat and excitement. A woman would have no chance with eyes like that,
and then he would be cruel. He would use his prick like a
weapon and his hands to overpower.

'Not my business if it didn't achieve what you wanted.
That's what you asked for, that's what I did. Got in, started it,
got out.'

'How did you get in?'

'None of your business. She's not a careful woman.
Whoever she is.'

Not a flicker of amusement, or scorn. Alan breathed
evenly. JT and his florist friend might watch where Sarah
lived, but not every minute of every day. Couldn't possibly
clock every visitor to the block, isolate who went through the
front door to which flat they visited. The watchers could
only guess from whoever appeared at the window. Alan never

stood by windows. JT was powerful, but not subtle or omnipresent. If he had an idea that the old man he faced was an intimate acquaintance of his victim, it would have registered long before now.

'So what do you want this time?' Alan asked, feigning impatience, keeping trembling hands in pockets.

'Want to know how you did it. You said it wasn't possible, not a small, containable fire.'

Oh God, even in this state Alan found he wanted to explain how he had done it. There was always that little touch of vanity, and he hated ignorance.

'Usually it isn't possible. Only this time it was. The room, and the layout of the place, perfect for it. Got candles everywhere, and solid doors and the right kind of floor . . . The set-up made it easier, made it look like an accident, didn't have to use petrol, nothing.'

He was giving too much information. Shut up.

'And she wasn't there, was she? How did you know she wasn't there? How did you get in?'

Alan shrugged, made himself sit up straighter, hands still firmly in pockets.

'How I get in's my business. You don't need to know. Locks are there to be picked, the alarm's so old, it couldn't have been working. I only went in to recce, took the opportunity. It was perfectly obvious she wasn't there. You can tell by a woman's bathroom. If she'd been there, I wouldn't have done it, come back another time. Anyway, you wanted it sooner rather than later, so I did what I could. You want your money back, or what?'

'So it was easy. Anyone could do it. All you professionals are frauds. Not sure I need you, you know. I've been reading up more of the science. I've learnt.'

JT sat back, nursing a teacup, which looked ridiculous in his large hands. Alan tried to think of him as a harmless ponce, squinted at him to try and make him seem smaller, but he seemed to swell. Big head, big face, big hands, all the more sinister for the manicured, shiny nails. He could feel the difference in their years. JT leant forward, and smashed down the cup.

'She goes somewhere else, this tart. And I know where she goes. I've got her on the run, I tell you. But that piddling fire of yours didn't work like it should, 'cos she isn't scared yet. I wrote, gave her numbers, but she doesn't make contact. And that old bitch, Mathewson's widow, she threatens me. I tell you, the tart's easy to follow. Got her, last Monday. She swans along, looking at things, all the time in the world. She's easy to follow.'

Alan remembered. Easy to follow, sauntering, always look-ing left, right and sideways, not suspicious, simply curious. He loved walking with Sarah. She could see what he did not always see, she was wide open. He could feel his hand in her pocket, and wanted to whimper.

'Look, I've done what you wanted. Just say what else you want. Or fuck off.'

Sheila came back into the room, just checking, a bit anx-ious about it being the time to get rid of the tea stuff and encourage more serious drinking. She smiled at Mr Julian Tysall. JT smiled back.

'I think she likes me,' he said. 'Charming lady.'

Alan said nothing. JT spread his legs wider. Alan hated men who did that, airing their balls and taking up space for two, and the thought of this man touching up plump, grate-ful Sheila made him sick. A temporary distraction. JT's face was too close. He kept his voice low, so Alan was forced to lean closer. Alan kept his eyes on the tablecloth and noticed an old stain.

'She goes to Golden Street, just near here, would you believe? Walks it. Is she looking for rough trade, or what? What does she want in a crap place like that? And it didn't work, that fire. She's had a day and a half to come running. But she might just go away. Hiding. We have to do it again, soon. But I don't want that flat damaged any more. It's my flat. So I thought we might have a go at the place where she stays. A house in Golden Street. That way, we can scare her rigid, and not damage *my* house.'

'We? Another little fire? *We?*'

'Another grand? I'm getting close, I know it. If you won't, then maybe I shall. After all, like I said, you've told me all you know. I've got itchy fingers. And then there's the black widow, Dulcie. Should have thought of her first. Maybe should've started with her. Maybe do both. Then she'll have to come to heel. Silly of the old lady to write to me again about her *daughter* . . .'

He was talking to himself as much as to anyone else, rehearsing his lines out loud. His weakness was in needing an audience. Alan was depressed by his own ability to guess what such a man would think or do. Word for word, it was what he had tried to explain to Dulcie yesterday. He felt dizzy.

'I could put the word about, *Al.* Mention in the right quarters how our Al never paid tax, no stamps, no cards. Not entitled to medical treatment when he gets old. Could lose you this job, at least.'

The smile revealed fine white carnivorous teeth. JT admired his own nails. Alan shifted in his seat, eyes down, processing damp ideas, like treading mud, nodded, looked up, all blue-eyed innocence.

'Don't know Golden Street. Near here? Give us the number and I'll go and check it out. Only I don't want you coming here again.'

'Tonight?'

'Maybe. Don't phone, either. Meet me at the caff, not here.'

'I want you to go tonight.'

'I'll go when I can.'

'Don't hurt her, old man. Just the property. I need her. I envy you really. Must feel great. Like an orgasm, is it?'

The rain eased and stopped, with a hint of warmth. Always warmer when it rained. Golden Street welcomed Sarah with slick pavements and an aura of light round the old lamps, the only sound her own heels clicking on the pavement and the background traffic round the square. She was confused, and did what she did, compartmentalised the shocking sight she had just seen and put it away for further consideration, just like she put unsuccessful shoes to the back of the wardrobe. She detoured round the square, which smelt earthy and fresh. Too wet to sit. Seven o'clock felt like midnight.

In fact, in one way, she looked forward to Henry's house in Golden Street. Under her care it had gathered a little dust in the last week, but in comparison with her own flat, in its current condition, Henry's maisonette would be its own study in harmony. Clean where her own felt dirty, in every corner, regardless of where the fire had touched. Walking down the rain-washed street, thinking how wrong her first impression of it had been, and how pretty it would be with the minimum of sympathetic renovation and the removal of plastic and scaffolding on the far side, she felt a lessening of the tension, as if it was indeed a home. Even with Mrs Celia Hornby squatting above it.

There were no lights in the upstairs flat as Sarah went up the steps to the front door, unlocking it now with the ease of practice, and making as much noise as possible getting into Henry's place. She slammed the door shut behind her, before prowling round the territory, tidying up a little, as she somehow imagined Henry would do. She made the bed she had left in such a hurry the night before last, and recovered her mobile phone before she took off her coat. The mild rain had raised the outside temperature, while the central heating system was set to cope with frost, and the place was stiflingly warm. Sarah wondered where the thermostat was. She was achingly tired, and restless.

Pausing in the hallway, looking at it all again with fresh eyes, admiring Henry's exquisite taste, she saw his apartment for what it was. The painstaking reconstruction of a shattered life, an artful selection of things collected and preserved in order to give meaning to an existence which had lost it. A home created as therapy, an island fortified against ugliness and failure. As Henry said, it was everything to him: all that was left of what felt like an ineffectual, middle-aged life. If he had achieved nothing else, he had at least nurtured and preserved this, his single source of pride. No wonder he had lost his nerve when it appeared to be threatened.

Which begged the question she had come to solve. Was Mrs Celia Hornby a real threat, or was she simply miserable, lonely, insecure and poorly, all of which conditions were likely to make a person less than pleasant? Sarah could never quite understand the saintly temperament which was heroic in the face of pain. It was far more natural to scream and spit, behave badly and selfishly. Saints were the stuff of myth.

Also, it was easier to be nice if you were popular; why bother at all if no one liked you anyway? The shunned shunned back. The vast majority had good in them, if only someone bothered to look. Or so she had always tried to convince herself because, although with a couple of notable exceptions, like Charles Tysall, her life had proved her own thesis. Psychopaths were rarer than sad, self-destructive souls, perpetrating their own delusions and mistakes. Decency was in the majority: human beings reacted to one another in accordance with their own preconceptions. With his history, Henry would be aggressively suspicious of anyone who invaded his space. Perhaps it was all an escalation of nothing between him and his neighbour. Perhaps Sarah herself was naïve, although her life had not given her cause. She was an optimist.

It had been silent when she came in, until she heard the footsteps. Deliberate, and painfully slow, one foot placed after the other as if it was a heavy-footed toddler, learning to walk. She tried to think what activity could be associated with footsteps like that, what task could create such clumsy, irregular, *bang bang bang* movements. Cleaning, moving an object, a strange form of exercise, or mere seeking of attention? Her determination to see the woman as sad rather than bad began to fade. Mrs Hornby was making this sinister noise for the hell of it. Sarah went down to the lower ground floor, which was even warmer, and opened the doors to the garden. The fresh smell was a blessed relief, until she saw Henry's cat. Elegantly dead, stretched alongside a pot of rosemary, as if dreaming of summer. The feeling of cold, damp fur was repellent.

Leaving the cat for so long would have been another matter for conscience, although she had left more than enough food, and Henry had said the animal would cope, was a hunter by nature, prone to augment its diet with birds and mice. He was very unsentimental about his cat, admiring its beauty, deploring its greed and encouraging it to roam wide through the hidden gardens behind the street. But it was his cat, and he was not going to rejoice in the fact that it was dead.

Surrounding the cat was strange litter. A hammer, a heavy pan, bits of grit, what looked, in this light, like pieces of minced meat, either thrown from over the wall, or dropped from above. The walls were high; above was more likely. There was no blood on the cat, no sign of a wound. It had succumbed to a blow, to poison, to something, or perhaps simply succumbed. It was a hunter, but an old cat. The light from the kitchen was kind; it appeared content. Sarah looked up. From the lit window two floors above, Celia Hornby looked down. Sarah could make out a face with a wide-open mouth, trying to speak.

She raced up the stairs to the front door of Henry's flat, ran into the turquoise hall and up the main stairs, white-hot with anger, breathless when she reached the landing, ready to punch her fist through the door. Steadied herself, stopped. The glass panel in the door was already broken. A gaping hole with jagged edges framed Mrs Celia Hornby's pale face, backlit by the hall light. She came closer and opened the door.

'It wasn't me,' she said. 'It wasn't me. Oh, thank God it's you. Thank God. You've got to help me.'

'What have you done? What the hell have you done? You—'

'Come in here, *please* come in here.' Celia grabbed her arm and tottered down a short length of corridor, bypassing piles of old newspaper, cans of paint and sacks of rubbish, opening the next door, which led into her living room. A very different layout to Henry's. Sarah shrugged off her hand, but followed, still shaking with rage. Celia shut this door behind them, muttering, 'I didn't do it, I didn't do it. It was Boris, he wanted Boris.'

The room they were in was lit by a single low-wattage lamp on a table. There were very old wooden shutters at the two windows, closed against the night, hiding the light from the street. The floor was old oak, with a dull gleam. It seemed that Celia took her advice from magazines. There were mountains of them, stacked into piles, a lifetime's collection. There was a day bed in the corner, with a blanket thrown over it, a glass of water on the floor, and a single armchair, facing a TV on a low table. Nothing else, except a hanging rail, stuffed with clothes, near the door and an ornate gilded cage on a tall stand, with the cage door open and Boris the bird standing forlornly on a perch inside. Avoiding Celia's voice and her eyes, Sarah looked at the ceiling. There was an ornate central rose, from which hung a bare bulb. A small and elegant room, full of lovely old wood, designed for elaboration, and currently used as if it was a box, for storing a person and a bird. Mrs Hornby sat heavily on the day bed. She held her neck at an odd angle, and twisted her body to stare at Sarah.

'I was dancing with Boris,' she said, very loudly. 'My therapist told me I shouldn't dance, but I do, sometimes. He likes it. He sits on my shoulder and we waltz. Then I heard you downstairs. Oh, thank God it's you. I thought it was him. He's going to kill me. I'm going to die, aren't I? I can scarcely move. I won't be able to run away. Is he coming back? Tell me he isn't coming back.'

The voice rose to shouting. She had been crying, and now she was shaking, pitifully. The spartan room, the grit on the floor, the transparent disability would have wiped out anger to replace it with pity, if only Sarah could have forgotten the cat.

'He's going to kill me,' Celia repeated.

She must mean Henry, Sarah thought. Celia was certainly right to fear his anger, but could it really be that they were both equally, irrationally afraid of each other? It was ludicrous.

'The cat, the poor cat. You were throwing things at it.'

Celia shuddered and cringed.

'It climbs up the creeper. It comes after Boris. I pushed it off the ledge, and threw things at it. Then it lay there, and I chucked food at it, but it didn't move. I can't get out into the garden. *He* won't ever let me out into the garden. There's no way out for me. What am I going to do? I saw him in the street. He came up to me and shook me. I ran away, even though I can't run. Got up here and slammed the door so hard the glass broke. Then it hurt so much I couldn't move. Oh, he's going to kill me.'

Sarah detested hysteria.

'No he won't,' she said crisply. 'Henry hasn't it in him to hurt a fly.'

Celia looked at her blankly, then folded her arms across her chest and began to rock back and forth. The guttural sounds she made could have been laughter. Her nose dribbled.

'Henry?' she shrieked. 'Who's Henry? I don't want Henry. I want Boris.'

Eleanor was right. Henry was right. The woman was paranoid, as frightening as she was frightened. Wicked: ridiculous in a silk peignoir under a brutal dressing gown, with shoes on her feet. It was the ridiculousness of her appearance which made pity intervene. No one should live like this. One last try, then.

'Henry would never hurt you, you know. Whatever you do. He wants to be friends. Be a good neighbour.'

Celia stopped moving. Keeping her head averted, she spoke to the wall.

'You stupid, stupid bitch. You wanted Boris too. What do you bitches know? You don't know anything. How can you know? Beautiful creatures, loved by men and one another. I was betrayed, I tell you; I was sold. I offer her love, and money—'

'Who, Mrs Hornby, who?'

'The beautiful sphinx who promised to make me better. I'd give anything to anyone who would touch me. She showed me photographs of myself. She laughed at me. She said, look at what you really are. She destroyed me. And he'll kill me, and I shall die never knowing what it was like to be touched. There's only Boris. I thought he was coming for me . . .'

The rambling died into silence. The room smelt sweet and airless, like the lair of a sick feral animal. Could a cat climb so far up a wall full of winter branches for such a snack as Boris? Had Boris attacked its owner? Could this arthritic lump of self-pity be human as well as paranoid? Whatever had brought her to this, surrounded by old magazines, living like this in a house with a good address from which she emerged immaculate, might have been her own fault, might not. Sarah stared at her, and then down at the honey-coloured patina of the floor. Her brother the aesthete would have rebelled against ever covering such a surface with carpet. Who knew anything about the interior life of another?

197

Maybe all Celia Hornby's ambitions were pure, not that it mattered. Misery was misery. All she said was, 'Can I get you anything? You look very tired.'

'Yes, very tired. I am so very, very sorry about the cat. And everything.'

She lay back on the day bed, raising her feet on to it with difficulty, pulled the blanket around herself.

'You could get me a cushion. And more of the brandy.'

There was not a hint of a scent that Celia had been drinking. She smelt of soap, and perfume, and fear. Sarah went from the room to the kitchen, then to the bedroom, via the doors which led off the lobby. It was a small flat, a fraction of the house. The bedroom was a bed and a wardrobe. The kitchen was a stark cupboard of a place, with no trace of alcohol to be found among the packets of food for Boris.

There were no cushions. There was no brandy. Sarah ran downstairs, pillaged Henry's supplies. There, there were silk cushions and plenty of brandy. She came back with a cut-glass tumbler, full to the brim, and one of Henry's linen napkins.

'There,' she said. 'Probably not the quality you're used to, but not bad.'

She propped Celia on three ivory silk cushions, and with her arms around her, helped her to sip. Celia did so, greedily. Then she closed her eyes.

Sarah detached herself, hoping this meant sleep. She forced herself to kiss that damp, papery forehead. It was not love. It was all she could do.

'You need sleep. See you in the morning.'

Celia opened her eyes. 'Stay with me,' she whispered.

'Yes,' Sarah lied. And left.

She could not stay here. Downstairs, Henry's flat was still

oppressively warm; the cat was still dead, the place was stocked to the edges with possessions, and she screamed with the desire to run, far and fast, escaping that misery upstairs, malign, tragic, deluded maybe, spiteful, but pitiful, and there was nothing, absolutely nothing she could do but wait and listen. A slug of Henry's wine, taken like water. A moment of standing still and realising she could not go, or not for ever, but she could go for a while, and come back. It was not the middle of the night; it was merely dark. The wilderness of central London was better than this. Go out, and walk. Go sit in the square, come back. Come back sooner if the square is locked. Don't forget keys.

Golden Street was empty. Locking the door behind her, she noticed the man on the other side of the road, lingering. She began to walk, and then to run towards the traffic noise of the square. Let it be open. Let her sit in it on a cold bench until this mindless feeling of grief passed, and then go back. The boots clipped the pavement, noisily. They were shod in rubber, did not slip. She reached the square, waited to cross the road. Always look left, right, and right again.

She saw him, striding up from the left from the direction of Hotel Row. He was walking at his usual pace, hands in pockets, slightly hunched. The road cleared in front of her, allowing her to cross. She wanted to continue running, but she waited instead until Alan drew level.

He smiled. He always smiled when he saw her, then frowned.

'Sarah, love. You forgot your coat.'

'Shall we walk?' she said.

CHAPTER TEN

'Here, you'd better have mine.'

'Should I take anything from you?'

He shook his head, and draped his coat round her shoulders. A coat already warmed by another body was irresistible, better than being embraced.

'Then *you'll* get cold.'

'Not yet I won't. Once round the square? No, you shouldn't take anything off me, doll, but maybe you must.'

There was no more than a smattering of people in the square: a lonely sweeper of paths, marshalling litter, stacking it into bags for collection in the morning, and a couple of shifty lingering male identities, shuffling youths or men in hooded sweatshirts, watching for chances. Seekers of shelter, looking for love or money; no London square was free of these. The gates would close in half an hour; those and the sleek black railings would never deter the determined in the height of summer, but summer was far away. At this hour, the square was mainly the resort of persons and their dogs, taking a last walk before retiring for the night. Small dogs, city canines on leads, giving a hint that life behind the big closed doors and immaculate façades of the grander houses surrounding the square was both more varied and more ordinary than it seemed. Inside those rooms were children and animals, pets and grandparents, juggling for space with businessmen in suits, just as it always had been. In Regency days, the residents of the square would have paraded with parasols and the streets would have smelt of animal dung.

Alan's coat was ridiculously large, sloping off her shoulders and reaching her ankles. She explored the pockets surreptitiously as they walked.

'Shame you forgot your coat,' Alan said. 'Still, as long as you've got your bag. And your keys.'

Once round the square was enough. Rain threatened again; people and dogs began to melt away, as if on some prearranged signal. He had the uncomfortable feeling that JT was watching, and knew it was impossible. JT was far away by now, but all the same he was tongue-tied, wanting to begin, while not knowing where to start.

'Why did you do it, Alan?'

He shrugged his shoulders, feeling lighter without the coat. Winter or summer, he was never without a coat.

'It's my living, doll. And if I hadn't done it, someone else would and made a hell of a mess.'

'Who is he, Alan?'

He shook his head, and shivered. 'Can't tell you that. Lips are sealed, for a bit. I've got orders, you see. I've just got to keep you out of his way.'

'You sound so melodramatic. Doesn't suit you. And maybe I already know who it is.'

She may as well be flippant. The warm coat, the events

and sights of the evening so far made her giddy. 'And I do think that if you were prevailed upon in some way to set fire to my bathroom, you might have warned me in advance, and told me how to put it out.'

'It was rather spur of the moment. I knew you weren't there.'

'And that makes it better?'

He was silent. They walked round the plinth of the equally silent fountain.

'Look,' she said, 'you're getting cold, so if you aren't going to enlighten my darkness and trust me at all, I'd better go. I left a neighbour in a bad way and promised I'd stay, even though I didn't. I could be doing a lot more useful things than this.'

A fire engine wailed round the square, followed by an ambulance, so frequent a city sound it was unremarkable, background music.

'In Golden Street? Please don't go back to Golden Street. Please *don't*.'

'I have a choice, do I? Believe me, my own place doesn't feel particularly welcoming or safe at the moment.'

He stood in front of her, one eye weeping, his voice almost comically earnest.

'It is, Sarah, for now it is. It's the safest, believe me.'

'I don't,' she said. 'I'd like to, but I can't. If you can't talk to me, do get out of the way. I'm sick of being excluded from whatever's going on. If I can trust you after what you did, why can't you bloody well trust me?'

She walked faster, aiming for the side gate to the square. He was overtaking her when a youth stepped into his path. Nothing unusual: they had an instinct for him. Simply one of the sweatsuit brigade, with a grey hood flopping over his head, making him anonymous and amorphous, man or boy. Tea leaves, Alan called them: cockney for thieves, see? But one of a kind with whom he was always gentle, emptying his pockets if ever he was asked, as she did. Talked, never bullied. They could be you or me, he said. Family. Neither of them recoiled. The boy was not aggressive. He was whining and scuffing the ground with his feet.

'What did you do with my dog, mister? I want her back.'

He came closer, poking his face at Alan, unconvincingly threatening. 'I want her,' he repeated. 'It's cold without her.'

Alan placed his hand on the boy's chest, and pushed him away.

'Fuck off out of it. Dog's got a good home.'

'Where is she, mister? I loved her, wanna go and see her. Can I? Can I? Can I? Feel bad about her. Is she all right? Where is she?'

The wheedling voice scared the birds.

'Course she's all right, son. With a nice old lady called Dulcie.'

The words were out of his mouth before he realised.

'It's not fair,' the youth muttered, backing off. 'It's not fair.'

'Best luck that dog ever had, son. Here.' A note changed hands with dizzying dexterity, first in one pocket, then in another. The boy melted away. A brief encounter.

'Dulcie?' Sarah said. '*Dulcie? My Dulcie?*'

'Oh fuck,' Alan said. 'Yeah. Your Dulcie. She wanted a dog. What's the matter? Think you've got ownership of your friends?'

She was so paralysed by the anger, she found it impossible to say anything. She shrugged off the coat and let it fall on the ground into a puddle left by the rain. Looked round for her own direction, completely disorientated. Go back to the main road and the junction with Golden Street. What were they doing? By what strange conspiracy did Alan know Dulcie and the man he sat with in the hotel, all of them together, as if reshaping the fate of a naughty child, giving her lessons about luck and fear they considered she did not understand, without telling her? The man in the hotel, sitting opposite Alan, bearing an uncanny resemblance to an old enemy, a more youthful Charles Tysall than she had ever known, but still, that man, and Dulcie, whom she would have trusted more than any person alive, right in the middle of some plot to teach her something. Bastards. She was utterly bewildered, but most of all, hurt. What did I ever do to you, Dulcie Mathewson? What did I do? It felt like being laughed at behind her back, patted and told she did not understand. Her response was childish: walk away again.

'Sarah, it's not what you think.'

'Don't ever dare tell me what I think.'

He might have said it, might not, as he stared at her in the lamplight, one eye streaming, before she finally moved. Backing away, then turning away, not running but moving fast. He could see the disgust and the disappointment in her eyes, encompassing them all.

There was nowhere else to go but back to Golden Street. He followed her, for a few hesitant steps. Julian Tysall had unhinged him. The boy had unhinged him. He had never so much regretted opening his mouth. He was a fool. Also angry. He hated it when women walked away. This was not the time. Then he went back for the coat. The coat had money in it. By the time he had retraced his steps, she was out of sight.

She would only go back to Golden Street. Standing at the

same crossing where he had met her, he thought, what does it matter if I am a complete idiot? What does it matter if I'm an old has-been, with all my old glory days gone and not much nerve left? You're only as good as what you do next. And me and her, we always have to do *something*. The coat was uncomfortably damp, but the purpose of a coat was to have pockets. It would have been quite a find for a homeless boy, since Alan carried his life in his pockets. Patting the sodden sleeve, he had an irrelevant memory of how he had once pinched a coat hung over a rail in a department store, while the owner was trying on another. Put it on, sauntered out with it, found two hundred quid in the inside pocket. A dream find, for a good-looking boy; never did it again, but was fond of coats ever since. She was ahead of him, but he did know where she was going. A red-haired woman in a dress and boots was easy to spot. Then, as he turned into Golden Street, he caught the scent of it on the damp air, and began to run.

Eleanor phoned to apologise, knowing it was useless and would make everything worse, but it had to be done. She had to make herself say the words, *I am sorry,* even if it was way too late, and could never make a difference. Yesterday evening, Celia Hornby had driven her too far. *You aren't making any money, are you, darling? There's room in my house. You may have to come and live with me.*

And she had lifted Celia's head up from the massage couch, by the hair, and made her stare at the enlarged photo of herself on the wall, in that yellow bobble hat and the lacy underwear, with all that blobby fat in between, and said, *With you? Who the hell do you think you are? I'd rather die.*

205

Eleanor was looking at the photo on the wall, to punish herself. It showed how Sasha's operation had left an ugly scar all right, puckered with flab. Face it, Sasha should never have been a surgeon. She was too contemptuous; she always knew best. She would have left anyway. Stop thinking that; think of what you have done. Remember Celia Hornby's face collapsing as she studied her own photograph, and saw herself as she really was. Photos did that far more effectively than mirrors. Her made-up face looked dreadful, crying like that. It crumpled, and stayed so. She had shuffled into her clothes, clumsily, still crying as she left.

It was not for Eleanor to face anyone with their own delusions or ugliness, or to cripple and destroy, and she knew she had done both. Sitting on her own massage table, with the silly stars on the painted ceiling, she phoned to say sorry. To say, you have had your revenge. You have made me betray every professional principle I have ever held dear. You have made me far worse than yourself. For whatever I've done, you've had your revenge.

'Yes.' Celia's thick, sleepy voice answered her, full of the usual unfriendly suspicion. A relief; at least she must have stopped crying.

'Celia, I'm—'

'It's Boris. He just went. He's gone. Why did he fly? My God, he really can fly. He's come back for me.'

Then a long, unearthly scream. Followed by a roaring sound, disconnection, and the loud buzz of silence.

The fire was quietly spectacular, and voracious. Sarah drew level with the house as the first of the upper-storey windows exploded, releasing smoke to billow into the night air. The sound of glass shattering on the ground below was the loudest noise; the rest was like the deep, impatient breathing of a hungry animal, creeping through dry undergrowth. Then flame followed smoke, so that the two windows of the top floor looked like carefully designed blocks of red and orange, mesmerisingly unreal. Smoke seeped through the roof, but it was the savage colour of the devouring flame which hypnotised. Sarah seemed to be hesitating, grasping her bag as if keys would materialise into her hand, standing at the bottom of the steps, looking up, unable to move. Alan grabbed her and dragged her to the other side of the street. The second window cracked; glass fell in heavy shards, breaking into smithereens, cascading down the steps. *That's her room!* Sarah was screaming. The solid front door looked unscathed and impenetrable, insulting in its indifference. Mrs Hornby would have been asleep. Could she hear screaming? Don't, he said; don't. He punched out 999 on his mobile phone, but already the sirens were close. Someone always saw it, someone always called. Sometimes, as he knew, the first 999 caller was the one who had started the carnage. Someone who might give a wrong address, keep rescue at bay. Smoke curled up through the tiles of the roof. He looked on, and watched her looking, her face pale in the eerie glow, dazed by it, unbelieving, as if it was a thing of newly discovered beauty.

He could see the top storey was well alight, burning merrily. A three-truck fire, the first in situ, and how he had always admired their speed. Someone was shouting at anyone who would listen, *is there anyone in there? Yes,* Sarah was yelling. *Yes.* Alan kept a firm hold on her, found himself muttering, *there* was. In an act of superstition he crossed himself, watched with relief as the first shower of water fountained into the air and hit the building with a sickening sizzling sound. No time for finesse. He pushed Sarah further away. From other doors in the street people began to emerge like slow, dazed insects, uncertain of the crisis. His face felt burned, his back cold.

'Come away,' he said. 'Come away. It's over.'

'She wouldn't have been able to move. She couldn't move. I said I would stay with her.'

Oh, for Christ's sake. Women. He screamed at her, his voice soundless over the noise, pulling at her arm, wanting to wring her neck.

'Get out of here. Get the fuck out.'

'No, she might—'

'Be alive? She's dead. Come ON.'

'No.'

He slapped her across the face, hard. Her eyes cleared, came into focus, looking at him as if she had never seen him before.

A straggled crowd was gathering. The fire engines blocked his view of the bottom of the house, but he could see above that, black smoke rather than flame emerging in a state of indignant fury from the upper windows, as if stating a protest. Sarah went with Alan, sidestepping the people, letting him take her, moving automatically. Thinking with shaking horror, *what have I done? What have I done?* And the secondary thought, a shameful relief, *Alan could not have done this. Alan came from the other direction. He was with me.*

They were back on the main street, walking unsteadily towards the hotels. She was suddenly freezing cold and shivering. The rain began again, spitting at them, in prelude to a downpour. She stopped, tugged at his arm.

'There isn't anywhere to go. There's nowhere safe.'

'Not in this world, doll, but somewhere a bit like it. We've got to talk.'

'Talk? What the hell's the point in talking?'

It was then that she realised he was hustling her along, as if ashamed to be with her, trying to push and pull her out of sight, keeping his own head down. The second realisation was that he was even more unsteady and disturbed and weepy than she was herself. Needed consoling and direction just as much. Somehow, it calmed her. Made her remember you could only do one thing at a time.

'Yes, we need to talk. Understatement of the year.'

She did not know quite how they came to be here.

A dream. A wonderful, quiet place, above the world.

There was one habitable room on the top floor of the hotel. He had fashioned it so, from the relics of serviceable furniture stored in all the other rooms, from three piled mattresses, a wobbly chair, three old duvets, after he had implored Sheila to get rid of all this flammable stuff, knowing she would do nothing of the kind, since she still dreamt of a safe little fire, larger than the last. Fire was worth money. Everyone's current fear of the place, and the newly secured door, allowed him to nest up here, like a migrant bird, like some fucking little pigeon in a loft. They sat; he in the chair, she on the mattresses with a duvet on her knees, and the small window open, neither touching each other. She could hear the crackling of fire, like tinnitus in her ears, and behind that, Celia Hornby, screaming. Surely she would have screamed? Perhaps she had been asleep: she was not used to brandy. Perhaps smoke had done the work long before fire. If only. She thought of the wretched yellow bird, flying into the oncoming flames. They did that, didn't they, had to be guarded from fire. Maybe it flew out of the window. Were the windows shut? She had left the living-room door open. The sound of the screams she had not heard were stuck in her head.

Between them were two paper cups and a bottle of whisky, worst treatment for shock, temporarily effective. Sarah was relieved that the cups were paper. Her teeth would have rattled against glass, bitten it. Shock faded; corrosive sorrow remained. Alan took off his damp coat. It was warm and airy up here. Secret and safe, because it was empty. Nothing in it anyone needed any more. He was talking.

'I didn't think in a million years he'd actually *do* it. And never so soon. He's playing games. I can't get inside his brain. What the fuck did he think he was doing? Proving something to *me*? Proving he can do it better? Must have used gallons of petrol, get it going like that.'

'Who, Alan, *who*? You aren't making sense.'

'Julian Tysall, mad sick bastard.'

'The man you were with downstairs?'

'Christ, Sarah, he didn't see you, did he? He's bad, he's—'

'Just like his father,' Sarah said. 'He *looks* like his father. Daddy had looks. Do you think you could begin at the beginning?'

He stared at her, uncomprehending, and chewed on the paper cup.

'You're the beginning,' he said. 'And the middle. And the end. You've got his dad's flat, and he wants it back. He's really turned a corner here, Sarah. He won't stop there. I should've treated him with a bit more respect. Should have seen he was on the brink.'

It didn't make sense yet, but it was beginning to. The

sound of the rain lashing against the window began to dis-
lodge the other sounds. Then Alan giggled. Grief, hysteria,
worry, giggling, all part of the same thing.

'I tell you what, if I'd been security-man me, and seen me,
just now, downstairs, I'd have stopped myself, if you see what
I mean. God, we're a mess. If anyone had seen us coming
through the foyer, you without a coat, they'd have thought I
was a drunk punter, sneaking in a tart.'

'They'd have got that completely right, wouldn't they?'

They were both giggling. Giggling without end, laughing
like children when someone says 'bums', awful, disrespectful,
remorseful, nervous giggles, cathartic, scared, childish, necessary, exhausting. Then they were both on the mattress pile,
wrapped in a duvet, hugging as if there was no tomorrow.
Giggling and sobbing: kindred activities. They were alive,
and finally, mercifully, dozing into something like sleep.

'You didn't kill her, Sarah.'

'I didn't stay with her, either.'

'She wouldn't have known.'

'Henry's house . . . What do I tell him?'

'Henry's house doesn't matter.'

'I was supposed to be looking after it.'

'I love you. I never meant to hurt you.'

'I know.'

'Dulcie,' he said. 'Got to tell you about Dulcie.'

She sat up. 'Just at the moment, I think I want to kill
Dulcie. Only the rest of the time I'd happily kill *for* her.'

'She's a piece of work, that Dulcie,' Alan said. 'Doesn't
need any underpinning herself, even if her house needs
rewiring.'

★

Keeping a young dog was exhausting, Dulcie thought. The thing liked to play. It was a huge distraction. Not popular at yesterday afternoon's committee meeting, even if it was on a brand-new lead with a very distinguished collar. There had been a dog in this house, once. Another stray which Ernest had abhorred, because it was Ernest who was house-proud about details and resented the incontinence, extremely. Not a devoted young bitch like this, which howled outside the door of the meeting. Since it was an animal charity, they had to put up with it. Tough.

Ernest, who would have hated it, would also have loved it. They would have *played*, for God's sake, if only Ernest had ever learnt to play. Not his forte. Dulcie threw the ball for Bimbo, who raced across the coffee table, scattering everything en route, paperwork flying, back before she had time to think, waiting for more, and more and more. Nothing would ever be enough, until the creature was old and wise, a fate Dulcie would not wish upon anyone. Looking around, she realised how much she had come to hate this house. It was so restrained. It needed much more colour. She had stuck with it for Ernest.

Enough of him, enough of everyone. She piled up the paperwork, thinking that maybe Bimbo had done her a favour by messing it all.

The wonders of gin, as well as its disappointments, were always a surprise. Such promising stuff when taken out of doors, while indoors it made her first so bright, and then so cheerless, that it showed up the obvious with disturbing clarity. Yup, the deeds which left Sarah Fortune as titular owner of her own apartment were very much intact, a matter of public record, indeed. Anyone could look them up. The correspondence which had led to such an arrangement, the notes, well, perhaps they were better not seen. Such a lot of them. It really was high time to get rid of it all. A completely bogus will by the old judge, for instance, manufactured and largely copied from the original, good enough to produce for Sarah's brief inspection, simply in order to explain how it had all come about. She had not really looked; she had never had an eye for that kind of detail. The *alleged* instructions from Charles Tysall as to his specific bequests, rather than the broader brush of his intentions, certainly did not bear close inspection, although they had passed muster at the time. Oh Lord, Dulcie and Ernest had been *good* at this. The power of attorney had been entirely genuine. It was always amazing what you could do if nobody stopped you doing it, especially if it looked right. There was an irony in it, too. Charles Tysall's secret flat was perfect for a single woman. Dulcie had gone there to look it over. Although she did not wish to speculate why it was secured the way it was, the place was about as solid as a fortress, bristling with discreet locks and precautions. Perfect. That way Sarah could secure it against her dubious friends, as Charles had needed to secure himself and hide from his numerous enemies. Personally, Dulcie thought such measures a waste of time. A strong door and a good insurance policy were all that did any good. She supposed it might be a bit different if you were expecting anyone violent, which in Charles's case was highly probable. If you hurt people for a hobby, there came a time when they felt inclined to retaliate. The opposite followed: if you had never done anyone any harm, as she knew she had not, you had every right to feel safe, as she did.

Dulcie sipped the gin and tonic, wondering yet again how it never tasted quite the same at home, even when it was ten times stronger than mean pub measures.

At last the dog was asleep. She looked at it fondly, and completed the task of reshuffling all the paper into the two piles she had originally created, one labelled *preserve*; the other labelled *destroy*. Bimbo was lying belly up, tits in the air, charmingly defenceless, spark out, and Dulcie felt the same way. She copied the dog's pose, lay on the floor with only slightly more decorum, certainly more clothes, and looked at the ceiling. There was a different viewpoint on everything from the floor. Such as the fussy feet on the armchair, otherwise invisible, the denser colours of the settee fabric nearer the floor, where the sun had no chance to fade it, the chipped edges of the tiles on the gas fire, which Ernest refused to change. The ornate moulding at the edges of the ceiling, the single socket supporting three plugs on an adaptor on the far wall, the dust clinging to the bottom of the curtains, the base of the old lampstand. From this angle she discovered, not entirely to her surprise, that she disliked what she could see, down to the last mote of dust and shade of colour. Ernest had liked it the way it was, hated spending money on things he would not notice.

Dulcie heaved herself to her feet and went back to the now warm and ever more disappointing gin and tonic. She chose her thoughts wisely. It was not disappointing, it was *disappointed*, to have been left alone. Right. *Destroy* what was to be destroyed. Destruction was easier said than done. What did you do with paper? Shredders were useless. Bonfires were better. The garden outside was wet and cold and the neighbours would complain. The small stretch of grass would be good for a dog's lavatory, but Bimbo was a street dog: she could only *go* on concrete. Feed the paper to the gas fire? She had tried that before. Dangerous. Leave it. No, tear it into pieces, put it in bags to go out with the rubbish.

Dulcie felt faintly idiotic, sitting on her hummingbird sofa, tearing up paper, dividing the torn pieces between separate polythene bags, so that no one would ever piece them together. It was not quite the behaviour of a mature woman with an invitation to three receptions and a Buckingham Palace garden party on her mantelpiece.

Blow me, if it wasn't two hours since midnight. No wonder the dog was still asleep. She needed to make a list, but it was too late. Sleepy. Leave the door open in case the dog wanted to follow her upstairs; she was *not* going to have it on the bed. Bless it. Leave the lights on in case it woke up and couldn't see. Stub out the last cigarette, very carefully. Phone everyone tomorrow.

Dulcie believed in trouble-free sleep. Up until now, even when Ernest was having heart attacks and dying, she could will herself to sleep. Scold herself into it, shut her eyes tight, count sheep, blank out everything, demand that it take her away. It was one's duty to sleep, because one was useless without it, and if one lay still enough Morpheus arrived. And if one woke up before the prescribed hour, one did not move; one waited for normal service to be resumed. It was a knack which anyone with a snoring spouse simply had to learn. After a brief reprimand to herself for not even bothering to fully undress – it was cold after all, the heat had been off for hours, and it would save time in the morning, when there was so much to do – she slept. The old house creaked around her. She loved the sound of the rain outside, and thought of hats.

Odd, to wake up so hot when she had been so cold. Swimming in sweat when she never normally perspired. Should have washed, she felt dirty, sniffed at her own armpits, looking for the source of the smell. Really, she told herself, you are turning into a perfect slut. What was that

215

smell? She willed herself back to sleep. The rain was still hitting the window. She knew every sound of this house. No, it was not rain. A scrabbling sound, like the time long ago when they had been overrun with mice. She felt the beginnings of unease blossoming into a fear which made her squeeze her eyes shut. There was someone there, a burglar. Stay calm, pretend to be asleep. The smell increased. The sounds were louder, more insistent. Rats, not mice. An army of vermin, creeping up the stairs towards her. Scratch, scratch, then whining, becoming desperate and insistent. The dog at the door.

It hadn't done that before. Slept outside the door, but did not try to get in, content with proximity rather than intimacy. A good dog. It sounded as if it wept. Dulcie threw back the covers, marched to the door, and flung it open. The dog cannoned into her legs, whimpering and clawing. She saw the view beyond it and wanted to faint. Smoke, choking smoke, blurred what she could see. A pall of smoke, as thick as wool, not drifting, not moving, sinister and threatening in its implacability, a fog.

Her bedroom faced the impressive stairs and the hall which led to the front door. The door seemed a very long way away, scarcely visible. The old carriage light, suspended from the ceiling to light the hall with an unforgiving, overbright light, simply glowed. It frightened her more than anything because it looked so unfamiliar. As if it was not one of Ernest's cheap stock of hundred-watt bulbs, randomly used everywhere, but a distant, unfamiliar gleam in a fog, like a lighthouse light, blurred and uncertain. She began to cough and then to choke. She shut the door.

Always so careful about fire. Switch stuff off, close down the house before bed. Turn everything off. Remember what to do. The sight and smell of the smoke made her retch. Dulcie tried to remember what she was supposed to do. Stay where you are, shut the door, do not rush towards the source of the fire. Get out of the nearest window. She went towards it, coughing, eyes streaming, banging her hip against the washbasin. Jump out of the window? Not such a long way down. The dog was frantic, cowering and whimpering, terrified. Dulcie paused for a minute for a trembling sigh. There had been many a time since Ernest died when she had wanted to die too. Maybe this was the time. It was horribly tempting to simply go back to bed and wait. She could open the window and jump into the back garden, or just wait. Pretend it was not happening until it did. Smoke got you first. She would die before the flames.

But not like this, skulking in a bedroom. Smoke was seeping round the door. At least throw the dog out of the window. She went towards it where it hid under the bed, grasped it by the short tail, pulled it towards her and tried to stroke it. The dog was strong, squirmed like a mad thing, bit her arm. She could not carry it towards the window. It was demented with fear. You poor sod, she thought. I got you into this. You woke me up. Dogs run from fire. If I run, you follow, get it. And you woke me up. She picked up the damp towel which hung by the washbasin, draped it over her shoulders and round her mouth, and opened the door. If she could get down to the front door, the dog would follow.

Dark swirling blackness, the stuff of nightmares. The light had gone out. The wood of the banisters was hot. It was a descent into hell, with nothing to see.

She felt for the wall instead, and went on, down, down, down. The stairs were endless. She tried to make herself count them. Then she tripped over the dog, fell, rolled to the bottom, losing the towel, picking it up. Lay there, winded and choking and gasping. The door was just visible. Looking back through the smoke, she could see flame in the living room, and an eerie glow coming from the kitchen. It seemed suddenly pointless to do anything else but stay still.

Goodbye, dears. Nice to know you.

Then she heard the dog, howling.

Chapter Eleven

It was misty and warm when Sarah went back to Golden Street in the early morning, dressed in a man's suit jacket and a silk scarf over a frock and high-heeled boots. No odder than anyone else in Bloomsbury. Better you than me, Alan said. You're less suspicious. They could be watching out for a fire-raiser coming back to look at what he's done, and he's always a man.

'Always?'

Ninety-nine times out of ten. Unless the fire's all about love and revenge, it'll be a man. Walk past. There'll be someone there, hanging around, still. Waiting for experts to finish or arrive. Something like that.

Always a man. *They.* Us and them. They were authorities, uniforms, investigators, the whole phalanx of persons Alan could never approach, and, implicated as they both were, Sarah could not either, pushing her further to the outside than she was, creating another swathe of potential enemies, from what might have been allies, if not friends.

Misty and sweet, melted rain suspended in droplets. Not quite light. An ambulance waited outside Henry's house, a driver and a woman standing by the open doors at the back, talking. The street was eerily silent; voices carried. The lower windows of the house reflected the daylight which struggled over the rooftops opposite. The front door was ajar. Sarah walked with preoccupied speed until she wheeled to a halt at the bottom of the steps. From there, she could smell the familiar smell, distinctive, cloying, destructive and musty. Toadstools and swamps and rottenness. The driver quickly stubbed out his cigarette, as if caught in a sacrilegious act, regarded her warily.

'Big fire?'

'You could say so.'

'I used to know someone who lived here. Is everyone all right?'

He coughed, looking at the half-done cigarette on the ground at his feet with regret.

'Not quite. Best you move along, if you don't mind. There's a body up there, miss. We're waiting to collect, when they're finished.'

'Finished?' she echoed, purposely stupid.

'Experts. Forensics. They take their time, they really do.'

He stamped his feet. Warmer today, but not warm enough for hanging round, waiting. Sarah nodded sympathetic understanding.

'Wasn't it an accident, then?' she asked.

'No,' he said. 'Not really.'

She waited, knowing full well that talking to a stranger was a way of passing dead time.

She would have to tell them. She would have to come back and confess knowledge, but not yet. The key to the door was burning a hole in her pocket, as she stayed, and watched, until the body came out of the house, a tiny, huddled thing, covered in plastic and strapped to a gurney. Sad and impersonal, a thing receiving gentle treatment which was still too businesslike for the living. She felt obliged to stay and watch, as if it could make any difference that someone did, recalling, irrelevantly, an old legal maxim, one of the few she remembered, *There is no property in a body,* and it was only as she watched that Alan's intense fear of Julian Tysall began to crystallise, take real shape, infect her own bones and creep under her skin. Here was the evidence of what he was willing to do, simply to intimidate. He was doing this because he could. She could picture his excitement, smell the sweat of his anxiety, feared him too. And felt herself, like an ailing fighter, a boxer, punching at air, ducking and diving, so that the monster he had become could strike at someone else smaller, instead, and felt wretched because of it.

Then, as she walked away, knowing she would never come back, she thought of Charles Tysall. Like father, like son, one of those old adages which all too often proved true, making her pause, remembering with awful clarity the vanity and the careful obsessions of the man, the fastidiousness as well as the malice. Revenge and ambition were well honed in Charles Tysall. He would never have done anything so random or full of personal risk as starting a fire, unless a specific, immediate result was guaranteed. He did not gamble on uncertainties, or expose intentions. He came up behind his quarry, like a shadow. She remembered him, too, when she had found him sick and dying, realising how he was just another man, whom no one should ever have feared. If Julian Tysall had indeed inherited the temperament of his father, he would never have done this. There were easier, far less dirty

221

ways to make fear work. Charles Tysall would have been as ruthless as this, but far more discriminating.

Better go home and tell Henry. *Always a man. Never a woman, unless for love and revenge.* It occurred to her that the starting of a fire was something Henry could have done, because Henry would certainly know how, and wanted rid of his neighbour, and she realised with shame that she was only thinking that at all because she would rather it was anyone other than Julian Tysall. Henry could put out a fire. He could not ever start one. She really only wanted the culprit to be anyone who had nothing to do with her, or those she had made her own responsibility, because she would prefer it if her current state of sadness was not complicated by the thorn of conscience. Unadulterated regret would be, by present standards, a luxury.

None of this was quite Henry's business. Henry had to know. Henry was utterly objective.

'I'm sorry, Henry. Very sorry.'

'Did they say a petrol bomb?'

'Not exactly. They couldn't be sure. Just a lot of petrol, siphoned through that big letter box. Plenty of it. Petrol-soaked sheet or something. No one would have noticed anyone lingering there for a while. The place reeked of petrol.'

'And the door to *her* flat was open?'

'No, broken, the glass in it was broken.'

'And other windows open up there?'

'Yes, the kitchen window, I think.'

'And you left the living-room door not quite shut?'

'Yes, I think so. I was going to come back.'

'And the windows in mine are still OK? And the door to mine's shut?'

'They told me no one's got into yours, Henry. The paint on the hallway side is all blistered, but the door stayed closed.'

'Fireproofed on the inside,' Henry said, proudly. 'Did it myself.'

He was sitting upright on a kitchen chair, with his hands clasping his knees. He did not ask about the cat. She decided she would not mention the cat until he did.

'It would have gone straight up,' he murmured. 'Straight up those damn stairs, to her. There's a colossal draught when the door's open. How very, *very* obliging of it. And the fire brigade there so soon, makes *such* a difference. Are you sure she's really dead?'

'I saw . . .'

'Fine, fine. Well, the Good Lord giveth and he also taketh away,' Henry said, and smiled. The smile was unnerving, all the more so for seeming entirely sincere. He began to laugh; she watched, hoping it was a symptom of shock, hysteria rather than downright callous joy, because she really wished to continue liking and respecting Henry, even if only in parts. He lapsed into silence, curiously relaxed.

'Now that,' he said, 'is what is vulgarly known as a result. I couldn't have done it better myself. Oh, do take that look off your face, Sarah. I'd be a hypocrite to pretend I was sorry my neighbour had perished. You're entirely right in what you suggested a few days ago. Yes, I did let Celia Hornby transmogrify herself into an ogress, in my own mind. I credited her with powers to wreck my life she simply didn't possess and wouldn't have had if I'd only looked at her, stood up to her, and not let myself be intimidated beyond reason. Granted, I failed to see the wood for the trees. That's what happens with people you fear. They feed on it, in your imagination, like a fire with oxygen, and grow into their own legends. But that aside, she was a thoroughly unpleasant, malicious bully. They do exist, you know, even with their reasons and excuses. Of course I'm glad she's dead.'

Sadness was different to guilt.

'You'd better go round, Henry. Do you want me to come with you? We could both go.'

He stirred out of a dream, stared at her blankly, and repeated that slow, triumphant smile.

'Oh, I don't think so,' he said. 'Not for a little while. It's the smell, I've had quite enough of those smells. Nothing's going to get worse in a few hours, and they're bound to think I did it, you see. The truth is, they could very well have been right. In fact, I'm really rather ashamed to have left it to anyone else. I could do with an alibi.' He leant down and patted the aircast boot he wore with the ease of an old shoe. 'This'll help, of course. And so will you. I was here, with you, mending your house. Recuperating. I shall go back after dark. I've been away for a few days, haven't I? Couldn't cope with questions, really.'

She looked at him, realising, not for the first time, that she would never understand the complex, logical reactions of men.

'Why ever would anyone think it was you, Henry? It's your house.'

'Two-thirds my house. Fire goes up. And people might think it was me, because I told her that's what I'd do. I screamed it at her in front of a whole street. And I told her husband.'

'Her *husband*?'

Henry shrugged, not only triumphant but exhausted.

'Ex-husband. Man called Boris. Called to see her when she was out, got me. I shouted at him, too. Said if he couldn't control her, I'd burn her house down.'

He raised the mug of coffee she had made before beginning on the news, as if proposing a toast. 'So, *thank you*, whoever the hell you are.'

'Henry, she was also afraid of you.'

He turned bleary, slightly tearful eyes on her, with the same rather awful smile.

'Is that so? I must have become another of those legends, then, because I never did anything else than shout and hide. Whoever could be frightened of me?'

He caught her expression.

'And you would actually like to think that I might have sneaked over to my own home and *done it*, simply because I know how fire behaves? So does your arsonist. Clever, clever man. Of course I'd never have done it. Far too much respect for property and far too scared. You have to be brave, to start a fire. You'd just rather it wasn't this man who wants something from you. The one who goes to such lengths to take care of you at the same time. Always waits till you're out. Bet that makes you feel good. I forgot to tell you. Your friend Dulcie rang. And someone called Eleanor.'

Alan steeled himself to answer his mobile. He had come to hate it. Once, it had been his most exciting possession, the password to his universe. Now, he detested it. Dreaded JT's voice, but the voice he heard was tired and sick, throaty, and female.

'Alan? It's about the dog. Seem to have lost it. You've got to find her.'

225

Dulcie Mathewson's booming voice, turned to a whisper. A memorable voice, pleading. He could feel the pit of his stomach, ready to drop into his shoes, and made himself speak loudly.

'It's that Dulcie M, isn't it? You lost the dog already? So soon? You bad girl, you. Not fit to look after anything.'

There was an explosion of coughing. He was standing in the laundry room of the hotel. Things went missing from here, all the time.

'You're so right, you know. Can't take care of anything. Naked, in the street, I ask you, at three in the morning. House went up in smoke. Dog ran away. Not sure where I am. Sarah's not at home. Very worried about the dog. Wondered if you were free.'

He kept calm. He was ice.

'Where are you?'

'Chelsea and Westminster. In a fucking queue. I've got no money.' Her voice cracked. She began to whimper. 'And no home. And no dog.'

'Are you hurt?'

There was indelicate snuffling, which touched his heart.

'My *pride*,' she said. The voice sank to a tearful whisper. 'My *hair*, I've got no *hair*. I don't want my son to see me like this. I want Sarah. I want someone to take me to Sarah.'

He could not have stayed still anyway. Fuck the job. There was only one thing he could do. In the taxi, cursing the traffic, hating the sunlight which made the skin on his shaking hands look grey, patting the pockets of the coat to check his cash flow, Alan made a single discovery which increased the pounding of his heart. The flick knife had gone.

He made the cab detour past Dulcie's elegant house. As was. Not a window left; he fancied he could smell it. A roof and walls, stinking in the mocking sunlight. Too many coppers to stop. Wouldn't be able to speak anyway. Concentrated on one thing, such as why Mrs Dulcie Mathewson had not immediately contacted the son whose photograph had adorned her mantelpiece, why people like her, with money and houses and a rank in the world, were as badly off as anyone else when it came to a crisis. Wanting the one they trusted by instinct, even a stranger, rather than the ones they were supposed to love. It gave him a brief sensation of pride, in a morning of unparalleled bleakness, that Dulcie had picked on him. He was addicted to being trusted. Trusted to set a place on fire, trusted never to tell a secret, to do what he said he would do, never to grass, and above all, being trusted by a woman. It took the edge off the nightmare.

JT had had time to start that fire. Nineish in Golden Street, three in the morning in Kensington. No problem. He had made his point.

He had discovered it was fun. Fucking orgasmic.

There was no hierarchy in a hospital queue, except that dictated by the nature of the injury. Bleeders and screamers went first, without deference to age. The patient patient, able to sit at least half upright and not yet at the door of death, was left behind. Dulcie had sent the nice lady officer away, after using her mobile. Couldn't think with her sitting there, even if she was kind. Convinced her that her daughter was coming along in a minute. People always believe me, she thought to herself, with a touch of bitterness, especially when I say I'm fine. Or when I say I'm right. I wish they didn't. I'm not all right, or even right. I wish people did not believe in the myth of me.

★

Sarah's flat, please. No, don't talk. My throat hurts. I'm numb. What could a doctor do for me? Bring Ernest back? Bring my home back? What have I done, Alan? What have I done?

When I get to Sarah's I'll be able to cry. I hate to be seen crying, not my kind of entrance. This taxi must be costing a bomb. Have you got enough?

It was a bad day for sunlight and spring promise. The sun was impertinent and determined. It hurt the eyes in the mid-afternoon, which was the time of day when Sarah's living room was at its lightest and brightest. Yesterday's rain would have suited the sombre mood, and the disparate company gathered inside, in various degrees afraid to go out. This, they agreed, was the safest place. Dulcie wept first and then slept in Sarah's room. Go away, Sarah told the men. Go away. They went and returned.

Dulcie was shocking. Dulcie was not supposed to cry like a baby, nor to be seen without make-up, dressed in a paper suit, her hair a singed frizz, her body a series of livid bruises. Nor to be so helpless, so bereft of authority and dignity. So unable to stop talking, even when it hurt. Sense and non-sense, whispered. So reduced, she seemed as small as Celia Hornby's body. Holding on to her hand, Sarah wished she could pray. Wished she could be grateful for a miraculous lack of burns. As if the burns were the point, rather than the grief. She shushed and coddled, and listened and watched as Dulcie's eyes closed into tranquillised sleep. Liver spots on the back of her hand: surely there had been none before? Dulcie was no longer ageless; she was old. But still Dulcie, talking, even in sleep, muttering: Alan said he would, that

Tysall man, what's his name, but he couldn't you know, not if he's his father's son. I shouldn't use big lightbulbs everywhere. All those plugs on one socket and all that paper lying around. Ernest should have spent the money. The dog, the poor dog. I must find Bimbo.

Sarah, I do love you.

And I you, more than anyone.

The sunlight seemed to last for ever, mocking at despair. Then, as evening arrived, the light went and the rain came down. Soft rain, heard through the open window as the traffic sloshed on the wet road below, and she waited.

The two men came back, like hunter-gatherers, with food. And with them, a nervy, dirty dog.

In any other room, any other city, house, road, place, Henry would have found Alan detestable. Despised him for everything: the el machismo swank he still possessed, the clothes, the facial scar, the contempt he carried with him for possessions, class, money, anyone with a uniform, the fact he was a hired hand, a cockney wide boy, a thief by any other name, a moving unit of harm, a threat, a bandit of sorts, and above all, far too masculine, a contrast to Henry's own effeminacy. All of that he could work out, plus the fact that Alan would have scared him witless, but for the fact he handled Dulcie like porcelain, admirable in its own way and more than he himself could have done, because women like Dulcie scared him as much as his own mother. But then a certain fascination intervened. A sneaking respect for a big man with nerves half shot to hell; an appreciation of another about to fall apart, but hanging in there. A recognition of weakness and strength which might complement his own, and a smidge of self-interest. And what the big man did not know about fire was not worth remembering. All these years in the business, and Henry had never once talked to a real live arsonist.

Alan, on the other hand, would have detested Henry in any other context. Precious little poofter, masquerading as a man, no height, not much in the way of looks, funny way of speaking. Obviously fussy, wringing his hands, collector of all that stuff in Golden Street, got taste, he liked it. Maybe the automatic dislike died when he realised he had once slept in the bloke's bed in that little house. Or maybe it was Sarah's introduction, as Dulcie fell into her arms. Alan, this is Henry, who put out the bathroom fire for me; Henry, this is Alan, who started it. Explain yourselves to one another.

Really? Henry said. How jolly clever. Do you know, that was the most *considerate* fire I've ever seen.

It was easy, after that. They were, after all, experts.

'*Very* crude fires,' Henry was saying, after they returned. 'At least mine was. Anyone could have done it. Petrol through a letter box after dark?'

'No, you're wrong, mate,' Alan argued. 'Least I wish you was. Anyone could *not* have done it. Anyone could have got themselves that result by a freak accident, if everything else was right, such as a broken window pane, or an open window, or her being asleep, so there's a delay in the 999, but otherwise, a result like that, well, it's tricky. Trust me, H, this shit didn't care what got destroyed. Whole house could've gone as far as he cared. No, he's pumping in the petrol at yours like planting a fucking bomb. But he waited for Sarah to leave, because he wants her healthy, so it must be Julian Tysall. Could've been you, though, since it got the result you wanted.'

'My place is a bit of a mess,' Henry protested. 'And I expect my cat is dead.'

Alan had never cared for cats, nor Henry for dogs. When Alan walked down Dulcie's road and found Bimbo shivering in a gateway, both Henry and the taxi driver had managed to avoid protest. Cash did it for the driver; sheer excitement for Henry. Bimbo was currently absent in the nether regions of the flat. Henry admitted to himself that despite the circumstances, he was enjoying himself when he should not; rejoicing when he should have been otherwise. All very well for me. He sobered up, and looked at the broader picture. He was actively pleased that Mrs Hornby was dead; he could not bring himself to regret it in any way. It freed him. If that was bad, bugger it, until Alan, who varied between loquacity (Henry's definition) and an awful sombreness, reminded him of the corollary. Mrs Hornby being dead meant someone had murdered her.

'Water damage, and the prospect of a lot of building works over your head? I don't call that much of a mess. The point is, Julian Tysall is a killer, who might enjoy it. An absolutely loose fucking cannon. I know he wanted to do it.'

'We don't know if he actually *tried* to kill Mrs Mathewson,' Henry said. 'She just happened to be *there* when he had a go at setting fire to her house. He probably had no idea of the effect. Bet there was petrol. Such common stuff. Shame we couldn't get in and smell it.'

'It had to be deliberate,' Alan said. 'She told me coming over she'd had a gin or two. Certainly didn't double-lock. No burglar alarm, cheap smoke alarms with dead batteries.'

Henry tut-tutted, and said, oh dear.

'So anyone with a bit of muscle could've got in. From upstairs or downstairs, or garden, wherever. But the main thing she said which clinches it is there were two seats of fire. She's in the hall, wishing she was fucking dead, and there's fire in the kitchen behind and fire in the living room to the side. Two fucking fires, I ask you.'

Darkness was mercifully complete. Sarah's living room was best after dark, shabbiness and makeshift hidden, careful lights, the magnificent curtains at odds with the rest, fully drawn, as if at the beginning or end of the play.

'Could it be one seat of fire and the fire flashing over?' Henry suggested, not believing it.

'No way. It's got to go up and over the hallway, down a corridor, find something to eat, and drop. It would have gone up, not left. Starts from either one end or the other. She'd never have got through the hallway if it had flashed over. She says the light fitting was still there, and the light, just before she crawled through, but there were flames in the kitchen *and* in the living room. No, there's two seats of fire. The kitchen, the living room. Dead giveaway. This bastard couldn't be too sure. Just in case one won't work, he does another. Now, what does that tell you?'

Henry was nodding. If I'd met this chap in a pub, Alan thought, I swear to God I'd have punched his lights out, long since. As it is, I quite like him.

I found the dog; I found the dog: did something right.

Henry had donned his specs and looked like an owl.

'It tells me amateur but thorough,' Alan said. 'He doesn't believe the first ignition'll work, in case the fire goes out or something, so takes his petrol backstage or frontstage, gives it another whirl. Just to be sure. Probably goes from front to back, and then out, silly wanker. But the only trouble is what's gone down here. Starting fires is addictive, and that's what's happened. You do one once, you can't wait to do it again. Think JT's lost sight of what he wanted. He just likes it. I mean, I know what he means. So he'll do it again, won't he? We need a drink.'

'Oh, I couldn't.'

'I could.'

Moving behind Dulcie, Sarah was reflecting that it was humbling to understand that the presence of a dog could make so much more difference than anything else. Dulcie Mathewson needed men and dogs to restore the will to live. She sailed into the room like an unsteady yacht battling against a gale with full rigging. It made Alan want to cry. Reminded him why he loved women. Made him shiver, for what could have happened. Gave him courage. He looked at his watch. Jesus, ten o'clock, the long dark day a rehashed memory. His hands were steady, though. His coat lay over the sofa. That was what he meant by relaxed. Taking it off. The pockets were lighter at the end of an expensive fourteen hours. He had lost the need to sleep.

'Just a large one, dear,' Dulcie said in her cracked voice. 'But not gin, for God's sake.'

Dulcie was swathed in a series of shawls, with a bright blue towel wrapped round her head and shaped like a turban. A dressing gown, almost meeting in the middle, a paisley shawl of orange and black over one shoulder, mingling with another shawl of peacock-feathered Liberty print, wrapped closely round her neck. The colours clashed. Following behind was the brushed brindled dog, with a scarf of feathered silk petals in rust and black trailing from its mouth, remarkably coincidental with the colour of its tan coat.

'I'm the Queen of Sheba, and the dog did it,' Dulcie

croaked. 'Red wine, please. We have to think out what to do. ALL of us. Really, darlings, I knew the wiring was bad when we moved there forty years ago.'

She was a piece of pathetic magnificence, and only Sarah knew how faded. Henry stared, open-mouthed. Wishing he had risen from the ashes of his own fire like this. The treacherous thought came to him that he could slip away from this mess whenever he liked. Any time now, in the morning, after a drink. He could go home whenever he wanted. Dulcie turned basilisk eyes on him. The pain and the determination made him flinch.

'Who are you?' she demanded.

'A friend,' Henry said, longing for the safe room, and knowing that he meant what he said, strangely relieved by it.

She squinted at him. 'Ah, yes. She told me. Good. Perhaps we can rely on you to bring a little rigour into this conversation. I need food.'

Cold, unappetising food. Plastic ham and vacuum-packed cheese, a stale loaf, nuts and crisps. Inedible for a smoke-filled throat.

'I'll stick to drink,' Dulcie said. 'Now, does anyone have any suggestions? Only I would like to say that my fire was an accident waiting to happen. I'd overloaded the circuits, story of my life. It could have happened any time, and anyway, I half wanted it to do just that. Probably willed it.'

They looked at her, not listening. She was still a natural chairwoman, so that not even grief or trauma could knock it out of her for long.

'Are we all up to speed?'

They nodded. It was more or less true.

'Only I'd like a bit of constructive thinking here, since Sarah's being silly.'

'Sarah often is,' Henry said.

Dulcie Mathewson, the magistrate, glared at him. She could say it; he could not. The dog lay at her feet like an acolyte before a monument. Henry detested dogs, and thought, for the first time, about his cat. How nice of Sarah not to mention it.

'Since you asked,' Henry said, 'we should go to the police. *I* have to go to them eventually anyway. Or they'll come to me. Am I to deny having any idea of who started *my* fire?'

'You don't know who started *your* fire. Are you always so possessive about everything? I *know* what caused mine. That damned old coffee maker, the lampstand. I've been warned about it over and over.'

The poor old dear was in denial, Henry decided.

'We all know who started it,' he said.

'Well, forget it in my case, because it doesn't apply,' Dulcie ordered. 'But no, we don't go to the police because we may expose Alan to questions, and we can't risk that, and I'm afraid we may also expose me. Anyway, my experience as a magistrate tells me that they're pretty useless and highly uninterested in matters of property, although perhaps not so useless that they would fail to look at how Sarah came to own this flat, and I'd rather they didn't.'

'They're interested in murder,' Sarah said.

'Which they'll investigate to the best of their ability,' Dulcie added. 'Let them. We don't stop them. It's up to me . . . us . . . to deal with Julian Tysall.'

'It's up to *me*,' Sarah said quietly.

'That's why she's being so silly.' Dulcie addressed the two men as if Sarah was not in the room. 'She's gone frightfully moral. *She* thinks that the best thing to do is exactly what Julian Tysall wants. Give him this flat. Sell it to him for tuppence. Let him have it, in other words. As if he had a right to it.'

'It did occur to me,' Sarah interrupted mildly, 'that he does have some moral rights to this place. Not legal, but moral. His father casts him aside, leaves him nothing, and his father owned this. Put another way, he's got far more moral right to it than I do.'

'Murderers don't have rights,' Alan muttered. 'Any more than arsonists. They could be said to have given them up.'

'I'm not sure I want it any more,' Sarah said. 'It's quite different enjoying a place because it appears to have been granted to you out of honest affection, a highly flattering, generous legacy of love, if you like, and even that didn't feel entirely deserved. But to know I have it because of a sleight of hand . . .'

She glanced at Dulcie, checking how well she was holding up. 'Well-intentioned, I'm sure. But to know it was Charles Tysall's? That he might have lived here and made it into a citadel with all these locks, and a safe room? To know it was never intended for me? It means it can never be mine.'

'Doesn't mean you give it away to a killer,' Alan said. 'Fucking hell, sell it and give the money to charity, if that's what you think. Two wrongs never make anything right.'

'You can't *give* it away,' Henry wailed. 'Where would we go? Where would your friends go? *We* need this, even if you don't.'

Sarah hesitated, spread her hands.

'I'm talking about damage limitation. Look at the damage he's done. He's reduced Alan to a shadow. Made a proud man afraid. I can't bear that. Destroyed Dulcie's foundations.'

'He didn't destroy any of *my* foundations,' Dulcie snapped.

'I keep telling you, it was my own bloody fault. No one came in, you idiots. *I* would have heard, Bimbo would have heard . . . It was alight before . . . must have been smouldering . . .'

'He's killed, and he's not going to stop,' Sarah continued. 'So if giving him what he thinks he deserves is what it takes to stop him, that's what I'll do.'

'Over my dead body,' Dulcie said. 'After all my trouble.' She was getting tired. The façade of recovery and authority was slipping. She clutched at the stem of her wine glass.

'But it won't stop him,' Alan said. 'It will just make him worse. What did money and power do for his father, Sarah? Make him a good man? Or encourage him? Think of that. If Julian Tysall gets what he wants this time, you only give him the means and the stepping stone to get out of his gutter and spend the rest of his life hurting people. You'll just be taking him off your back and putting him on to someone else's, and he's got a long way to go. Very responsible, that is.'

She could see that. It made complete and frightful sense. She had always considered him wiser than herself. Alan got up and paced the room, as if measuring it.

'Got to be neutralised,' he said.

'Supposing we burn *his* house down,' Henry suggested, feeling faintly frivolous.

'It's a dump, he rents it. His fucking grouse is that he hasn't got a house to burn down. Funny how houses make people vulnerable, isn't it? They're supposed to make you feel safe.'

Alan stopped talking. It was easy to feel strong, among allies. He thought of how he would feel when JT turned up at the Marchmont caff in the morning.

'Man like that? The only way's to kill him. Or take away his looks. Yeah, that might do it.'

237

'He didn't,' Dulcie was repeating wearily. 'He didn't. I'd been warned about it. The insurance man said, he told me . . .'

'Take away his looks,' Sarah repeated, slowly. 'Are they really so important?'

'Too right they are. It's women who cope with losing looks. Man like that wouldn't. Any more than I did.'

'I see.'

She always listened to him. She listened to him intently.

He thought of the missing knife, which he had flourished once, and never, ever used. Never had the bottle or the inclination, never saw the need. He remembered, as he did every day, what violence had done to his childhood, how he had admired it; that was where the rot began. He shuddered at his own helplessness.

First time in memory, there were people he cared about, and he was fuck-all useless.

'. . . that the wiring in both rooms was dangerous,' Dulcie finished. 'Told me that I had three months to fix it, or they couldn't insure me. A time bomb, he said, especially when it was cold and everything was on . . . didn't know which was worse . . .'

'Neutralise,' Sarah said, as if experimenting with the word. 'To render harmless. Defuse. Could mean persuade him, compromise him, render him vulnerable. Disarm him. Distract him. Give him something else he wants. Hmmm. There must be other, gentler ways to reel him in. Towards the sense of domination he craves. The satiation he wants. The respect. He's only a man.'

The others were slower to understand. Dulcie stared at her, and began to struggle to her feet in protest, fell back with the effort.

'*No*,' she said. 'Sarah, NO.'

238

She began to cry. 'Will you listen to me?' she whispered. 'It was an accident.'

'Like father, like son,' Sarah said. 'His daddy had a terrible weakness for red-haired ladies. Had to have them. And in the end, that ruined his life too.'

'You can't go to bed with him,' Dulcie wailed. 'He'll hurt you.'

'Why not?' Sarah said. She glanced obliquely towards Henry and Alan. 'It's a very good way of beginning a dialogue. And you seem to forget, that's what I do.'

She looked closely at Dulcie.

'I do listen, love, I heard you, promise. Time for bed, isn't it? He's not coming back tonight. Safer than houses, here.'

CHAPTER TWELVE

It was an uneasy dawn.

Alan thought he knew her better than anyone else, but he did not know her at all. None of them did. And yet they were all going to do what she wanted. They fell into line like raw recruits.

Henry agreed to take Dulcie and the dog to Dulcie's son. Dulcie did not protest. She had no fight left in her. Henry was to go on, with Dulcie's signed authority, to blag his way into her house, make an inspection. Then he was to go home, to Golden Street. His own obedience amazed him.

Alan went from the hotel to Marchmont Street, thanking his stars that Sheila was off with the accountants for the day. Out in the fresh air, he felt as naked as a newborn. Bring him, Sarah had told him. That's all you have to do. Invite him to tea. Fetch him to that quiet, private place.

Sitting in the empty caff, he had no appetite for breakfast. The smell of it made him wince. He felt like a fucking pimp. Yeah, yeah, do as you're told, bring the geezer along. For what? So that she could smooch all over him, suck his cock, stare into his big blue eyes, seduce him? Was that what she thought? But that was what tarts did. Tweaked cocks and stroked balls. Exactly as she'd done to him. Only it was different, with him, wasn't it? No, it wasn't. He looked at his ragged fingernails. For fuck's sake, whassermatter? It *had* been different. She had made him feel real. Proved his fucking manhood, taught him looks didn't matter, trusted him as she did now. Accepted him as she did now. Taken him straight off a Park Square bench, knowing fine which particular muscle a humbled man needed to exercise; knew that what he really needed was belief that some woman, any woman, might have him, the way they had before. Might actually want what was left of him for an hour or two. And she did, she fucking did: she wanted his company, for God's sake. It's a lovely day, she'd said. Let's go for a walk. Walk and talk and love, or was it the other way round? He could not remember and wanted to remember every detail of the summer before, to prove it wasn't the same. Tried to think of the way it always seemed as if she had all the time in the world. Course, there were all the other blokes, and it had never crossed his mind to be envious. Most of his previous women were safely married, bored wives, and he hadn't envied the husbands, had he? Do you have any rules, Sarah? he'd asked her once. Yes, I have to like you, she'd said. Otherwise I can't do anything other than flaunt it. He told himself, pull yourself together, Alan. This isn't about you.

He was drinking bad coffee. Not like Dulcie's.

I got that fucking dog back. That's all I'm good for.

He was angry with her. It was jealousy troubling him, gnawing his gut, shoving some of the fear out of the way. JT and Sarah: Jesus. Envy, whatever it was, shouldn't matter. He should simply be afraid for her. As it was, he was angry at her stupid thinking that she could neutralise the bastard by being sexy, for God's sake. Don't kid yourself, Sarah: you're gorgeous, but don't flatter yourself that much. It doesn't work with all men, do you think we're all so stupid? Don't think sex will work with JT, even if does with most of us silly sods. God, I hope he doesn't turn up. Can't face it.

There he was, Julian Tysall, holding his coat away from contact with the tabletops, not in a hurry. Something odd about him. He was somehow smaller than he had been in the hotel, two days ago. There was no room in the Marchmont caff for him to spread his legs and air his balls, or for showing off a good suit and clean cuffs, like in the hotel bar. It made a difference. Here, they had to sit with knees together under the table, like prim old ladies; that was it. No, he was definitely smaller. Settings could make a man grow. Then Alan had the uncomfortable thought that maybe it was his own imagination which made him remember JT as a bigger man than he was, as if he had grown in his own memory, in accordance with his recent achievements, into a fearsome giant, like something in a film. As if, over the last twenty-four hours, since Alan knew what he had done, he had swelled, only in memory, and had now shrunk to his true size. Like Popeye, before and after spinach. Or maybe a man who set fires without caring if he was caught had to be big, because he deserved respect. Only he wasn't really big. He was average size, with a poncy name and still startlingly good-looking.

'You didn't answer your phone,' Julian Tysall said.

'Didn't I? Sorry. I was busy.'

Julian Tysall smiled, fleetingly. It whispered across his fine features in a flash of white teeth, before leaving.

'Busy? I'll say you've been busy. Christ, I heard you were quick off the mark, but not that speedy.' He was shaking his head in slow, admiring wonder, tapping the pepper pot on the table for emphasis.

'First you were going to scout out Golden Street, so you said, and next thing I know the bloody place has been burnt. Are you making up for lost time, or what? Then, yesterday, I decide I'll go in person and try and put the fear of God into the widow Mathewson, and what do I find? Alan the fire-raiser has got there first. Never knew anyone so quick to take up a suggestion. Two fires in one night, you must have motored, or got help. More than I dreamt of. I thought, who helped you, old man? He's the one I need. Then I thought about what you did with the first one in *my* flat. You were just going to look at the place, work out how to do it, next thing I know, it's done. The thought really is the same as the deed with you, isn't it? But I hate to tell you, you went a bit far, 'cos no one was supposed to die.'

That last bit did not seem to bother him much. He placed loosely clasped hands on the table, linking his fingers. He was, Alan realised, excited and nervous, trying to keep himself still. Perfect, artistic hands, with the same translucent fingernails polished to a professional sheen. Such a strange vanity for a man to be so proud of his hands. The white fingers repelled Alan as much as worms. He focused his absolute fury on the hands. *Bastard, bastard, bastard.* The sheer front of the man took his breath away and made him splutter.

'So that's your game, is it? You're saying it was *me* did it? That I started two fucking fires in one fucking night? How the fuck was I supposed to do that?'

'Oh, calm down. Thought you'd be proud of it. I did
wonder. I suppose even a pro can get carried away with
enthusiasm. I don't need to know how you did it, do I, but I
do know it had to be you. Who else? You pinched that letter
from the widow, don't think I didn't notice. Are you always
so keen to get ahead of the game, or are you just anxious to
please? Or did you think I'd pay you a bonus? Couldn't possibly compromise myself by paying you anything at all, could
I? Not to a man who murders old ladies in their beds. I knew
you were good, Al, old man, but not Superman. What on
earth happened to your coat?'

Alan's coat was ruined. The sleeves seemed shorter, the
rest of it sagged and it was grubby with dog hairs, and he was
suddenly conscious of it. Old man with shabby clothes.

The manicured hands arranged the salt and pepper pots
on the table, and began to fondle a paper napkin. Then abandoned it, reached into his inside pocket for cigarettes, jittery
but controlled. Alan could not raise his eyes. He felt beaten.

'I didn't. I fucking didn't. I don't do women.'

'You mean you didn't but you do now? Needs must. You
didn't see me, did you, when you went back for the dog?
That dog you had last time we met here. Did you lose it
when you started the widow's fire?'

What fucking new hell was this? This was the story, the
cunning bastard. It was never going to be his fault, nothing
would ever be JT's fault. He would always invent an alternative scenario which left him out and absolved him, just as he
had invented his so-called rights to Sarah's flat. He would
believe in his own invention completely, and the fact that it
was not true had nothing to do with anything. Stick him in a
witness box on oath and pain of death, he would still believe
it. He would forget the truth as if it had never been. The gall

of it choked Alan, even more than the knowledge that looking like this, JT would be believed and he himself never would be.

'But seriously, old man, it was bloody well done. Sorry I can't pay you. Matter of principle, you see. But I promise I'll be careful about who I tell.'

Alan looked at his own hands, turned them over and thought he could see his pulse, kicking him awake. All right. Go with the flow, let it be, choke on it. He managed a swallow of coffee without spitting. Remember why he was there. If this turd had convinced himself that he, Alan, was the new version of middle-aged Arson Superman, then he might go for this too. In his experience, congenital liars were good at absorbing lies, and a bloke was always easier to fool when he was winning.

'All right,' he said. 'I'm a fucking miracle-worker, OK? More than you thought, as a matter of fact, much more, but then I like to surprise. I've done even more than you know about. She wants to meet you.'

'Who?'

'Sarah Fortune, of course. Who else did you think I fucking meant?'

This time he met the blue eyes, rounded in astonishment. 'How . . .'

'It was you who said you don't need to know how. She spotted me, see? I do like to do a job thoroughly, so I talked to her. You're right: I've changed my mind about not doing women. She's out of her mind. You were spot on that the best way of getting to her was that Mathewson woman. That did it. Shame, really. It was a nice house.'

The eyes blinked naked incredulity. It was not going to work.

'All right,' Alan said wearily. 'I ain't a miracle-worker. I knew her once, Sarah. Same old underworld we live in, see? I paid for a shag once. So that gave me a bit of a start, see what I mean. Trust me, I know her. She's only a tart, but she loves the old lady and she doesn't want any more burning. She'll sign whatever you want. She's running shit scared. Says get it together and she'll do it. She's asked you to tea.'

'Tea?'

JT lost his incredulity and roared with laughter. 'Tea? TEA?'

The caff fell silent. The waitress arrived.

'Yes?' she said.

'Yes,' said Julian Tysall. 'YES, yes. When?'

When he cupped his chiselled chin with those manicured hands, he looked like a boy who had just won first prize. A winner who knew the next prize was round the next corner. He would believe anything now.

'She wants it very private,' Alan said. 'Just you and her, and whatever paperwork to start the thing rolling. So I've fixed up a place, OK?'

Alan went back to the hotel. Things were sloppier in Sheila's absence, and he was giving a bad example of absenteeism. So he made his presence felt for a bit, sitting in the foyer, watching the guests check out late morning, doing a patrol, so everyone would know he was around. There was a big business conference beginning at noon in the basement meeting rooms. A lot of men in suits, milling now, for coffee. Enough to keep the wolf from the hotel door. In the afternoon the foyer would be more or less deserted, and then crowded again when they finished. He could not think why it mattered, but it did. Crowds or no crowds, what difference did it make? He went up to the attic floor, tidied up, sat on the bed and tried to think this through until he could not think at all. He went back to his room and tried to brush his coat into a state of decency, and then, unable to stand the great indoors, went back out into the blustery day.

If only he knew what was in her mind. Words spoken in the early hours of the morning were simply words. He thought she had a plan, but really she was thinking out loud, making it up as she went along. She had been so definite, though. You must not be seen with Julian Tysall, she told him, especially not in the hotel, where everyone knows you. You stay right out of the way. I know the way upstairs. Why would he hurt me? He needs me. *What are you going to do, Sarah?* It's my fight, she said, it isn't yours. Get him to the foyer, and then just stay out of the way. Make yourself seen somewhere else. Give yourself an alibi. Henry will do.

And then her questions. How long could a person stay up on the attic floors before anyone noticed?

Days, I suppose. Why do you ask?

Did I?

Will you listen to me, Sarah? It won't work.

I always listen to you, she'd said. You know more about men than I ever shall. You said, go for his looks. I want him dead. It would be easier for everyone if he was dead.

The fountain was on in the square, the wind buffeting the water sideways, blurring the effect, throwing damp spray into his eyes. The cold of it stung. He touched his face, wiping it with his hand, and realised that he had not thought about his face, the burn, the watering eye, for days. Not noticed it in the mirror either, not wondered about its effect on others. Well, glory be. That was something. He fished in his trouser pocket for a handkerchief. None there, now that was slipshod. Automatically explored the other pockets. Money, yes, important bits of paper, yes, wallet with old photo of his mother, yes, flick knife, no. She had palmed it, while wearing his coat in this very square, just like he had palmed her keys. She had that damn knife.

He thought he knew what she was planning to do.

She was not going to seduce Julian Tysall. She was going to kill him or scar him, all because she had listened to Alan, the way she did. She could easily kill JT for what he had done to Dulcie. Dulcie counted for more than anyone. All of them, all the men, were in a queue behind Dulcie when it came to love. Dulcie was family. What had he done? Promised that JT would be in the foyer, and that he himself would stay away.

What if she did kill him?

Henry reached his own forlorn front door in the middle of the afternoon, highly perplexed, and feeling very strange indeed, desperately wishing for company as he entered the place like a thief with his own key. All right, a superficial survey of the outside yesterday with Alan, as well as a superficial analysis of the fire itself, informed him that his own portion of the building might well have survived with everything inside it intact, but one could never be sure. The one thing which puzzled him most was the strange feeling that he did not really care, either way, or at least did not care to anything like the extent he thought he might. He was more curious than chafing at the bit. More interested in the interi-

ors of other people's houses than he was in his own, just at
the minute. Oh dear, it was almost liberating. He did not
care what it was like in there, provided *she* was not upstairs.
After all, her death was entirely fitting. Kind people like
Sarah might try and imagine that Mrs Hornby had not been
wicked, but she was. Living with her upstairs had been like
being squashed by an enormous toad. No, he had not *imagined* the malice. It was as if the fire had cleansed the place of
an evil ghost, and in comparison to what it had been like to
live there before, the prospect of clearing up the mess seemed
no great problem, but possibly an opportunity. He looked
down at the unbecoming grey of his aircast boot as he
inserted the key in the door. Really, he could sprint in this.
Breaking the dear foot and being mistaken for someone who
could not have needed rescuing as much as he had then may
have been one of the better things to happen, although it
might be best not to tell anyone that. Fire destroyed; fire
redeemed. *C'est la vie.* He would not miss the cat.

He pulled back the shutters in his living room. Not quite
the same, but good enough. Fire was mercifully selective. So
was the fire brigade. If there was no fire to put out, they
didn't come in, and they hadn't. Their presence was marked
by the streaks of water on the wall, stains on the ceiling more
prominent than those which had been there before. It would
be the same in the other rooms. Fire went up, water came
down. The old sofa was damp to the touch, the carpet would
be damp. It smelt bad, and would, of course, smell worse.
Fungus would grow. Everything in here would need treatment. That was what insurance was for. He would be able to
do everything he had ever wanted to do. Possibly even buy
back upstairs. He felt giddy with relief, before he remembered everything else, and even then the relief did not quite

go away. There was, after all, plenty to celebrate. Such as not hurting any more, a feeling that the worst was over, eroded, just a little bit, when he stopped to think, and realised he would rather not have been excluded from whatever ultimate plans had been formed for what was going to happen today.

He sat down on the damp sofa, to recapitulate. Remembered Sarah's face as she had got shrivelled Dulcie Mathewson to bed, hushing her like a child in a pram. That face of Sarah's was harder than nails. Dulcie would never be the same, of course; he could have told her that. What he could not conjecture was what Sarah might do to anyone who had done what had been done to Dulcie. Death would not be good enough, unless it was slow. Sarah would err as much on the side of brutal revenge as she did on the side of such undiscriminating generosity as she had been foolish enough to show to him. Surely. He was absolutely sure that Sarah Fortune could hate as fully and efficiently as she could love. If he himself were that Julian Tysall, he would go away and lock himself into a safe room, straight away.

Fire brigade water and tumultuous rain had converted his garden into a damp morass, in the midst of which lay the cat. He buried it, dispassionately, in the raised flowerbed at the side. Always knew Celia Hornby would kill it. Again that little stab of rejoicing. It would not do. It was vaguely immoral.

He should not feel this way, especially in the light of what he knew. At least when *they* came (how quickly he had come to think of them as *they*) he would not have to lie. Because he did not know who had started the fire which had killed Celia Hornby, any more, after visiting Dulcie's wrecked house this morning, than he knew who had started that. In the latter case, he told himself, shovelling earth on to the cat, no one. Dulcie's analysis could have been entirely right. No petrol. It posed a slight, but only slight, moral dilemma, such as did this Julian Tysall fellow deserve what Sarah was going to do to him?

He went back up to the hallway, to collect the note left there urging him to get in touch with *them*. His fine sense of smell detected lingering traces of petrol. There was a shallow pit near the door, where the carpet was scorched down to charred wood beneath. The stairs leading upwards were incompletely scorched, with patches of the original colour faintly visible. The flimsy banisters were partially intact, some of the uprights burned into charred sticks, others standing as they were, supporting fragments of handrail as if doing their duty. It was as if the fire had bounced and pounced, nibbling on titbits as it was forced on to greater things, like a dog on a lead dragged reluctantly from a scent in order to find a better one. The whole thing was fetid, as if brown mud had cascaded down the walls. Water doing battle with smoke, displacing fire. The seat of the fire was here; the real work of it elsewhere. For the first time ever, Henry could see that fire could also be a friend. There was absolutely no way he was going to go upstairs, towards that patch of light he could see through the gloom, like the hovering of a ghost. Scenes from Dulcie's house interposed themselves in his mind. Her fire had been less kind, but it had come from within, not from without.

As he stood, Henry heard a tentative knocking on the front door, which made him jump. There was a temptation not to respond, but to scuttle back inside his own place, almost out of habit. But he could guess who it was. A public knocking on a discoloured front door in broad daylight could only be neighbour or police. He thumped his way towards it, quite absurdly pleased that the fanlight above the door was still intact. It was high time for the police to arrive, so that he could put his hand on his heart and say, *I really do not know.* Without embellishing it by saying, someone else thinks they know. Officer, I have absolutely no idea who started the fire. Yes, I did not like her upstairs, but I could never have done such a thing unless in my sleep.

Suddenly he felt terrified all over again, paralysed. Swept with a sense of déjà vu, when a knock would make him want to run and hide. In case it was her. Then sense intervened. He steeled himself to open the door, because, after all, on the other side there could only be a man. With a couple of legs and arms, only a man. What was the worst he could do? You could not set a house on fire twice. Or do what had already been done.

He was right that it was a man at the door. A not unfamiliar man, although Henry could not quite remember where he had seen him last. Big late-middle-aged bloke, looking sad, rather than bad. So sad he was crying, and repeating, sorry, sorry, sorry, I shouldn't have done it. Henry knew he was entering another zone when he looked over the man's head from the superior height of his top step, looking out for *them,* and at the same time pulled the man inside. He had never wanted to shield anyone in his life, but now he did. Boris, Celia Hornby's husband.

Parting from Dulcie, being alone, allowed Sarah to dwell with the rage and make it work for her rather than against her. The rage had begun when she first saw Dulcie. The first instinct was to scream it out loud, and then it left her cold, with the effect of an icy shower. Sharp, clean rage like this was useful and had to be harnessed while it lasted. The space of her empty flat, now they were all gone, was also useful. She had hated sending Dulcie to her daughter-in-law, but most of all she had detested the fact that she had given Dulcie orders and Dulcie had obeyed, talking all the time. It *was* an accident, Sarah, you know my house. It was, it was. Yes, I know, I know, go to sleep.

The flick knife lay on the bed. An evil thing: press the button, and from an object as anonymous-looking as a tin opener there sprang a lethal blade. Once upon a time Sarah's brother had played with one of these, and showed it to her to frighten her, taught her how to use it, practising on a hapless oversized soft toy which between them they had ripped to pieces, but that was a long time ago. Her brother's possession of it had terrified her then, until she realised it had also terrified him. Scar his good looks, Alan said. Take his pride. Like taking all of Samson's strength by cutting off his hair. She picked up the knife, activated the blade and slashed, underhand, into empty space. Then she let it drop on to the cover of the bed. She had tidied the room assiduously, just as she had tidied the whole of the apartment, not wanting a mess when she came back. During the morning, in the sweetness of isolation, she had answered the phone messages, renewed contacts, caught up with her own routine obligations, spoken normally as if life was going to go on as before, because it was: it had to.

Sarah was haunted by visions of the interior of Dulcie's home as she had seen it last. By the time she had passed on to the real dilemma of the early afternoon, she found she was less in agreement with Alan than she had been the night before, and knew she could no longer afford to be influenced by his judgements. A man did not become all-powerful just because he was feared. Julian Tysall was only a man.

Accidents happen. She would know better when she saw him face to face, worked out how like his father he really was.

Speaking at length to Eleanor made all the difference, as well as making both of them feel useful. It was good that Eleanor felt she had to make amends for something. She really did want to help, because she needed to do something with that conscience of hers; she insisted that there was no risk, but then Eleanor was totally unafraid of men as a result of never having desired them. It was only women she feared.

The real dilemma was what to wear and how to look. Sarah was a chameleon; she could adopt any number of demeanours through the medium of clothes, shoes, hairstyles, expressions. Something a little slipshod, perhaps. Sexily waifish. Distressed but revealing; upholstered but fleshy. Or like mourning, pale and defeated. She laid out all the clothes as if she was dressing an actress for scene three, and finally decided on the coat, secondly because it was cold out there, and firstly because Dulcie had given it to her.

She was glad it was the old coat she had left in Golden Street.

Stay away. One more turn around this fucking square, and he would be dizzy with walking. Yes, she would kill him. A woman who lived with the careless style of a Sarah would have to be able to do that, for sure. If not kill, at least defend herself. She would know a trick or two. And she had so many motives for hurting him. He was his father's son, for starters, the bastard son of the man who had created those little scars which made him close to her, and in the quarters where Alan had grown up, before it all changed, you were always your father's son, fair game for revenge from three generations back, let alone the one. Daddy's sins were not what anyone would call a head start in life. So number one, there was that, enough to make her hurt him. Then there was what JT had done to Dulcie, he kept going back to that, in some jealous recognition of a greater affection. Women loving women: they were supposed to hate one another. The sisterhood was stronger than the brotherhood ever was, if only he'd known. Like family. And, fuck it, this order to *stay away* was entirely for him. It was him she had in mind. She simply wanted him out of the way, in case anyone later made a connection between him and Tysall. It could not be Alan who steered JT through the foyer into the lift and up to the attic floor, because she was bloody determined no one would ever make a connection between them, or at least not on this date. Showed that she was planning something more than a naked chat. She listened to him. She'd been listening to him when he had said, scratch him, hurt his looks. She had been listening hard when he said, a man like that won't fall for sex, or he'll take it and hurt you, and it won't make no difference. Has his pride in his face and his privates. Like I did. Everything radiating out from his eyes and his groin.

Less of *like I did*. Less of *me*. JT is *not* like me. I never, ever had hands like that. Hands were for getting dirty. Alan was resting his own hands on the back of a bench, gazing at the fountain, which was undisturbed by anything but its own graceful upward progress, falling and cascading back into the ground from which it flowed. A contemporary work, unlike the grandness of Trafalgar Square and Nelson's Column, where water fell from a great height, bounced over details and cupped pools, offset the carved heads of lions and landed in its own sculpted basin. This was simply water, rising and falling, delighting and distracting with its own sound. Part of a playground, rather than a monument. The bench on which his own hands rested was wrought iron, leaving a residue of London dirt and damp on his palms. He liked to touch metal. He could feel the calluses on his hands when he grasped a railing; it was like scratching an itch. There were things deeply ingrained in his hands he would never remove. You needed Swarfega and bleach to get rid of petrol. You did not get rid of that perfume for days.

Would Sarah feel good if she hurt him?

So when did Julian Tysall find time yesterday to be so free of scent and get his fingernails done? Those dreadful mani-cured hands were guarded like a pair of rare species of something. Not a sniff or a stain, when he turned his palms up in all innocence. No way had he got them dirty. Gloves, then. Gloves weren't the point, or they were. Alan had always despised them himself, and couldn't see an arrogant bastard like that bothering with them either, not without plenty of practice. He was smaller than he looked, too.

Alan removed his hands from the back of the iron bench where he had rested them for cooling, and turned back his cuff to look at his watch for the twentieth time in four hours. Four fifteen. Alibi time. Suppressed the thought that there was no way a wee runt called Julian had stood and poured petrol through a letter box in Golden Street with hands like those. He did not want to be wrong, and he knew he was. And then get inside another house, and do it again? Don't make me laugh. And it was for the second house, the second fire, that Sarah would seek revenge. Look, Sarah, if you kill or scar a bloke, it's you who stays scarred. They get away with it. They get better; you don't. Bloke who did my face in died of cancer, anyway. He wiped his own hands down the side of

256

his trousers and went to Golden Street. Henry would do, she said, for an alibi.

'We could have a fantastic salon up here,' Eleanor said. 'Needs a bit of work, though. All this crap, all this room. Makes me want to spit. All this empty space and the rent I pay. Where do I wait? Can we go through it again?'

'No. You heard me first time. If it doesn't work, use your imagination.'

'But not to hurt him?'

'I have to see what he needs first.'

'OK. Go and fetch him.'

The woman Julian Tysall met in the foyer of the Belvedere Hotel surprised him. He had seen Sarah Fortune from the distance he kept when following her through London, which he had found extremely difficult to do, although he would never have admitted it. She never walked at an even pace, or ever too fast for this kind of pursuit; it had been his own self-consciousness which had impeded him. Keeping in sight of her red hair was easy; acting nonchalantly, as if he had another purpose, was not. It was only when he realised that no one would notice that he became bolder and better at it, realising he could take his eyes off her for more than a second, especially when he had known where she was going. Practice made him feel less foolish, and it was the fear of making a fool of himself, following a woman like a lovesick boy, which had slowed him down, initially. There had been no love in it. He hated her, from his distance. Face to face, he still did, but it was harder, on the brink of victory, to feel it with the same intensity. From a distance of three feet, touching distance, she was so much smaller than she had seemed. He had seen her first in the autumn, coming out on to the street from the big front door which should have been his, dressed rich, in purple and green, frighteningly flamboyant. A high-class hooker, dressed to order, someone's artful party piece, and that was his abiding image, although he had never seen her like that again. Today she was like a neat little bird. The grey coat he had seen before, but not in detail, covered her from neck to ankle, leaving on show only a small pale face with enormous anxious eyes, and a massive quantity of hair, which moved as she almost curtsied to him. It was only later that he wondered how she had known immediately who he was, as he came through the revolving doors, awkwardly, tripping on the carpet and regaining control of his briefcase, to see her emerge from behind the urn of flowers and come towards him. She had a white handkerchief in her hand, and dabbed at her eyes as she spoke, haltingly.

'Mr Tysall?'

'Yes.'

'I'm sorry. This is all very painful for me. I don't want to cry in public, so I've got us a room upstairs. Is that all right?'

Her voice was low and pleading. She was no higher than his chest, stood back from him, looking at his face, then looking away, timidly. Very, very nervous. He could have broken her in half.

'Whatever,' he said, and followed her, swaggering across the empty foyer into the lift, looking to see who watched. No one. There was no one else in the lift. It moved slowly up the floors. A small lift, making them stand close. He did not notice at first when she began to undo the coat, until it was unbuttoned and hanging open. There was a glimpse of black bra, spilling bosom, suspenders and black tights, tanned flesh, spike-heeled boots. She was smiling at him, still nervous.

'I thought,' she said, 'we could at least make this pleasant.'

Red hair, big tits, his fantasy. Like his mother. Like all his father's women. Screwing the woman who had screwed his father. It had always been his fantasy.

After that, he ceased to notice where he was going. He was a winner, all the way. Why not? It was finally his turn, and a winner takes all. He hesitated as they went through the fire door, but she was shrugging off the coat entirely, so he still followed. He scarcely noticed the room he was in. All the excitement, the scent of victory, was with him. He hated her; he wanted her mouth on him. She wanted it too. She had her hands on the zip of his trousers, looking up at him imploringly. Please, she said, please. God, she couldn't wait. The bitch.

What he remembered next was an intense pain in his neck.

And that, for a little while, was all he remembered.

He came to, hearing voices. The room seemed dark. The smudge of daylight had faded. Two voices from one person, one a shadow of the other. The deeper voice saying, he won't stay like this for long. The effect's only temporary. Quick, then. She, they, were doing something to him, moving him about, as if he was a featherweight. His limbs felt free; he was lying down and he was cold. There was a candle burning near his face. Too close. And Sarah Fortune, leaning over him stark naked, bosom level with his face, still anxious, talking to him.

'You aren't hurt, are you? Speak to us, there's a dear. Like you said, we really need to talk.'

He put his hand up to his face. It paused at his neck, feeling the rough texture of a swathe of material. The material felt soft and solid: a thick restraining bandage.

'Don't worry about it,' she said. 'You can sit up, slowly. If you would.'

He drew his arms up and propelled himself from the horizontal to seated. The mattress on which he lay sagged; he lurched sideways, righted himself. She was sitting in an old plastic chair, facing him, cross-legged, as naked as birth, with only a coat round her shoulders. He placed his feet on the floor, took his weight on his hands, and realised he too was naked. She spoke to someone behind his head.

'I was right, wasn't I? He's only another man.'

There was a disembodied voice from far away.

'I told you it was Boris set that fire. Celia drove him to it, she said on the phone. *He* never could.'

His hands moved to cover his balls, protectively.

'Will you look at that?' Sarah said, staring at his groin. 'Lovely hands he has. Gamblers' hands don't get dirty. Just like his father's.'

He knew he was tethered by a leash. The voice behind would yank it, break his neck. He could not move, remained staring at her.

'My clothes,' he croaked.

'You took them off,' she said, with the utmost gentleness. 'Don't you remember?'

'You don't mean it,' Alan said.

'Yes, of course I do.'

'But she'll kill him.'

'So? Sounds like bloody good riddance to me, from what

I know. Besides, it won't have anything to do with us, will it? We're far, far away. Nowhere near the incriminating scene.'

'Tell me again.'

Henry sighed. His deliberate manner of speech, that of the expert witness, or a teacher at school, was infuriating. He could not hurry it. Alan looked at his watch. It told him nothing but time. Five in the afternoon, dark, and raining again. He hated Henry's house and its redolent smell, and he hated Henry being right.

'He called, Boris, the *ex*-husband of that bitch upstairs. I gave him tea and advised him to say nothing. I doubt he'll take the advice, so few people do; such a ridiculous thing, remorse, especially over someone who makes your life hell, which she'd certainly done to him. Poisoned his wife's mind, he said, wrecked the marriage. Mind, I was always better on science than human nature. I told him to get home and forget what he'd said, soonest. He'll probably confess, like nice men do. A whole bed sheet, twisted first, soaked in petrol, fed through the letter box. Left a tail sticking out, then lit it with a lighter. Burned his fingers a bit, poor soul, that'll be a give-away, *awfully* conventional method, but he did wait until no one else was in, and he did seem to know about stairwell draughts.'

Alan wanted to smash the ornaments on the mantelpiece. Instead he formed one hand into a fist and wrapped his other palm firmly around it, and exerted pressure until the outside knuckles were white.

'And as for Mrs Mathewson,' Henry went on, 'well, I can't take credit for finding out about that. The insurance investigator was already on the job. Used to know him, as a matter of fact. I might just get a job. Fact is, Dulcie is massively underwired. She had a hundred-and-fifty-watt spotlight touching her curtains, far too powerful, left on for hours. That was the seat in there. As for the kitchen, he reckons it could be an old burnt-out coffee percolator left on for ever without water, melted. Whole ceiling gone, just above. No sign anyone came in. No accelerant whatever. If that were me, I'd say it was an accident waiting to happen. She did mention that, didn't she?'

'On the same fucking night?' Alan shouted.

Henry shrugged. 'On any night when she'd had a gin too many and failed to turn things off.'

Henry sipped his tea. They were in the kitchen, where the smell was least, the streaked glass doors open to darkness.

'So,' he said. 'It might *not* have been him. That's good, isn't it?'

Alan went out into the back garden and spat his tea at a grave, without knowing it.

'No, it's not good,' he called over his shoulder. 'Because Sarah doesn't know it. And Sarah's with him now. Taking what you might call an entirely inappropriate revenge.'

Henry took the empty china cup from Alan's hand and placed it in the sink. Then he put on his jacket, which had been draped neatly over the back of his chair. Alan looked at his watch. Five thirty. Time for drinks.

'Perhaps we'd better go then,' Henry said. 'You should have phoned me earlier. You should have trusted me, you know. I'm frightfully selfish, but not all the time.'

Chapter Thirteen

'Where are my clothes?' he asked.

'Long gone, I'm afraid. Out the window. Who needs them? Good-looking man like you.'

He could feel the ligature round his neck, held his head straight, waiting for pain if he moved. He was sure that the ligature was attached by a wire to an unknown hand, ready to tweak the lead and agonise him. He could not sit upright on the sagging surface. It forced him to take his hands from his groin and brace himself on his thighs, so he would not move his neck.

'Eleanor refuses to tell me how she did that,' Sarah went on. 'It's a trade secret known to massage therapists and a few others, like policemen on riot duty. I don't want to learn it, any more than I want to carry a knife. So I left it at home. *My* home. Do you want me to tell you about your father?'

He was too terrified to nod. He knew he would be choked if he nodded.

'Well, in the end, he was just a man. You don't want to be

like him, you really don't. Far too good-looking. Couldn't bear to be refused. He made his demons. You don't want to go that way.'

She turned towards the other voice, her face beautifully savage in the light of the candle she held aloft, so close to his face, the better to examine him.

'I think we can deal with this fairly quickly, don't you?'

At five forty-five, the hotel foyer was full.

The conferees from the basement rooms were up on ground level, as noisy and thirsty a group of men as Sheila could have wished. Mid-thirties, mid-level, staring at futures and still proud with it, strutting, wanting to celebrate the end of a long day and wanting to stay put, because the rain poured down outside, like water released from a dam. Falling in buckets. Those stumbling indoors not going anywhere either. The plinth of the flower urn was festooned with umbrellas. They sat in the bar with spread legs, boasting; they stood round the flowers with drinks in hand, and they were not going anywhere. Dark out there. Wet.

Alan was just inside the revolving doors, listening to the noise levels, pushing his way to the lift, when the whole room began to go quiet. A hesitant quiet, starting somewhere and rolling through. He stayed where he was, taller than most of them, shaking the rain from his hair, Henry behind him, both of them wetter than sewer rats and breathless.

The hush had begun when the man, wearing nothing but a feathery silk scarf round his neck, came out of the lift, followed by the woman with her hair in a neat chignon and wearing a smart grey coat and high-heeled boots. She prodded him towards the desk with polite excuse me's, making him take a long route through the crowd of men. Gradually, only gradually, heads turned. Alan skirted round the foyer crowd, at the back. One of Sheila's acolytes, better trained than most, spoke to the woman in the grey coat, a mild discussion until the redhead raised her voice.

'You don't understand. There are NO complaints. Except about this man. HE brought me here, and he hasn't even got a room. Took me upstairs to a dump, and then he *COULDN'T EVEN GET IT UP*, and doesn't want to pay, either. Look at him. LOOK AT HIM.'

The deathly silence crawled round like smoke, until every head was turned in that direction, drinks held steady, not swallowed, listening for the noise as she slapped a wallet on the desk. Silence and whispers.

'I wouldn't. even WANT his money. I've got my pride. Sorry for him, really. Better get him a taxi, could you?'

She parted the crowd of men, smiling to left and right like a bride coming out of church. It was so quiet then, they could hear the click of her heels on the faux marble floor. She paused to pick up the best-looking umbrella leaning against the flower urn, examined it briefly, and disappeared through the revolving door into the night.

All heads turned away from the door and swivelled back towards the man at the desk. People, men and a sprinkling of women, stood and jostled and craned their necks to see. The naked man presented pink buttocks. The woman behind the desk was smiling at him and shaking her head. The man picked up the wallet he was handed, and went to follow the same route as the woman in the coat. The crowd parted easily, the path already made. Someone began a slow handclap. Julian Tysall passed through, walking drunkenly, staring down unseeing, looking for nothing but the door. His face was the same face, stricken but unscarred. Alan held his breath and gazed, like everyone else. Everything about Julian Tysall was small. Everything an illusion. His hands were bunched into harmless fists, dangling by his sides. He fell into the revolving door. Alan felt sorry for him, began to go after him. Henry held him back.

The water lapped round them.

'I'm not sure the punishment fitted the crime,' Sarah said to Eleanor.

'Oh yes it did. He sought to expose and was exposed.'

'He hadn't actually done much, had he? Dreamt, gambled . . . nursed a grievance.'

'Blackmail, threats, a small, containable fire? No, not much. He was punished for his intentions. For what he wanted to do. And we didn't hurt him at all.'

'I wish I knew how you did that hold on the neck.'

'I'm not going to tell you. It would be entirely irresponsible of me. I can only say that it requires the patient to be totally distracted by something else.'

'You were fantastic. You're a marvellous friend.'

'You thought of it. It could easily have gone wrong.'

'A gamble. The power of auto-suggestion,' Sarah said. 'Funny, put something round his neck, and he thinks he's restrained. Didn't know about that, really I didn't. It was only a silk scarf. I loved it, too, shame. Immobilise for three seconds, take away the clothes, and he stays immobilised. Powerless. Would we be the same?'

'There was also the threat of retaliation by fire to his skin.

266

Probably we would be the same. Fear works better than injury. Let me guess. You were making him fulfil your own worst fantasy, weren't you? Such as walking naked through a crowd.'

Sarah kicked water at the shallow end of the pool, and considered.

'That isn't my worst fantasy. Come to think of it, I might actually enjoy it. I was just thinking that if only some woman had done that to his father, his father might not have turned out the way he was. Before he had time to take power for granted. OK, so men called Tysall, men like the Tysalls, may have certain proclivities, as Henry might say, or expectations, at least. But then they get made into something else as soon as others start to fear them. And then people like us, we give them the power, we make them legends. Simply by not stopping them, by retreating, running away, standing back. They get bigger, we get smaller, until they seem invincible. And then we do what they say. Or become desperate and wreck our own lives by committing the wrong kind of revenge.'

'Too much philosophy, Sarah. You mean like I did to Celia Hornby?'

'Yes. Don't let her wreck you now. That would be giving her real power.'

'Now there's our real mystery. Was she bad or sad?'

'Do you mean, do we know if she was abused and driven to be like she was, or was simply like it? Don't know. Let her simply be dead. And by being dead, she may have done exactly what she intended. Ruined her husband's life.'

The blue ceiling glowed. The water subsided.

'They'll be closing in a minute,' Eleanor said. 'We'd better go home.'

'I don't want to go home. Where is it?'

'Where the heart is. I felt entirely at home in those attics,' Eleanor said. 'What an awful waste of space. Do you think you did enough to our young man? He wasn't really so small. He just looked and felt it. Why do men mind so much?'

'Oh, I think we did enough. Because they really do mind. About *feeling* small. And they rely far too much on clothes.'

Towards the end of May, when the weather was fine, Mrs Dulcinda Mathewson, that being the name on the invitation, waited at the door of her house for the taxi which would bring her guest for the occasion to meet her. She was allowed just the one, security-checked in advance. That might have limited her choices, since she found she preferred persons with previous convictions, but the choice had already been made. The best companion for such an occasion was necessarily female, since a man would not appreciate the hats. Someone would have to stay at home with the dog, and someone would. Someone who did not mind that home was scarcely habitable, and only just hygienic, with little more than an incomplete roof, a working bathroom and one small other room to make it so. Still, progress was swift. That was what money could do, and she was claiming the rank of age, like their dear Queen herself. Dulcie spent time at her reconstituting wreck of a house every day, to admonish an astonishing number of people in her querulous voice. Something wrong with the larynx made her whisper with a strange sibilance, but it seemed to have an effect. The infirmity appeared to scare them even more than rude health. It was, Dulcie thought, a splendid exercise in how to continue to fool some of the people some of the time. They still believed she knew what she wanted. There was no comfort in losing the power in one's voice, except the realisation that there really was no necessity to shout.

Pink, she told Alan. Like raw plaster. I should have dark pink everywhere. Like the inside of a throat. No, no, no, he said. Creamy white, like your unburned skin. Blue, like your new hair. Cool lilac, like the bush surviving in your garden, where no fire went, same colour as the suit and the hat. Thanks for showing me yourself. You look a million.

Looking a million while feeling like shite was proof of what it took to make a lady. As a test of stamina, that would do. And it was a very nice hat. Lighter than the feathers of a bird, broad-brimmed to protect sun-intolerant skin, it was finest straw and felt as if it was a mile wide. You did not kiss a person who was wearing this hat, but you might bend inside the shade of it to discover who she might be, and what she looked like. There were lilac flowers on the top too, and all round the brim, as if she cared. She was beginning to wonder if it was too wide to go through the door of a black cab, couldn't be arsed really, and where she had learnt that disgusting phrase, she could not think. There was a bit of a fog over her eyes at the minute, but it would clear. Paint the whole sodding house white, then. Give me a bathroom from paradise, with jungle plants and a shower and fish in a tank, and everything. Conscience said she should be giving the money to the poor. They'll get it when I die, she said, and she suddenly found herself saying, not yet, not yet, not yet. Too much to do, including this. She had always wanted to go to a Buckingham Palace garden party. As a republican, Ernest would not have approved.

The cab arrived, obedient to directions, suitably impressed by the passenger. The hat fitted through the door, the stick

269

was disobedient to instructions. Dulcie wavered and wanted to go home. The entrance they chose was in Buckingham Gate. There's a coincidence, Dulcie told Sarah. Same name as your block, dear.

A mile west of here, Sarah said. There are lots of Buckinghams in London. Wasn't the Duke of Buckingham the favourite of King Charles? He had great looks and no inhibitions, that Buckingham, the most powerful man in the kingdom once.

Dulcie had considerable respect for Queen Elizabeth the Second, on several counts. First for never really putting a foot wrong in all these years, shaming everyone with her sheer consistency, as well as for being mightily good at throwing a party. She could show them all how it should be done. Although it might not be difficult to run a party on this scale if four thousand people turned up in hats on a good, warm day, with scenery like this and five hundred staff. Dulcie wanted to throw away her stick, but, cautiously, kept hold.

It was silly to call it a garden. It was a sodding great park with delightfully uncultured spaces. A boating pond as they came in, an acre of untamed woodland and scum-filled water. Pathways, summerhouses, not all perfectly main-tained, gigantic beds of conventional cottage-garden flowers, tall stems competing with nasturtiums and weeds and rooted foxgloves, and all that came in with the wind, just like any other garden. It had scarcely rained since March. How absolutely bloody inconsiderate of it. They came through the woods into the mown meadows of the lawns, the rear of the Palace dominating the distance. Progressing forward, the ambling ranks of guests passed one cheerful bandstand after another. Dulcie and Sarah decided they would take the

Palace exit when they left, just to see inside. What on earth would it be like to live in a place so large when one was, one-self, so small? Awful, Dulcie said. Back in the taxi, Sarah Fortune and Mrs Dulcinda Mathewson had placed bets on what colour Her Majesty would wear today. Faced with crowds as intensely interesting as these, they forgot the wager. Queen and entourage were distant specks on the Palace veranda, fascinating, of course, but not as much as the rest of the crowds.

Such organisation, too. Milky-white marquees the size of churches, fast-moving queues lining up to be served in quick succession by the waiting dozens, tea and cucumber sand-wiches on the first round, miniature cakes and scones with jam and cream on the second, ice cream on the third. Not a loaf or fish in sight, and equally miraculous. Not that anyone was there for the food, only for the crowd. A breathtakingly comprehensive crowd, enough to fill a dozen London squares. Frock coats and pinstripes for most of the men, making them universally handsome, and a dizzying varia-tion of dress among the women. Some wore clothes fit for a wedding, some looked as if they had raided the wardrobes of relatives and friends. Some looked as if they had taken up a frock at the last minute, lost the iron and rescued the obliga-tory hat from the back of a cupboard. Every walk of life: librarians, social workers, animal rescuers, Red Cross doers, hospital nurses, army wives, lesser diplomats, cleaners, rub-bish collectors, manufacturers, teachers, lords, ladies and long-serving minions, refreshingly ordinary: no one was in the least afraid to stare. Sarah and Dulcie found seats under an awning, and when their eyes beneath the shade of the hats grew tired of gazing, they talked as if they were somewhere else entirely. Catching up, again.

'Of course, I should have rewired the house twenty years ago,' Dulcie was saying. 'I wonder who does the Queen's? Even she has fires. Anyway, it's wonderful having Alan to oversee everything. Even more wonderful that he'll stay on once it's finished. I hope you don't think I've stolen him from you.'

'He was never anyone's to steal,' Sarah said. 'And besides, we still . . . go for walks together.'

'That's all right, then. It was very convenient him getting sacked just when I needed him, and very unfair sacking him for an incident in the bar he could hardly have controlled.'

'I think it was rather more a question of him making himself available,' Sarah said. 'He's in his element with you. Mending and fixing, as opposed to burning things down. Says he's found his true vocation. And he didn't leave his job on bad terms. He still has influence there. My friend Eleanor has taken over part of the attics. Generating income, I think it's called. The hotel gives her a captive audience. Which . . . I don't know why it reminds me, Dulcie. I never did find the real Henry.'

'Oh, that's all right, he found me, didn't I tell you? It's just as well you found the other one instead.' She turned back to crowd-watching. 'I really think the men are the winners in the dress stakes, don't you?' she said. 'Apart from the Indian women in the saris, and the African headdresses, that is. Nothing like a uniform to make a man look good, but the clerics really do get first prize.'

There were colourful clerics littered among the multitudes. The most stunning combination, they agreed, was a posse of priests with coal-black skin and white hair, wearing scarlet cassocks down to their hidden shoes, the whole ensemble offset by wide purple sashes. No male competition really came close to that, except maybe a Canadian Mountie, and a Royal Navy man in full white, with vivid gold epaulettes catching the sun.

'It isn't fair,' Dulcie said. 'If we did that, we'd be accused of overdressing.'

The bands played, distant and near, and the hours passed. When it was time to go, they stood on the veranda of the yellow palace, and watched the elegant hordes marshalling themselves for the way out, moving along as if there was all the time in the world. Below where they stood, the Gurkha band played, and as the crowd thinned, they began to belt out 'The Stripper'. In automatic response, each passer-by, whatever age, gave a brief, enchanting shimmy of the hips.

'And what about you, dear?' Dulcie asked, wiggling herself in response to the sheer infection of the music. 'Are you going to reconsider this career of yours? I'm probably only saying it because I'm feeling so ancient myself, but I feel it my duty to point out that you aren't getting any younger.'

Sarah looked down at a group of distinguished men passing by below.

One of them, grey-haired and ruddy-faced, walking tall, paused in surprise to wave extravagantly towards her with delighted recognition. There was more than one nice elderly judge. Sarah grinned and waved back, rather more discreetly.

'Neither,' she said, 'are they.'